# Between
# the Sheets

Books by P. J. Mellor

PLEASURE BEACH

GIVE ME MORE

MAKE ME SCREAM

DRIVE ME WILD

BETWEEN THE SHEETS

THE COWBOY
(with Vonna Harper, Nelissa Donovan, and Nikki Alton)

THE FIREFIGHTER
(with Susan Lyons and Alyssa Brooks)

NAUGHTY, NAUGHTY
(with Melissa MacNeal and Valerie Martinez)

ONLY WITH A COWBOY
(with Melissa MacNeal and Vonna Harper)

UNDER THE COVERS
(with Crystal Jordan and Lorie O'Clare)

Published by Kensington Publishing Corporation

# Between the Sheets

## P.J. Mellor

APHRODISIA

KENSINGTON BOOKS
http://www.kensingtonbooks.com

APHRODISIA BOOKS are published by

Kensington Publishing Corp.
119 West 40th Street
New York, NY 10018

ISBN-13: 978-0-7582-3818-4
ISBN-10: 0-7582-3818-5

First Kensington Trade Paperback Printing: February 2010

10  9  8  7  6  5  4  3  2  1

Printed in the United States of America

For Andrew and Shelley

# Acknowledgments

Many thanks to my fabulous agent, Jennifer Schober, and my editor, John Scognamiglio. Words can't convey my appreciation.

I also want to thank all the people who helped with the technical aspects of this book, especially Rob Hancock at Sea Sports Scuba. Any mistakes are all mine.

# CONTENTS

# REDD HOT

# 1

―――――――

"Oh, yeah, baby, that's right. Bend it, work it." Connor O'Brian slouched deeper into the leather bucket seat of his rental car and groped for his binoculars, his gaze locked on the woman in the red power suit across the street.

He visually caressed the trim ankle flexing above the black stiletto as she attempted to right the REDD HOT PROPERTIES real estate sign in the front yard of the beach house.

His gaze licked the length of tan leg exposed by the tight, short skirt while he mentally urged her to bend over a little farther. He was betting she wore a black thong.

When it became apparent she would not cooperate, his gaze took a leisurely trip along the gentle swell of her ass, shown to perfection, thanks to the tight skirt and the angle of her leg. The flair of her hip had his heart racing.

"Turn around," he urged in a hoarse whisper. "I need to see if the front is as delicious as the back view."

Her spine stiffened, and for a moment, he wondered if she'd heard him. She glanced left and right, then back over her shoulder.

He held his breath. It whooshed out when she again bent to her task, a clump of long, shining dark hair falling across her face, this time giving him a direct view down the plunging neckline of the black-trimmed red jacket. With each movement, her perfect breasts jiggled in an intriguing manner.

She straightened again and swiped her forehead with the back of her hand. After a quick glance around, she stripped off the jacket and tossed it over a purse and briefcase a few feet away, then resumed her struggle with the sign.

Connor swallowed and adjusted the hardness pressing against the fly of his cargo shorts. Tank tops had intrigued him since puberty, and the form-fitting, wrapped black version the woman wore had just become his favorite.

He swallowed and swiped at the sweat trickling down his temples. If he turned the engine on to cool off, she might notice him.

He wasn't ready yet.

Andrea Redd brushed a strand of hair away from her sweaty forehead and glared at the sign. She'd sunk a million signs just like it over the years. She'd be damned if she'd let this one get the best of her.

The strains of "Five O'Clock Somewhere" filtered through the air above the sound of nearby waves. Abandoning her battlestation, she trudged to her purse and fished out her cell. "What?"

"Isn't that a lovely, professional way to answer your phone." Her assistant Lisa's droll voice echoed in her ear. "I know you prob don't want to hear this, but BFD, because we have a little, um, situation."

"Stop speaking in text-messaging jargon. It annoys me."

"Again, BFD. Everything annoys you lately." Lisa huffed out a sigh. "Do you want to hear what I have to say?"

"Do I have a choice?" Andrea balanced the phone on her ear and attempted to right the sign.

"We lost him."

"Who?" *Please don't let it be the new client,* she silently prayed. While business was good, it had been better. She'd planned to get back in the game with the next sale.

"Connor O'Brian. Remember? The guy we were supposed to be meeting at the airport this morning? Hello? IDK, is any of this ringing a bell?"

"Of course it is; don't be a smart-ass." She lifted her hair, allowing the ocean breeze to cool her neck. "What I don't understand is how in the hell you could lose him. My God, isn't he ancient, like a hundred or something? How difficult is it to find a doddering old rich guy? The airport isn't that big!"

"There you go, making assumptions again. All I know is the driver stood with the sign until everyone was gone and no Connor O'Brian."

"He has to be somewhere. His hotel? Did you check there?" She thumped the sign, which immediately fell over, so she kicked it for good measure. When had her life taken a wrong turn?

"Of course I checked." Lisa's voice brought her back to the conversation. "If he's on Mustang Island, he hasn't checked in yet."

"Great." Andrea sighed and glanced around. Was there a man in the car across the street? A second glance revealed nothing. "Well, keep trying to find him. We can only assume he'll show up for his appointment this afternoon." She added a quick thanks to her assistant and disconnected.

Connor slumped lower in the seat and held his breath. He could have sworn the woman looked straight at him. A buzz vibrated his hip. He pulled his cell from the holster. "Hello?" he said in a low voice.

"Where the hell are you?" His friend and financial advisor, Bill Farnsworth, bellowed. "I came to have a drink with you before your flight, and you were nowhere to be found."

"Bill, I was only going to Mustang Island. I think seeing me off was overkill."

"Not for you. It was for me. I wanted to make sure you actually left town this time. I need a break."

"You poor slob. I know managing my finances is a real drain on you. Wait! Isn't that why you became an advisor?" He could feel his muscles tensing, so he focused on the shapely behind of the woman and took a deep breath.

"Don't be an ass. You're my friend. I enjoy working for you. But I need a life, too, you know. I'm hoping you'll meet Miss Right and get married and have nine kids. And if you spend just five minutes a day with each child, it will free up forty-five minutes a day I can have all to myself. Is that too much to ask of an old friend?"

Bill was right about him needing a vacation, Connor realized as he pressed the disconnect button after the call. Granted, looking for vacation property wasn't technically it, but it was as close as he was able to get at the moment.

"That son of a bitch!" Andrea slammed down the phone on her desk, then fumed while she checked her nails for chips. Bad enough that Rich, her ex, was still mucking with her life, chipping a newly manicured nail would be the final straw of her lousy day.

"Problem?" Lisa peeked around the door of Andrea's office as though afraid what she might find.

"If Richard Redd was here right now, I'd cheerfully strangle him." Slumping back in the smooth burgundy leather desk chair, Andrea closed her eyes and rubbed her aching temples. "Then I'd castrate him with a dull butcher knife, just for fun."

"What'd he do now?"

"Stole another damn listing. The Hendersons just told me they decided to go with him instead of Redd Hot Properties." She opened her eyes to see Lisa edging into the room, mail in her outstretched hand, and sighed. "Lisa, relax. I've told you before—I don't blame you for anything he does. Or doesn't do."

"Thanks to my mother's dip into the shallow end of the gene pool, before she had the good sense to marry my dad, I'm still related to the scumbag."

Andrea regarded her best friend and ex-sister-in-law with a smile. "Well, at least something good came out of me being married to him. I met you."

"BFF. That's sweet." Lisa glanced at her watch. "But if you don't get a move on, you'll be late to meet Connor O'Brian."

"Connor O'Brian?" Andrea shifted some papers on her desk and scrolled through her appointment list. "I assume you found him, then?"

"Yeah, turns out he took an earlier flight and rented a car. He called while you were out." She motioned to Andrea's phone. "I sank all the data for you. With traffic, you need to leave ASAP. Like now."

Andrea retrieved her purse from the desk drawer. "The preapproval letter is in order, right?"

Lisa chewed on her lower lip. "Well, not exactly."

"What is it . . . exactly?"

"Not here yet. But I'm sure it will be, any time now," Lisa rushed to assure her. "Ray wouldn't have referred him if he didn't have the money."

"True, but you know my policy. I don't waste my time on clients without a preapproval of some kind." She dug in her purse, finally dumping the contents on the desk. "Where are my damn keys?"

"In your car, I assume. Remember? You sent it to be detailed this morning. It's out front."

"Right. I knew that." Andrea stood and smoothed her skirt.

"Pick all that up for me . . . please? I'm going to brush my teeth and do a quick makeup check."

"IOI." Lisa reached for the pile on the desk.

Pausing at the door to her private bathroom, Andrea turned. "What?"

"I'm on it." Lisa did an eye-roll. "OMG."

"Cut it out, Lisa." Andrea twirled. "Do you think I should swing by home and change? I wouldn't want to give the old guy a heart attack." She chuckled. "At least not before he buys a house."

Her assistant smiled one of her damn wan smiles, the ones that always made Andrea nervous. "No prob."

Closing her eyes and counting to ten didn't lessen the feeling of foreboding Lisa's smiles always conjured. "I'm not going to waste precious time with twenty questions." She leveled her gaze on her assistant. "If you're withholding vital information, I suggest you get your résumé in order because you're fired."

"NBD."

# 2

Andrea tossed her keys to the valet and strode through the revolving door of MacClairen's, girding herself for the inevitable feelings of inadequacy that always washed over her when entering the posh hotel. Logically, she knew it was a throwback to her less-than-fiscally-healthy beginning. A knee-jerk reaction.

Less than five minutes later, she breathed a sigh of relief as she stepped out of the private elevator onto the lavishly polished marble entry of the penthouse suite.

She could do this. A deep breath gave her oxygen-deprived lungs a moment to relax. Rolling her shoulders helped. It was a common occurrence; a lot of people held their breath on elevators.

Girding her business persona, she briskly tapped the polished brass knocker, pushing aside the niggling misgiving about Connor O'Brian's lack of preapproval. Surely it was an oversight. It would arrive any time.

The door swung wide, derailing her worrisome train of thought.

The young man standing in the open doorway cocked his

head as he perused her from head to stiletto and back again, his sun-streaked blond hair falling boyishly over his forehead.

He was gorgeous—she'd give him that—and he probably knew it. No doubt girls flocked around him like homing pigeons.

She preferred her men more . . . mature. Casual sophistication that came with age was very . . . reassuring. Comforting. You knew where you stood with older men. They knew how to play the game, censure their facial expressions.

Unlike the young wannabe stud before her, who was all but drooling as his heated green gaze licked her from head to toe, pausing at all the tingling spots.

Which was utterly ridiculous. She was too old to tingle.

She straightened and glared her fiercest don't-fuck-with-me look.

He had the audacity to grin, his teeth white and straight in his guileless face. His long finger pushed up a pair of rimless glasses she hadn't noticed until that moment.

"Hello," she said with what she hoped was just the right blend of professionalism and authority. "I'm here to meet with Connor O'Brian. Would that, by chance, be your father?" Please, Lord, don't let it be his grandfather. Old, she could take. Old, she could coerce into buying. Doddering made her feel, well, too guilty.

Surfer Dude leaned one T-shirt-clad shoulder against the doorjamb, crossing his arms over his impressive chest. "Actually, my father is Connor O'Brian, but—"

"Excellent." Andrea swept past him and set her briefcase on the tiled foyer floor beside a cherry hall table, determined to regain her self-control. She was, after all, a professional. "Please tell him Andrea Redd, from Redd Hot Properties, is here for our appointment."

"But"—he shrugged and closed the door, then leaned against it, his gaze never leaving hers—"my father is in Miami."

Shit. "I'm sorry. I don't understand." In heels, she looked directly into his eyes, which was one of the reasons she preferred stilettos: They gave her power. "Connor O'Brian just arrived on the island. He called my office to set up this appointment. Was there some kind of emergency or . . . ?"

A slow shake of his head had her struggling to concentrate on his words instead of admiring his assets.

"My name is Connor O'Brian, too. I'm the one who made the appointment." He opened the door, inclining his head toward the hall. "I'm ready to go check out beach houses. How about you?" The grin he flashed was unrepentant.

No doubt about it, she needed damage control. *Play nice,* her mind screamed while her mouth blurted out, "Let's go, *Junior.*"

"I thought you were going to show me beachfront property," Connor complained when Andrea Redd pulled her Mercedes 600SL to the curb after an uncomfortably silent ten-minute drive.

"This house has beach access." She opened her door and stepped out.

"It looks like it needs painting." He shut his door and glared at the forlorn-looking structure.

"It has that weathered look," she countered, striding toward the front door.

He shook his head to clear it of the lascivious thoughts the sway of her red-clad hips instilled and caught up to her as she inserted her card key into the lockbox on the "weathered" double entry doors. "I may not be from around here, but that," he said, pointing to the water in the distance, "doesn't look like the Gulf of Mexico."

She sighed and turned to pin him with her cool, crystal-blue gaze. "It's a lake, but it has all the amenities of Gulf property. It's really quite a deal."

"What makes you think I'm looking for a *deal*?" Did the

snooty brunette actually think he couldn't afford Gulf property?

"Nothing, Junior, although I have not seen the promised preapproval letter. I just thought it was a good deal and possibly might work for you." A fine brow arched. "Perhaps if you gave me an idea of your price range, I could better narrow it down."

Connor sighed and ran a hand through his hair, wishing he'd gotten another haircut before leaving Houston. He glanced down at his more-than-casual attire and again cursed Bill for not only convincing him to take the trip but also for replacing his normal wardrobe. No wonder Andrea Redd didn't take him seriously. As soon as they were finished, he'd go buy some decent clothes. Wait. His wardrobe shouldn't make a difference. Maybe Miss High and Mighty needed to learn clothes do not make the man. Besides, she worked for him, regardless of what he wore.

"Stop calling me Junior," he finally said, "please."

"I thought you said you and your father had the same name."

"We do. But no one ever calls me Junior. Ever." He edged closer to her, unable to stop the urge to inhale the flowery scent of her perfume. Okay, maybe he also got a perverse sense of pleasure in knowing his nearness disturbed her. He could see it in the way her clear blue eyes widened a fraction and the fact she took a tiny step back.

What had gotten into him? After Whitley's defection, he'd sworn off powerful, high-maintenance women. Hell, in fact, he'd sworn off all women. At least for a while.

But there was something . . . different about Andrea Redd.

And he intended to find out what.

Beneath his baggy cargo shorts, his cock stirred in an effort to tell him exactly what it thought about Ms. Redd.

He watched in fascination as her tongue darted out to lick her glossy lips, surprised to realize he wanted to feel that tongue, those lips, on his body.

It was his vacation, after all, pitiful as it was. And it was the first one in more years than he wanted to count. Why not?

Andrea forced her feet to stop retreating, locking her knees to keep them from trembling. Her heart raced, her breath coming in shallow huffs. Every nerve ending stood at attention. The whole situation was ridiculous. The man was young enough to be . . . well, at least her younger brother. So what if he oozed sex appeal? She was immune, thanks to her snake-in-the-grass ex-husband and waning hormones.

He looked down at her from his less-than-considerable height advantage, thanks to her heels. She fought the urge to clutch her lapels together like some shy virgin, irritated he had the ability to make her nipples tingle with just a casual glance.

She took a quick peek downward and bit back a smile. Obviously *Junior* liked what he saw.

Redd Hot Properties could use a sale. Unloading the heretofore unsalable unit she'd just unlocked would just be icing on the cake.

And, really, was a little harmless flirtation, both giving and receiving, going to kill her?

Thinking of possibly unloading the property made her wet. Oh, yes, she could definitely see the possibilities in playing nice. Mutual satisfaction could perform miracles.

Decision made, she released her lapels and took a deep breath, inwardly chuckling when Junior's eyes widened at her expanded cleavage.

She leaned in so he could get a better view, casually dragging the tip of her finger along the upper swell of her breast. "Since we're already here, why don't I just show you around? Who knows?" She turned, causing the tips of her nipples to graze his firm chest. A surprising streak of fiery awareness shot through her and renewed the dampness between her legs. What was wrong with her? "Maybe you'll see something you like," she finished in a breathy voice. No doubt about it, she'd already found something she liked, if her body's reaction to him was any indication. Hell, who was she kidding? If it would unload the property, she wouldn't be totally adverse to shoving her now-aching breast into his mouth.

She was reasonably sure he'd be receptive.

She ignored the light brush of his hand on her ass as they walked into the entry. After all, they were two consenting adults.

Well, she was, anyway.

# 3

Connor could barely walk with the monster hard-on. He half expected her to slap him when he brushed his hand across her firm backside.

She didn't.

Instead, she looked up at him with those blue, blue eyes as though daring—or wanting—him to do it again.

She stopped just inside the door. His eyes took a second to adjust to the dimness of the interior after the bright sunshine. At least, that was his excuse when he ran into her back.

Automatically reaching out to steady her, his hands gripped the soft curves that filled her suit jacket so enticingly.

Before he could utter the apology on his lips, she murmured, "Easy, Junior."

Did she just wiggle her bottom against his erection? Or was that just a figment of his sex-starved imagination?

Without a backward glance, she sauntered into the vaulted living room while he stood with his mouth hanging open.

Giving himself a mental shake, he walked toward her. Two

could play her game. His friends were always ragging on him to take a chance, indulge his baser instincts. A glance at his Realtor caught her giving him the once-over. She was obviously interested in showing him more than a beach house. At least he thought so. Wasn't she?

No doubt about it, he'd been out of circulation for too long.

Andrea could practically smell the testosterone wafting from Connor. Ordinarily, she kept business and pleasure separate. Besides being too young, he was not her type. But that didn't seem to dull the sharp edge of lust she felt just by being in the same room.

Her gaze took a leisurely journey from his bare, flip-flop-clad toes up long, powerful-looking legs to lean hips. A little thrill of excitement zipped through her, hardening her nipples, when she eyed the obvious bulge in his cargo shorts. It was stupid to react so strongly to his virility.

It could be professional suicide.

He stepped closer, the hardened tips of her breasts grazing his firm chest again, sending little jolts of electric awareness shooting to her extremities.

It could be worth the risk.

"What do you think? Do you like it?" Damn, her voice sounded weak and airy. "W-would you like to see the rest?" She bit back a smile when she saw his gaze was directed down her cleavage.

Now she understood the term *heaving bosoms*. Hers were definitely heaving, her breathing labored, while her panties grew wet. What was happening to her?

It was ridiculous.

Slowly he raised his hand to trail the blunt tip of his index finger between her breasts, down between the cleavage created by her push-up bra. His actions made her breath lodge in her throat, her heart race.

It was dangerous. The man was a client, not to mention a stranger. A young stranger.

"Oh, yeah," he said in a low, seductive voice as he dipped his finger beneath her décolletage to graze her turgid nipple. "I'd definitely be interested in seeing the rest." With that, he flicked the front closure of her bra open, palming her eager flesh.

It was beyond thrilling.

It was not professional behavior. She should push him away and cover herself instead of standing there, clamping her shaking legs together, while her thong dripped her excitement. And she would. Soon. It had just been so long since a man—any man—had touched her like that.

He bent and took her puckered nipple deep into his hot mouth, his tongue swirling around and around in maddening circles with each deep pull on her sensitized flesh.

Her breath hitched and she had to lock her knees to remain upright. She knew it was wrong to allow him to continue, but damn, it felt so good.

As a result, she made no objections when he tugged her shoulders free of her suit jacket and pulled her open bra off over her head, along with her tank top.

Against her will—well, it *should* have been against her will—her hands found the closure of his shorts. In no time, he stood before her, magnificent in his nudity.

He reached for her, and she went willingly into his arms, glorying in the tactile pleasure of her breasts pushed against the warmth of his chest.

She gave a little sideways movement, dragging her erect nipples back and forth against his, her stilettos making her close in height.

The heat of his erection nudged her abdomen, sending a thrill shooting through her that was out of proportion with her experience.

His mouth claimed hers, his lips soft at first, then harder, more demanding, as he took possession of her suddenly hungry mouth. His tongue swept her mouth once, twice, before she captured and sucked on it, earning a deep-throated moan. It may or may not have been from him.

Still kissing her, he hooked his thumbs in her now-unzipped skirt, easing it down over her hips to pool around her ankles.

He broke the kiss and stepped back to look at her as she stood before him in her stilettos and black silk thong.

It made her nipples pucker even tighter, if that was possible. She resisted the urge to cover her breasts with her hands. She'd worked hard to keep her body firm and fit. If the expression on Junior's face was any indication, she'd succeeded. Proudly, she straightened her shoulders, glorying in a sexual urge she'd thought deserted her.

Connor sank to his knees in front of her, trailing hot kisses from her breast downward.

Sun streamed in through the bay window, warming her back. He hooked his fingers under the strings on her hips and began tugging, his hot breath warming her front more than the sun streaming through to bare windows warmed her back. The sun . . . oh, no!

Her hands shot out to grasp his wrists.

Breathing hard, they looked at each other.

Although Connor had obeyed her nonverbal command, his fingers toyed with her damp folds while he waited, still holding the thin sides of her thong.

Andrea all but moaned at his touch, wanting nothing more than to sink to the dubious cleanliness of the carpet and let him take her away to a place she had not visited in a long time: sexual bliss.

She closed her eyes, gathering strength to stop him.

Her breath caught when he plunged his finger deep within her wetness. Goose bumps sprang up on every inch of her skin, her nipples puckering to painful points. She couldn't help herself; she gyrated her hips, grinding against his hand, pushing his finger deeper.

More . . . she wanted, needed more. And, Lord help her, she wanted it with Connor.

Connor must have taken her action as the go-ahead, because he resumed tugging at her panties.

Once again, she reached out and stopped him. "Not here," she managed to croak out of her parched throat, "someone might see us." She jerked her head in the general direction of the bare windows.

A frantic glance at the kitchen had her cursing the trend in open-concept designs.

Connor knew he was not leaving the house without fucking her. They'd gone too far to stop now. At least he had, and, judging from the wetness dripping down his hand, she was right there with him. "Bathroom?" Even in a house like this, there had to be a way of closing off a bathroom to gain privacy.

"The master is down the hall." Andrea pointed a shaking hand over his shoulder.

He scooped her into his arms, pleased when she wrapped her long legs around him, reveling in the feel of the stiletto heels scraping the small of his back, and almost ran down the hall.

"What?" Andrea said, turning her head when he stopped and cursed at the door of the master suite. "Damn open concept!"

Connor couldn't believe his—their—luck. The master bedroom sprawled right into a huge master bathroom that was totally open. "There's a door." He headed toward a narrow opening on one end of the bathroom. The rub of wet silk against his cock was delicate torture. If he didn't get relief soon, he'd explode.

"It's a water closet! We'll never fit in there," she objected, but he tightened his grip, stepping into the miniscule area and closing the pocket door.

There was barely room to slide her down his body. Each millimeter was excruciating. Sexual torture.

"My wallet," he finally gasped, "there's a condom in there. Damn! I can't believe I left it in the other room."

Andrea paused. Was it a sign to stop what they were doing? She glanced down at the shiny purple head bobbing against the trembling flesh of her abdomen. Hell, no.

"I'll go get it." She reached behind her, feeling for the recessed door handle.

"Wait." He pulled her tightly against his sweat-slicked chest. "Kiss me good-bye." He covered her mouth in a kiss that had her all but climbing up his strong body. She whimpered when he pulled back. "Hurry," he whispered against her kiss-swollen lips.

She surely broke the land-speed record, running to the living room and grabbing his shorts, practically tearing the pocket in her haste to get his wallet.

She paused, her natural curiosity warring with her sexual urge to finish what they'd started. Clutching the sun-warmed wallet to her breasts, she looked at their clothes, scattered in the afternoon sun on the worn carpet of the empty house. The sight elicited tingles that skittered up and down her labia, the result further drenching her thong and tightening her nipples. Tamping down all the reasons why it was a bad idea to continue, she pulled several condoms from his wallet, dropping it back to the floor.

Hell, she'd gone this far; she may as well finish what they'd started. She kicked off her shoes and ran back to the bathroom.

Connor was waiting for her, his erection bigger than when she'd left, if that was possible. He grabbed a condom, ripping the foil open with his teeth and sheathing his penis in record time.

Before she could comment on his speed, he grabbed her arm, pulling her into the little room and sliding the door shut as he lifted her.

Her knee bumped the door trim. "Ouch!"

Her head banged against the closed door when he slid her panties down and attempted to align his heat to her opening.

"Sorry. Here. Put your leg on my shoulder."

"I can't get my leg out far enough to put it on your shoulder!" She felt like crying. "This isn't going to work, is it?" Damn, she wished the needy ache between her legs would subside.

"I'm an engineer. I can make it work." He slid his warm hand down her leg, making her shiver. "Trust me." He grasped her ankle and gently lifted until her foot touched the closed commode lid. "Relax." He slid his finger up and down her folds, making them plump and moist again. "Look," he whispered, "look at how pretty you are down there."

She glanced down, intrigued at the contrast of his masculine hand against her most feminine parts. Parts that were open and fully exposed. It was wicked and decadent, thoroughly unprofessional and naughty, to say the least.

She loved it.

The heat of his fingers combined with the heat of his breath whispering over her erect nipples increased her heart rate, her breath coming in shallow pants while she watched him pleasure her.

He plucked at her engorged clitoris, causing it to swell and darken, her excitement making it glisten in the limited light from the tiny window above the toilet.

Her hips began moving involuntarily, in an age-old rhythm, seeking sexual gratification.

His finger slid into her aching folds, seeking the part of her weeping for him, and impaled her.

She found what she'd been seeking.

# 4

Andrea trembled in his arms, her flesh vibrating against his as her climax washed over his hand. Her knees gave way, but he managed to hold her up with one arm wrapped around her bare back, his finger still deeply embedded. His dick twitched as he indulged in petting her clamping, slick folds and kissing her forehead, touching her everywhere he could reach while she calmed down.

He wanted nothing more than to bury himself in her wet, welcoming heat. But he also wanted her to be with him every second, sharing the experience, the bone-deep satisfaction, the . . . Oh, man, what was he thinking? Well, obviously he wasn't, to even consider having sex in an empty house. With his Realtor. Worse, to attempt to have anything close to gratification while standing in a miniscule toilet area.

It wasn't that he didn't want her. Hell, yes, he wanted her. In fact, he couldn't honestly remember ever wanting a woman more than he wanted Andrea Redd. But he'd be damned if their first time was going to be in a cramped bath of an empty house.

He wanted to spread her out on the king-size bed in his hotel room, to feel the soft rub of her skin against his while he explored every delectable inch of her before finally sinking to the hilt in her honeyed sex.

He closed his eyes to block the erotic sight of Andrea, naked, with one foot raised high for his viewing pleasure, while he took deep breaths to try to calm down. If he continued looking, he knew he'd want to keep touching her. And it wouldn't stop with just touching. The thought of it made him shake with need. He'd been too long without sex, but even a sex-starved geek had to draw the line somewhere.

Shuffling alerted him to Andrea's movement. The cooler air wafting around his sweating torso told him she'd moved away from him. Well, as far away as one could move, given the confining space.

"Relax, Junior." Andrea's voice sounded harsh, detached, the breathy sexiness from just a few minutes ago completely gone. "I'm not going to ravage you." The sound of the pocket door opening shot through the little room. "Now, be a brave boy, open your eyes, and go get our clothes."

She gave a little shove, then a slight tap on his butt as he turned to exit the bathroom.

He wanted to assure her that ravaging was the furthest thing from his mind, unless it was him doing the ravaging. Actually, he wanted to tell her more than that, but she'd already pushed him out and closed the door again.

He looked down. What a waste of a perfectly good condom.

"You are such a nerd," he grumbled, stripping off the condom as he stalked into the living room. Bending to scoop up their clothing, he looked at the wadded condom in his hand. He would toss it, of course, but just leaving it lying around in an empty house wasn't going to work. Besides, it might damage Andrea's reputation or business if someone who knew she'd shown the house found it. After throwing on his clothes, he shoved it in his pocket. If he didn't find a better place, he could always dispose of it in his hotel room later.

His knock on the pocket door sounded timid, even to him, but the change in Andrea's attitude was a little scary. Not that he was afraid of her—it was just an awkward situation, and now that he thought about it, she was probably embarrassed. Which would account for the way her arm shot through the opening to grab her clothes before slamming the door shut again.

Seconds later, the door reopened and Andrea stepped out, looking once again like the consummate professional. Except for her bare feet.

The bloodred polish on her toes flashed in the sunlight. Lord, she even had sexy toes. He shifted to accommodate his renewed arousal.

She evidently noticed the direction of his gaze. "Where are my fucking shoes?" Was that a hint of tears in her voice?

Mute, he pointed toward the living room, swallowing as he watched her walk purposefully in that direction. Damn, she had a fine ass. The thought of how it had felt to touch the firm smoothness . . . No, he needed to stop remembering what had happened.

At least for now.

Andrea blinked back stupid tears as she fumbled with her shoes. What the hell had just happened? She'd worked damn hard to get where she was, and fucking a potential client just to get a sale was low, even for her. She'd never really minded being referred to as a wolf in her pursuit of sales. But this . . . It could have meant professional suicide. It could have led to disastrous consequences. It could have been . . . the most ecstatic experience of her life.

Eyes closed, she took a fortifying breath. *Don't be ridiculous. You've been working your ass off and haven't even had the time to consider recreational sex. You just need to make time for a hot sexual encounter. Something that doesn't require batteries. Soon.* She stiffened at the charged awareness when he touched her shoulder. *Very soon.* She opened her eyes, schooling her features against the emotions she saw in his boyish face. *But not with him, damn it.*

"If you're willing to take on a fixer, the owners might negotiate on price. What do you think about this place?" she asked, reaching for her briefcase. "Any interest in looking at the rest of the house?"

*Not unless there is a bed in one of the rooms for us to test drive.* "Nope. I told you I want property on the Gulf, not inland—"

"Technically, this is a beach house, with the lake right out—"

His eyes narrowed as he interrupted. "It's not the Gulf. And I have no interest in a fixer. Do you have anything else to show me?"

"If I knew a price range, it could narrow our search."

"Show me a house I am interested in purchasing, then tell me the price," he fired back, "and I'll tell you if I'll take it."

"Fine." Stalking to the door, she opened it, motioning for him to exit. "As soon as I lock up, I'll meet you at the car."

Effectively dismissed, he walked to the car. What had he seen in the fire-breathing she-dragon? He glanced back as she bent to replace the key in the lockbox, her red skirt caressing the firm cheeks of her smooth-skinned ass, an ass he'd been up close and personal with just a few minutes ago.

Well, yeah, there was that.

# 5

_____

The drive to the next property was made in silence while Connor averted his eyes from the expanse of leg exposed every time Andrea braked.

Damn, the little car's interior was hot.

Andrea leaned across him, looking at the addresses, her full breast threatening to fall out of her low-cut top. And into his waiting hands. No. He had to stop thinking about stuff like that.

"Here we are," she announced, turning into a wide, circle drive of a stucco home with a red tile roof. "I'm sure this is more what you had in mind."

She put the car in park and stretched to reach behind her seat for her purse. The action caused her jacket to gape, giving him a perfect view of the dark edge of her nipple.

Suddenly, what he had in mind had nothing to do with looking at houses.

He heaved an inward sigh and pushed open his door. But they were here to look at potential vacation homes. Unfortunately.

As they approached the door, Andrea rambled on about the landscaping and sprinkler system.

Even the swipe of her key card in the realty lockbox was sexy.

He shoved his hands deep into the pockets of his shorts to avoid reaching for her as she punched in the code for the alarm, just inside the beveled glass doors.

The entry floor gleamed in the setting sun streaming through the windows. To the left was a massive dining room that connected to a kitchen that could surely be used for industrial purposes.

The kitchen eating area wrapped around to a family room, its ceiling jutting up to the third floor.

The sight of Andrea standing by the French doors leading to the patio had him instantly hard.

"The backyard is adequate, with an infinity pool. Beyond it is a deep-water dock." At his raised brow, she hurried on. "Technically, the house is on an inlet, but that inlet empties into the Gulf." Her hand rested on the levered knob of the French door. "Would you like to take a look?"

He shook his head. "The house is empty, right?"

Slowly, she nodded, her hand gripping the door. "Yes, why? Is there a problem?"

"No, I just thought we should probably take the tour before it gets too dark to see." He glanced back at the kitchen. "Other than the recessed lights in here and the chandelier in the entry, I don't see any other lights." His gaze met hers. "Which way to the master?"

She pointed to the left. With a slight bow, he let her know he'd follow.

The sway of her hips as she walked ahead of him had him shoving his hand deeper into his pocket, pushing his zipper hard against his potentially embarrassing erection.

The master bedroom was huge, with a soaring perimeter-lit

tray ceiling. The pale lush carpeting pushed up along the edge of his sandals to caress the sides of his feet. He was sure it would be magnificent, as Andrea was saying, with furnishings, but all he could see was Andrea spread naked on a big bed in the middle of the room.

"Connor?" Andrea's voice jerked him back to reality. "Did you hear what I said about the master bath? Would you like to check it out?"

"Um, sure." He casually adjusted himself as he followed her through a double door.

"The double-vessel sinks are custom, as is the granite vanity top. The cabinets are solid cherry. There's a working sauna as well as a five-head shower with a steam feature. A separate water closet." She gave a brief nod in the direction of a closed door, and he wondered if she was remembering the same sexy things he was remembering.

She pointed to a recessed tub that could easily sit five or six people. "And, of course, a jetted tub."

"Of course." He'd like nothing better than to strip his Realtor naked and check out the tub. Which was why they needed to get out of the room. Fast.

When they finally had sex—and they would definitely have it—it was going to be on his terms and in a place where he could take all night to please her.

And from the slight frown on her gorgeous face, it would probably take at least that long.

Raking a hand through his hair, he turned and stalked from the bathroom. "It's getting darker; we'd better go out and look at the pool and dock."

"There are patio and dock lights," she said, but she doubted he heard her since he'd already disappeared around the corner.

She glanced at the big, empty tub and pictured herself and

Connor lounging, naked, in the churning bubbles, then shook her head. The property had been vacant quite a while. Selling it would be a definite coup. But would it be worth selling her body in the process?

Eyeing Connor's firm backside as he bent over the bubbling water of the spa on the patio, she leaned against the open patio door, enjoying the view.

It might just be worth it, after all.

With slow, deliberate steps, she walked up behind Connor.

He turned with a grin. "The spa's hot. Someone must have been here recently."

With a vague nod, she strolled to sit on a thick padded patio chair and crossed her legs, not bothering to tug her skirt back down when it crept up her thighs. The way Connor's heated gaze zeroed in on her legs sent a jolt of feminine satisfaction through her, dampening her panties in the process.

It was flattering. That was the only reason she felt flushed. No one had looked at her like that in a very long time. And to have a man that young and sexy take an obvious interest in her *assets* was, well, a thrill. It didn't necessarily mean she returned his interest.

Yet, if it helped seal the deal . . .

"Strip." Her eyes widened at the word coming out of her mouth, but it was too late to take it back.

Connor froze, then met her gaze. "Excuse me?"

"You heard me." She flipped open the button on her jacket and leaned back against the table, pushing her breasts a little higher by arching her back. Uncrossing her legs, she hitched one knee over the arm of the wrought-iron chair, praying she wasn't overexposing herself and playing the fool. "No one will see you." *Except me.* "It's really the only way to experience the feel of the pool and spa, by taking a dip au naturel."

He reached for the zipper on his shorts. "What about you?"

Shifting on the rough, all-weather fabric of the cushion, she couldn't resist running her fingers up the length of her exposed leg until she touched the dampness between her legs. "I believe I'll just watch."

He shucked off his shirt and unzipped his shorts as he stepped out of his flip-flops. "You like to watch?" he asked in a husky voice.

Her fingers stroked her aching folds, her heart pounding. She nodded.

His shorts and boxers fell around his ankles.

She made a slow visual journey up his toned legs, pausing at the sacks nesting easily by the most erect penis she'd ever remembered seeing. It seemed to pulse, its dark head shining in the lights of the pool.

When she could find her voice, she murmured, "Maybe you should take a dip in the pool to cool off, Junior."

"Join me."

Slowly, she shook her head, trailing a fingertip beneath the crotch of her panties, the feel of her excitement stealing her breath.

He stepped to the edge of the pool and looked back over his shoulder. "Okay. For now. But I like to watch, too."

He entered the water with barely a splash, slicing through it in sure, silent strokes.

It shouldn't have been so overwhelmingly sexy that it left her gasping for air, increasing the strokes along her slick folds.

He flipped to his back. The sight pushed her over the edge, nearly drowning her in the all-consuming pleasure of her self-induced climax.

His hands curved over the brick coping, then he hoisted up his lean, perfect body until he stood before her in all his sleek, naked perfection.

A thrill shot through her when he turned, and she saw the

swim had not cooled his lust. In fact, if anything, he looked even larger.

"Now it's your turn," he said in a low, dangerously sexy voice. "Strip for me, pretty lady."

She wouldn't consider it just because she was turned on. She wouldn't consider it just because Connor was the first man to sexually arouse her in a very long time. She wouldn't consider it just because she was almost desperate to make a sale.

But the total of all those things made an irresistible combination.

Slowly, she peeled off her jacket. The top and bra immediately followed.

She leaned back, eyes locked with his, while she squeezed her nipple with one hand and continued petting her clitoris through her wet panties with the other.

Connor made a sort of growling sound and took a step toward her, one hand extended.

"Come any closer," she warned, "and I'll put my clothes back on."

He stopped and dropped his hand. "Then take off the rest. I want to . . . see all of you."

She tsked and shook her head. "You're going to have to be more specific, Junior. I need to hear you say exactly what you want to see. And do." She spread her legs a little farther, pushing the scrap of fabric aside to tease them both. "Say it."

"Strip. I want you naked. I . . . I want to watch you pleasure yourself."

"Is that all you want?" Her fingers flicked her swollen folds. She bit back a moan.

"No. After you're done, I want to taste your pussy. I want to lick up your juices and suck your clit until you scream and come again."

"And then what?" She eased her skirt over her hips and then

shimmied out of her panties. Standing naked in her black stilettos, she kicked her clothing aside, then looked at him. "Don't you want me to touch you?"

"More than I want my next breath, darlin'." He walked to her, pushing her back into the chair, then arranging her legs on either arm. He gently dragged his fingers along the suddenly renewed moisture on her folds, then stepped back, pulling another chair until it faced her.

He sat down. "I like to watch, too."

Did she have the nerve to do it again? Then again, the idea excited her. Almost as much as the possibility of selling the house.

Money. The thought made her wet. She imagined rolling around naked in millions of dollars. Her hand stroked faster. Just the smell of money made her feel like coming. Money was power to a lot of people, but for her it was more. It was an aphrodisiac.

She peeked through heavy lids, her nipples tingling at the sight of Connor stroking his erect penis while he watched her masturbate. She licked her parched lips, wishing she could take a swipe of him. And she would. Soon.

Her breath hitched. Moisture drenched her hand as waves of pleasure washed over her.

When she could summon the strength to open her eyes, she watched Connor's strokes and the truth hit her. It wasn't pretty or even honorable. But it was the truth:

She would most definitely fuck for money.

# 6

Connor's legs wobbled, but he finally managed to navigate the steps into the hot, churning water of the spa. With a sigh, he sat on the slightly rough nonskid surface of the bench and waited for his heart rate to slow down before Andrea got into the water.

He'd about exploded watching her get off by herself, her engorged folds glistening in the indirect lights of the pool. He slapped a weak hand on the cool decking until he felt the edge of his cargo shorts and dragged them closer. It was imperative the condoms be close at hand.

Sure, he'd planned to finally get horizontal with Andrea back at his hotel, where there was a king-size bed and room service. But the spa proved too much of a temptation. It immediately became Plan B.

Andrea was still sprawled on the chair, her head thrown back, hedonistically basking in the afterglow.

He meant what he said earlier about wanting to taste her, suck her. But that would have to wait until he appeased the raging testosterone-crazed beast threatening to overtake him and make him the rutting animal his mother had always accused his father of being.

Raising a weak hand, he motioned to her. "C'mere, darlin'. I need you."

One of Andrea's eyes opened, and he held his breath, praying she wouldn't say something to ruin what could turn out to be a beautiful experience.

Instead, she stood and toed off her shoes before padding to the edge of the spa.

Through the steam, he could see she was smooth all over. What was it Whitley had called it? Not a bikini wax. Brazilian, that was it. He ran an appreciative hand over the smooth, soft skin as she lowered into the water. Oh, yeah, he definitely approved.

His hands shook so much it was difficult to roll the condom on, but he finally managed it.

He pulled her to him, covering her mouth in the most carnal kiss he'd ever given or received.

With their lips locked, he didn't pause to savor the feel of her smooth skin rubbing against his as he lifted her to straddle his hips. All it took was one good, strong flex and he was where he wanted to be. A part of him longed to take it slow and easy, drawing out each sexually anguished moment. But another part, the part screaming for release, promised to take it slower next time as his arms locked around her rib cage to begin a wild ride.

Warm water sloshed against his face and caressed his balls with each thrust. The roar in his ears drowned out the electric hum of the spa jets, the happy-sounding bubbles surrounding them.

Andrea's knees tightened against the sides of his chest. Her back arched. Had he not held her close, she'd have arched head-first back into the churning water as a low moan of satisfaction erupted from her throat, the tendons stretched taut.

His climax roared down on him, taking his breath while his heart threatened to rip from his chest.

Crushing her to him, heartbeat to heartbeat, he struggled to draw air into his starving lungs. His muscles vibrated, but he knew if he released her, he wouldn't have the strength to pull her up out of the water should she slide.

Andrea collapsed onto Connor's chest, her face buried in his neck while she greedily sucked in air along with the mouth-watering scent of the man she'd just seduced.

Sure, it had been an unbelievably unprofessional thing to do, but the climax she'd just experienced made it worthwhile. As her heart rate ceased its furious galloping, she frowned, trying to remember if she'd ever had an orgasm anywhere near the last one.

She hadn't. She was sure she'd have remembered something like that.

But now what? Did she simply slide off his still-impressive erection, get dressed, and continue the showing? Did she act as though they hadn't just shared mind-blowing sex? What exactly was the protocol? She stifled a laugh when she thought she could probably ask her lying scumbag ex-husband how he'd handled these types of situations.

She knew what she should probably do: turn Connor O'Brian over to one of her capable agents. But she also knew what she really wanted to do: slide right back into the spa and beg for more, which was totally ridiculous.

Andrea Redd never begged for anything. Or anyone.

Her back stiffened. "What was that? Did you hear something?"

Connor paused mid-nuzzling of her neck. "I'm not sure."

They didn't have to wait long. The chiming doorbell echoed in the empty house, its sound drifting out through the open patio doors.

"Oh, no!" Andrea scrambled off Connor's lap, all but leaping from the spa and skidding across the wet decking to grab her clothes.

He leaned against the spa, arms stretched along the tile, enjoying the view while he waited for his brain cells to reengage. Dang, the woman had a hot body. His cock twitched with renewed interest when she bent to pull her thong up over her wet legs. He wanted to say something, to tell her how special it had been or at least how great she was, but all he could manage to say was, "Don't bother putting them back on, darlin', 'cause I'll just take them off again as soon as I get my second wind."

A sarcastic comeback he could have taken. An incredulous laugh he could have taken. He could have even taken casual indifference.

But when she looked at him like he was something that just crawled out from under a rock, he found he couldn't take it.

"Don't even try to tell me you didn't enjoy what just happened," he warned, rising from the churning water and reaching for his shorts. "'Cause I'd just have to come over there and make a liar out of you."

He was right, of course, Andrea thought as a little thrill streaked through her at the prospect of exactly how he would accomplish such a task.

The doorbell chimed again, dousing any remaining embers of passion she may have been inclined to stoke.

Whoever was at the door was obviously not going away. Her car was in the driveway; they knew she was inside.

"For God's sake, Junior, get out of the damn spa and get dressed! Someone's at the door!"

Her train of thought was temporarily derailed as she watched him step into his shorts. If it wasn't for the very real possibility of being caught, she could think of several other ways to slake her lust with his willing young body.

He straightened and looked at her as though he could read her lecherous thoughts. "Now what?"

She straightened her suit and stepped into her shoes, taking a quick glance around the pool area to make sure they hadn't left any evidence of their tryst.

"Now we go back into the house and I answer the door." Thank goodness she hadn't replaced the key in the lockbox. If it was another Realtor at the door—which, in all probability, it was—they would have stumbled onto her and Connor's private sex show, quite possibly ruining her business.

"Should we turn off the spa?"

Shaking her head, she turned to take one last look before leaving the patio and winced. "No, but please dispose of the condom floating around in the middle."

Striding to the front door, she swallowed a groan. Even through the beveled glass, she easily recognized her rat-fink ex-husband.

Plastering on a smile that was more baring of teeth than a statement of pleasure, she swung open the door. "Rich! Fancy meeting you here. Unfortunately, I'm showing the property—"

"So that's why you didn't replace the key in the lockbox, huh?" Her ex swept past her, an older couple in his wake. "Please," he told the couple, "feel free to roam around, get a feel for the place. After all, if you act fast, it could be your new home!" He stepped close to Andrea and lowered his voice. "What the hell do you think you're doing? You have no right to hold the key, preventing me or anyone else from showing the property. I know you're probably desperate to make a sale, but this is low, even for you." He stopped and gave her a once-over. "How did you get all wet?"

"It was an oversight; I simply forgot to replace the key." Jaw clenched, she ignored his question about her suit while she looked over his shoulder for Connor. "If you'd kindly take your clients and wait on the patio for a few minutes, we'll be out of your way."

"No way. I know you. You're going to put pressure on your client to make an offer, which you will then run to the seller with before I can get anything in writing." He narrowed already-beady eyes. "You always were a conniving bitch—"

"Excuse me?" A familiar voice came from behind Rich. Andrea held her breath, hoping her ex didn't put two and two together when he saw the dampness clinging to Connor. Rich always had a sixth sense for sex. It was like he could smell it.

Rich turned. "Yeah? What?"

"I think you owe the lady an apology."

"Bullshit! I don't owe that cunt anything except a long hard—"

Connor's fist connected squarely with Rich's face, knocking him flat.

"Ow." Connor shook his hand, hopping from one foot to the other. "I had no idea it would hurt me, too."

"Good job, Junior. C'mon, let's get out of here before he wakes up."

Andrea concentrated on putting one foot in front of the other, then on fastening her seat belt and putting the car in gear.

It wasn't until she'd dropped Connor at his hotel and called Lisa to meet her for drinks that she allowed a smile to creep out as her mind replayed Connor knocking out Rich. Damn, she'd never had her very own knight in shining armor.

She liked it.

# 7

---

"A party spa," Andrea said an hour later as she took a sip of her margarita and leaned back in the pedicure chair. She looked over at Lisa. "Leave it to you to find something like this."

Lisa's nose wrinkled with her impish smile. "Isn't it TDF?"

"TDF?"

That earned an eye-roll. "Duh. To. Die. For."

"Nothing is worth dying for. Not even a spa that serves margaritas."

"You take things too seriously. Loosen up."

"You'd be amazed at how *loose* I've become of late." The thought of her *loose* activities that afternoon with Connor had her struggling to keep from squirming in the big chair. She took a long swallow of her margarita and must have breathed in because she choked.

"Drea, are you okay?" Lisa put down her own drink and reached over to thump her friend's back.

Andrea drew in a breath between gagging and coughing. "Yes," she sputtered, "just went down the wrong way."

After they'd settled back with their drinks, Lisa grinned over at her. "Okay, I'll bite. Exactly how loose have you been lately? What? Did you forget to enter something into your to-do list? I know! You didn't pick up your dry cleaning." She chuckled. "You rebel, you."

"Ah, no." Andrea waited until the manicurist finished laying the hot stones on her legs, covered them with a towel, and walked away before she answered. "Not even close," she whispered, then leaned a little closer. "I had sex."

Lisa rolled her eyes. "No offense, but I think you've done that a few times since I've known you. Although I did notice you have sort of a glow. What makes this different?" Her eyes widened. "No! You did not have sex with your newest client, Mr. O'Something?"

"You know perfectly well what his name is. O'Brian. Connor O'Brian."

"Yeah. Him. The old guy, right?" The twinkle in her eyes told Andrea her assistant also knew Connor was far from old.

"You knew he wasn't old, didn't you?"

Lisa took a swig of her drink and waved her hand negligently. "BFD. It's not like you're robbing the cradle or anything. I checked him out. You're not even five years older." She shrugged. "What harm did it do to let you think he was old for a while?"

"You have no idea."

"So." Lisa leaned across the space separating their chairs. "How was it? How was he? I saw his picture." She fanned her face with her newly manicured hand. "Whoa, baby. That's one showing I wouldn't have minded." She winked. "Not that I'd have *shown* him everything you did, boss."

Ignoring the innuendo, Andrea narrowed her eyes. "Where did you see a picture of Connor O'Brian?"

Lisa shrugged. "IDK. Maybe a magazine or something."

"A magazine or something. Right. Why do I think I was set

up?" She set her empty glass on the built-in tray on the arm of the chair and faced her friend. "You were the one who went over and turned on the spa at the Ocean Drive house, weren't you?"

"Hey, I was just trying to help. We both know property shows better when it's staged. Since the furniture is out, I thought the best selling point would be the pool area. So . . . did it work? Did he make an offer?"

"No. No offer. Not on the house, anyway." Connor's heated words, telling her exactly what he wanted to do to her, echoed through her mind, bringing a flush to her cheeks.

"Ooh! Do tell."

"There's nothing to tell, Lisa." She took a sip of her margarita. "Oh, get this! Rich just happened to come by to show the house while we were there. How's that for a coincidence?"

"Do you think it was a legit showing? Big brother has pulled stuff like that before."

Andrea thought for a moment. "You know, now that I think about it, the couple really wasn't the demographic for that kind of house." She grinned. "Now I'm really glad Connor decked him."

"RUK? He did that?" Lisa sighed and batted her eyelashes. "Our hero."

Trying to banish the same thought, Andrea raised her glass. "*Uno mas, por favor!*"

"Um, Drea? They're Vietnamese; it's doubtful they speak Spanish."

"Oh. I knew that." She ran her tongue around the edge of the empty glass, savoring every last taste. "But they still make a damn good margarita."

An older woman walked out with a sweating pitcher of margaritas, smiling and nodding.

Andrea and Lisa smiled and nodded back, holding out their glasses for a refill.

"So now what?" Lisa asked, settling back in the chair as she punched the massage controls.

"What do you mean?"

"Drea, it's a pretty simple question. Now that you've, you know, how do you plan to proceed? I mean, as the saying goes, once you've had sex, you can't go back to holding hands, if you know what I mean."

"No, I don't. Explain." Just the thought of having sex with Connor again brought a flush to her face that had very little to do with the margaritas. But maybe Lisa had a point. "Are you saying I should dump Connor as a client? Lisa, we need this sale, remember? I've already invested a lot of time, put in a lot of legwork."

Lisa snickered. "Not to mention other body parts."

"Very funny. I'm a professional. I can control myself and continue the agent/client relationship, following through to the sales contract."

Lisa sighed and set her glass aside. "Drea, I'm not questioning your professionalism or work ethic. We both know you excel in those areas." She shrugged. "I guess I'm just questioning your motive. Your true motive."

"I didn't have a motive. It just happened."

"BS. I've known you for ten years, and I have yet to see anything *just happen* with you. You plan every minute detail of your life. If this wasn't planned"—she held up her hand to stop Andrea's automatic protest—"and I believe you when you say it wasn't, I just have to question your subliminal motive."

"For the last time, I'm telling you, there was no motive! Subliminal or otherwise."

"Exactly." Lisa looked annoyingly smug. "I think there's more to it than hormones and opportunity. I think, on some level, quite possibly a primal one, you responded to whatever it is that's hardwired into Connor O'Brian's DNA."

"What! That's ridiculous. It was happenstance. Serendipity

maybe, even." Andrea paused, unable to control the warmth flooding through her at the thought of the *afternoon delight* she'd indulged in. But what Lisa was suggesting was preposterous, even for Lisa. "It was . . . I mean, it was just . . . well, unless I somehow thought it might sweeten the deal." Her mouth pulled down. "We see how well that worked."

Of course, though difficult to admit, she'd basically prostituted herself for the sake of making a sale; it was, in all probability, the essence of it. Would she do it again? Heated memories flashed through her. In a New York minute.

"Oh, give it up, Drea!" Lisa's voice brought her back to the conversation. "Admit it. It was to hell and gone more than casual sex."

# 8

---

Connor winced as he placed the ice bag on his bruised knuckles.

"Are you still there?" Bill's disembodied voice echoed in the hotel suite.

"Yeah. I just put fresh ice on my hand."

"Dude." Bill's laughter was in the word. "I still can't get my mind wrapped around you decking a guy. That's so un-Connor."

"Like I said, he had it coming. But the thing that gets me is it turned out he is the Realtor's ex-husband."

"Ouch. Bet that was awkward."

"You don't know the half of it." Damn. He wasn't the kind of guy to kiss and tell. Why couldn't he keep his big mouth shut?

Maybe Bill wouldn't notice.

"Oh, yeah? What's the Realtor look like? Is she hot? Hey! You two didn't . . . ?"

"Don't be a jerk. She's my Realtor, for cripes sake. I'd have reacted like that when any woman was treated that way." He flexed his aching hand, then had an immediate flashback to the way his hand had looked on Andrea Redd's porcelain skin.

And farther south. The image had his dick twitching, eager for more action.

No doubt about it, he needed to date more.

"Well, like I said, beware of a wolf in sheep's clothing. But, then again, maybe if she's hot and available, she might be persuaded to sweeten the deal a little. You know, you scratch her itch, she'll scratch yours? You're the efficiency expert. Think of it as multitasking!" Bill's laugh boomed from the walls of the empty sitting area.

"You're a real asshole, you know that?" Connor dropped the ice bag and walked to the speaker phone. "I'm starving. I need to order room service. Besides, this conversation is over." He pressed the OFF button, then stood staring at the phone.

What he'd told Bill was true. He really was hungry. But Bill had unknowingly planted the seed.

Had Andrea had sex with him simply to make a sale? More importantly, would she have done something like that?

Not that he really cared. Andrea Redd was not his type. If he had a type, which he did not. Not after his experience with Whitley. Maybe that was his initial attraction to Andrea, since she was definitely Whitley-esque. Maybe he needed to prove he'd moved on and was now immune to powerful women.

Then again, maybe he was an idiot, doomed to repeat past mistakes. After all, he'd never been the casual-sex, love-'em-and-leave-'em type of guy. It would make sense, in a perverse sort of way, that he'd read more into the encounter with his sexy Realtor than truly existed. Pathetic. That was him, lonely and pathetic—despite being touted as one of Houston's most eligible bachelors last year.

Change occurs only when the subject is open and conducive to it. A leopard may not be able to change its spots, but he could change the behavior that caused heartache by remaining detached. After all, sex was a physical response to stimuli. It was only natural for his response to be in direct correlation to Andrea's sexual aggression.

Still pathetic, but natural.

Appetite gone, he stripped on his way into the bathroom and stepped into the stinging hot shower, closing his eyes, willing images of Andrea's perfect, naked body from his mind.

His soapy hand slid to his more-than-semierect penis. Damn, he wished Andrea was here, wished it was her hand caressing him, stroking his balls.

His hips bucked at the thought, his erection jerking to attention.

He couldn't remember ever feeling the way he'd felt that afternoon. No woman had ever had the immediate effect on him that Andrea Redd had. Ever. The effect she obviously still had.

His breath hitched while his heart threatened to break out of his chest.

Just sex, just sex, just sex . . .

His climax came fast and hard, leaving his knees weak. He slid down the wall to sit on the floor of the huge shower. A shower obviously built with more than one occupant in mind. And he couldn't help but envision Andrea beside him, stroking him. Kissing him. Loving him.

Which was totally ridiculous. They'd had sex. End of story. Now it was his decision as to whether he continued looking at beach houses with her or switched Realtors. Or cut his losses and left the island entirely.

Regardless, one fact remained.

He was still alone.

Despite having world-class sex just a few hours earlier. Despite being pretty sure Andrea wouldn't be opposed to a replay. Or several repeat performances. Despite having just taken the edge off via masturbation.

He was not only alone, but he was also lonely.

# 9

Andrea willed away her tequila headache and glanced at her cell as she walked into the elevator of her office parking garage the next morning. No messages.

Like a fool, she'd slept with the damn phone on her nightstand, just in case. In case Connor O'Brian called. What was her problem? Was she reverting to junior high behavior?

It was stupid and asinine to mope around. She was a mover and a shaker. She didn't have time for . . . well, for relationships. Not that what she and Connor had shared was a relationship. Not that she'd want it to be. No, sir.

But the fact that she hadn't heard one word from him gave her pause. Had she just been a convenience? Had what they shared been merely a way for Connor O'Brian to get his jollies, relieve a little pressure?

She didn't want to believe it. She knew when a man was interested, and Connor O'Brian had been interested. More than interested.

The alternative was too humiliating to contemplate.

On the bright side, she noted, checking messages and e-mails at her desk, he hadn't canceled their morning appointment.

"Lisa." She leaned toward the edge of her desk, scanning her schedule. "Lisa!"

"I said what!" Lisa skidded to a stop just inside the door. "Must you yell like that?" She rubbed her furrowed brow. "One of us has the hangover from hell."

"I warned you about the Jello shots."

"Hey, they were free, since the bridal shower had canceled. No point in letting them go to waste. Anyway, you bellowed?"

"Yes. Did you put in the call for the limo for my morning appointment?" Thoughts of what she and Connor could do in the relative privacy of the back of the stretch limo owned by Redd Hot Properties had her all but squirming on the seat of the padded leather desk chair. Of course, it was only a fantasy. She knew better.

She hoped.

"IOI. Called after I got home last night. The driver will be here by nine." Lisa rubbed her forehead again. "If you don't need anything else, is it okay if I go home after you leave? I can switch the calls to my place."

"Hmm? Oh, sure. I just have the one client. Depending on how the showing goes, I may or may not make it back into the office today." Andrea stood and smoothed her black pencil skirt. She reached for the matching jacket, hanging on the visitor's chair. "If you don't want to be disturbed, just roll the phone over to the service and take the day off."

"OMG! You're not making a BFD about me leaving. You're planning something." Her eyes narrowed. "Spill."

"Words, Lisa, use words, please." Andrea paused by the brushed stainless framed mirror and checked her lip gloss. "And the only thing I'm planning is showing Mr. O'Brian some beach property in the hopes of finally getting him to commit to one."

She walked into the bathroom adjoining her office, discreetly closing the door.

"Maybe he'll commit to something else, something more, ah, personal!" Lisa's voice carried through the door.

"Don't be ridiculous." Andrea paused, then stepped out of her thong and stuffed it in her purse.

It had nothing to do with emotions. It had nothing to do with sex, even. She was determined to make a sale.

She had no intentions of having sex again in an attempt to sell a house. But she wasn't adverse to a little sexual teasing to get Connor's attention.

Hell, maybe if he thought they'd do it again, he'd be speedier about making a decision on a beach house.

And once he'd signed on the dotted line . . . Well, she wasn't adverse to letting nature take its course.

Assuming his funding was in order, of course.

# 10

---

Connor shifted from one sandaled foot to the other, squinting in the sunshine while he waited. Andrea Redd's assistant had called earlier to tell him a Redd Hot Property limousine would be picking him up for today's excursion. He wondered if Andrea would be in the limo or if she'd chicken out and turn him over to another Realtor.

He also wondered how he'd feel about that.

The sleek limo, its navy paint sparkling in the morning sun, glided to the curb. REDD HOT PROPERTIES INC. was discreetly lettered in silver paint on the door.

Connor bit back a grin when a man no older than twenty hopped from the driver's side and scurried around to open the rear passenger door. The driver wore a purple and green tropical-print shirt, baggy cargo shorts not dissimilar to Connor's own, and purple rubber flip-flops.

"Good morning, Mr. O'Brian?"

Connor nodded as he sauntered to the curb.

"I'm Cody. I'll be your driver today. Ms. Redd is already in the car."

"Great." He returned Cody's smile. "Let's rock and roll, Cody."

The cool interior and the smell of Andrea's perfume wrapped around him the second he stepped into the car. Although only twinkling lights lit the perimeter of the seating area, he saw her immediately.

And, even though he'd sworn today's outing would be strictly business, he wanted her.

Not good.

He slid onto a side seat, ignoring the long bench at the back where there would be plenty of room to sit next to his Realtor. Plenty of room to stretch out on the long, black leather seat. Plenty of room to do any one of the myriad sexy things popping into his fevered brain.

She motioned with the fluted glass in her long-fingered hand. "There's a carafe of mimosas in the bar. Pour yourself a drink. I thought we'd go over our itinerary for today, along the way to our first showing." She was quiet while he poured his drink, then patted the seat next to her. "Come here, Junior. It will be easier for you to see the pictures."

"No, thanks, I want to be surprised." He gave a tight smile and leaned back, his arm along the back of the plush seat in an effort to look relaxed.

Her eyes widened along with her smile. "Fine with me. It gives me more room to stretch out." She kicked off one high-heeled shoe and turned, propping her bare foot on the seat, her skirt riding up her slender leg.

Connor held his glass in a death grip. He knew he should avert his eyes, but they seemed to have a will of their own. And they insisted on feasting on the erotic sight before them.

Andrea gave a knowing smile and leaned back a little more, the action causing the smooth lips between her legs to part ever so slightly, beckoning him.

Connor gulped back the rest of his drink and sloshed some on his hand in his haste to pour another.

His gaze darted back to the luscious skin beneath Andrea's skirt. Swallowing, he grabbed a piece of ice from the bin in the bar and ran it along his forehead.

Good Lord, he was a dead man.

"It's okay," she said in a soft voice.

His gaze flew to hers.

She pointed downward, then stroked the spot he'd been desperately trying to ignore.

"It's okay to look." She canted her hips for his viewing pleasure. "Or touch." She dipped her index finger into her mimosa, then dragged it along the plump lips begging for his attention. "Or even taste," she finished on a whisper.

Tempting. To say her offer tempted him was a gross understatement.

The question was, did he have the strength or willpower to resist what she was offering? Did he even want to resist?

"I know you're interested." He followed her gaze to the pup tent in the front of his shorts. "I know you enjoyed what happened yesterday just as much as I did." She spread her legs as much as her skirt would allow, unapologetically stroking her moist core. "C'mon, let's play a little before we get down to business."

His Realtor disappeared. In her place sat a siren, offering him solace. Offering him sex. Her musky scent filled his nostrils, intoxicating him more than his recently ingested drink.

His mouth watered.

He slid from the seat to his knees on the carpeted floor, then slowly made his way to the back of the limo.

Andrea swallowed, holding still when all she wanted to do was squirm to ease the ache between her legs. An ache, miraculously, only Connor O'Brian seemed able to appease. Finally—

finally!—he was close. Close enough for her to feel his hot breath on her engorged labia.

It made her impossibly wetter.

She wanted to tell him to take her, suck her, do whatever he wanted to do to her as long as he did something besides look at her.

But a part of her resisted, wanted to prolong the sexual stimulus of being so close to getting satisfaction. Just the thought of what might happen had her poised on the brink of an orgasm.

Beneath her silk tank, her breasts ached for his touch, her nipples drawn into hard, stiff peaks of anticipation. She wanted to flick open her jacket to show him she was braless. To show him how her body reacted to his nearness.

But she didn't want to appear too eager, too needy. Power was the name of every game, and sex was the ultimate power game.

It was imperative she remain the one in control.

She dipped a shaking finger into her mimosa and again painted her swollen labia. "Taste me," she demanded, even though her voice cracked a little.

His green eyes met hers a moment before dropping to look beneath her skirt.

The air in the back of the limo seemed stifling. Her heartbeat echoed in her ears. A quick glance confirmed they were still hidden by the privacy screen. As discreetly as possible, she slowly reached until she could flip the lock, preventing Cody from interrupting them.

She bit back a groan at the feel of Connor's hot hands easing up her legs, pushing her skirt higher and higher until it bunched around her waist.

He skimmed his hands up and down her inner thighs once, twice, three times.

She clamped her mouth shut to prevent herself from demanding he give her some much-needed satisfaction.

Just when she thought she might scream her frustration, he nipped her clitoris with his teeth.

Her breath hitched.

He closed his lips over the nub, sucking it deeply into the wet heat of his mouth, his tongue swirling in maddening circles.

Her hips arched off the seat. She dug in her heels, clutching his head close, gritting her teeth and clenching her eyes shut in her effort to breathe and stave off the impending climax rushing toward her.

She might have succeeded had he not chosen that moment to slip one hand under her top, squeezing the hardened tip of her nipple at the same time his other hand slipped a finger into her.

What was a girl to do, faced with such a delicious onslaught of sensations?

Arching off the seat, anchored only by his hands, a guttural sound filled the back of the limo—it took a second to realize it had come from her. Nipples at attention and puckered in painful points, her uterus contracted violently, sending wave after wave of pleasure washing through her.

When her heart resumed beating, she opened her eyes. Connor was still on his knees, his hand still between her legs, his fingers still deeply embedded. Eyes bright, he moved his thumb, brushing her swollen, still-aching nub with the pad while staring into her eyes.

"Thank you," he whispered. His hand beneath her tank top resumed its petting of her breasts, his other hand still busy.

*Thank you,* she wanted to say, but her throat still refused to obey her commands for speech.

She tried to back away from the mesmerizing stroking of his hands but found her muscles too weak at the moment.

"Ms. Redd?" Cody's voice echoed through the car from the speaker.

She had to clear her throat twice but finally managed to answer. "Yes?"

"The first property is up ahead on the right."

"Thanks, Cody." She shoved her skirt down reasonably in place and then looked at Connor, who had taken a hand towel from the bar and was mopping up the evidence of her orgasm.

Cheeks flaming, she silently cursed her stupid decision to go pantyless. Whatever had she been thinking?

Connor reclaimed his seat perpendicular from hers as he made a quick adjustment.

By the time Cody rolled to a stop and threw open their door, all was in order.

"I'll buzz you when we're ready to be picked up," she told her driver as he helped her from the car.

"I can wait, ma'am, since I'm yours for the day."

"That's not necessary. Really." Her spine stiffened. Was that a smothered laugh she heard from Connor? She leaned closer to the chauffeur and lowered her voice. "Some clients have a problem relaxing and telling me what they really think of a property when there is someone waiting."

"Ah." Cody nodded and stepped back. "I understand. I'll just go get a coffee and wait for your call. 'Bye."

Connor stared up the steep circular drive at the red-tiled stucco monstrosity. "This house may be more than I need."

With a sigh, Andrea put her fists on her hips and glared at him. "How do you know? You haven't even seen the interior yet."

"True." He held out his arm. "Let's go check it out."

"I didn't mean to snap at you," she mumbled as they made their way up the drive.

"I know. Now tell me about this house."

"It's new, recently constructed, Energy Star rated. The floors are pretty much bare still. The builder is waiting for the buyer to pick out the materials." Bending to swipe her card in the reader, she waited for the key fob to dispense, then opened the beveled glass front door. "Any fixture or appliances you don't like can be switched out."

"I understand all that, but I'd kind of hoped to at least see a furnished model." At her quick glance, he said, "You know, to get an idea of how furniture will fit in here." He shrugged. "I'm sort of a visual, hands-on kind of guy."

The massive dusty cement entry opened up to a great room and an open-concept kitchen.

"No formal dining room?" He flipped the lever to turn on a stream of water in the kitchen sink. "Plumbing works."

In answer, she sighed and walked to a door at the end of the kitchen, opening it as she spoke. "There is a very nice walk-in pantry."

"But no formal living or dining room."

The pantry door slammed shut. "No! There is no formal anything. This is a beach house, Junior. What you professed to want, remember? *Beach house* denotes casual living."

He watched her chew on her lower lip. "What's really the problem, Miz Redd? I'd think maybe you didn't get enough sleep and it made you cranky, but you probably slept as much as me." He advanced, backing her against the snack bar. "You know what I think?"

Instead of answering, she glared some more and slowly shook her head.

"I think," he said, pinning her with his eager body, "you're afraid to be alone with me in this big ole house. Afraid you might not be able to control yourself and will rip my clothes off and have your wicked way with me again."

Her mouth fell open, but she recovered fast. "Is that the way you remember it? At the very least," she continued when he nodded, "it was a mutual thing. Something, by the way, I've never done."

His eyebrows rose. "Never? Huh. I didn't think you were a virgin yesterday."

"Don't be ridiculous!" She slapped at his hand, which was toying with her nipple, making it harden through her shirt. "I meant I had never, um, done something like that with a client." Her cool blue gaze met his. "It was inappropriate."

"Mmm-hmm." He trailed kisses down the sweet-smelling side of her neck, bumping his erection against her hips.

"Unprofessional," she whispered, arching her neck, her hands stroking his back beneath his shirt. "Unethical."

His mouth covered hers. Hearing how wrong it was to do what they'd done or what he planned to do again was not on his agenda.

Breaking the kiss, he lifted her to sit on the edge of the dusty granite counter and stepped between her legs. "Let's do it again," he said as he swooped back in for another taste of her tempting, lying mouth.

A little whimper escaped her as she pulled him tighter to her, the pointy heels of her shoes gouging his backside.

He reacted like a stallion that was being spurred into action. Sheathing himself at the speed of lust, he pulled her closer to the edge, flexed his hips, and impaled her.

They both groaned.

# 11

Andrea bit Connor's earlobe and tightened her grip as his lean hips slammed against hers, his penis buried deep within her aching body.

They could get caught. She didn't care.

She could lose her license. She didn't care.

She could lose the sale. Damned if she'd let that happen. She didn't care if she had to screw the guy 24-7, he would buy a damn house from her. Even if it meant she had to wear him down to do it.

Taking off her panties before picking Connor up had been an impulse. She'd had no intention of a replay of the day before. Well, okay, maybe some small part of her had hoped for it. She was only human. Sex of any kind was a distant memory. Sex like she'd experienced with Connor fell into a whole other category from anything she'd done before. She'd be a fool not to want it again. And again. For as long as it lasted. Hell, he was going to be in town for only a few days, a week at the most. If she were a man having sex with a willing female client, people would look the other way. People had, when she and Rich were married.

The way she saw it, if she was an equal in business, why not also in pleasure?

True, Connor was not only a client, but he was also significantly younger. It's not as though she thought it was love or even a lasting, potential long-term affair. She saw it for what it was: mutual gratification. A means to an end. Nothing more.

The last thought fled in the face of her climax rushing toward her, drowning her in such bliss, she wouldn't have been surprised to find herself floating above the granite countertop had she not been anchored by Connor's strong arms.

"Wait," she said on a breath. "More." She leaned back on her hands, not caring about the dusty surface, offering her now-bared breasts.

He sucked voraciously, continuing until she grew wet and slippery where they were still joined.

"More," she whispered again. "There's more house to, ah, see."

He wrapped an arm around her waist and lifted her from the counter, still embedded deep within her aching body. "Which way?"

*Any way you want, big guy,* she thought, then realized he was asking for directions for their house tour. Gyrating against his sweat-slicked skin, she pointed in the general direction of the master suite.

One second, lovely fantasies were flitting through her mind of exactly how she was going to show him the features of the house. The next second, he stumbled. They landed with a lung-squeezing thud on the paper-covered hardwood floor of the great room.

"Crap! I'm such a clod!" Connor's voice wheezed in her ear.

His teeth nipped the tendon along her neck, making her wetter. "Are you okay?"

All she could do was nod, thrilled to realize not only was it true, but also miraculously they were still joined. She gave an experimental gyration of her hips.

Connor groaned and flexed, driving deeper.

"What happened?" Not that she really cared, not when he was plunging in and out of her with such slow, deliberate and delicious movements. She loved the firm heat alternately filling and pulling out of her, the feel of his skin rubbing against hers. . . .

Her body relaxed for the first time in a long time while she allowed her hips to rise and fall in cadence with his, her breathing synchronized with each breath that ruffled the hair by her ear.

Adrift in sexual satiation, she was surprised when the first ripples of another climax began to tickle deep within.

Connor must have picked up on the clamping of her inner muscles, because he increased his tempo. What had been slow and easy, almost lazy movements picked up in speed to become hard, aggressive thrusts. Thrusts that drove her bare bottom along the dusty paper and pushed her hip bones against the hard flooring.

Breathing became heavier, then shallow pants, puffing in and out in time with each powerful surge of Connor's hips as he pounded into her eager, receptive body.

They reached the climax together. Her breath caught. Connor let out a sound somewhere between a growl and a roar of completion. He collapsed. Their hearts slammed against each other through their skin and ribs.

Connor wanted to speak, to tell her how special it was, how no woman had moved him the way she moved him. She touched him.

He paused, his breath lodged. What they'd shared went beyond sex. Did she feel it, too?

"Move," she said against his ear. "I can't breathe."

He adjusted his position but was determined to stay in their intimate alignment for as long as possible.

Beneath him, she shifted. "How did we end up down here?"

Embarrassment heated his ears. "I forgot to step out of my shorts. I tripped."

He braced, waiting for her to laugh at him or, worse, call him *Junior* again. With his penis still buried deep within her honeyed warmth, he didn't know if he could take it.

"Are you hurt?" She sounded genuinely concerned.

"No, just uncoordinated."

Her chuckle did funny things to his still-interested member.

"Your coordination seemed just fine to me." She smoothed her hand over his buttocks. "But maybe we should go get cleaned up and check everything out, just to make sure." The tip of her tongue traced the shell of his ear, making his whole body tingle. She lowered her voice to a husky whisper. "The bathroom is that way, Junior. Let me kiss it and make it all better."

Wiggling downward, she closed her teeth around one of his nipples.

Suddenly it didn't matter if she called him Junior.

# 12

Connor relaxed against the edge of the whirlpool tub and watched Andrea kiss and lick his eager cock. Oh, yeah, no doubt about it, he'd never been shown a house in quite that way.

He liked it.

But a part of him struggled to push aside the niggling doubts about her motive. He knew he wasn't the kind of guy women fell all over. Not even close. His was the kind of personality that had to grow on people. For that reason, he had difficulty finding and maintaining friendships. And personal relationships were even more difficult.

Was it unusual for a woman like Andrea Redd to fall into bed with a guy like him? Damn straight. But, as his grandmother used to say, every once in a while, even a blind squirrel finds an acorn. Regardless of the reason, at the risk of mixing metaphors, he wasn't about to look a gift horse in the mouth.

True, he'd never indulged in casual sex. But there was a first time for everything, and that didn't mean he couldn't enjoy it.

If he could just turn off his suspicious brain and stop remembering Bill's comment about the possibility of Andrea being a wolf in sheep's clothing. What did Bill know, anyway? It's not like his friend had been any more successful in personal relationships than Connor.

"Junior?" Andrea's husky voice brought him back to his current activity. She looked up at him with a look that told him she'd just spoken, while he had been arguing with his too-logical brain.

"Hmm?" He licked suddenly dry lips.

"Where were you? I don't like to play alone. If you're not interested . . ." She began to rise from the churning water.

"No! Wait!" He reached out, trailing his index finger down her perfect breast until he touched the pebbled tip. "I'm sorry. Please. Come back."

"Make me," she challenged. "I dare you."

"Okay, I'll take that challenge." He slid his arms around her, tugging her down, closer, until he held her flush against his excited body, his hands palming the firm smoothness of her buttocks. "I tell you what. I'll make you a deal. I bet I can make you come without touching you. And I can do it in under five minutes."

Leaning back to look him in the eye, she smiled. "You seem awfully confident, Junior."

"And stop calling me Junior," he said, kneading her ass, the movement causing her to rub against him in a very pleasant manner. "You have to play nice and give me a chance."

In answer, she wiggled against him, rubbing her smooth folds against his erection. "The clock is ticking. Go for it."

Flipping her until her back was against the end of the tub, he moved to one side, placing one of her long legs along the edge of the tub and the other resting on his shoulder. "Relax." His hands stroked up and down her inner thighs once, twice, three times, until he felt her muscles soften against his palms.

They watched as the jets fluttered her swollen labia.

It was very erotic, but Andrea still craved the touch of a

man's hand—Connor's hand, to be specific—and, later, other male body parts to sufficiently get off.

"Connor, this is all very nice and interesting, in a bizarre kind of way, but I—oh! Ah-ah-aah!" Back arched, her nipples tightened into painful points while the powerful jets pulled every last shuddering ripple of her climax from her.

She slid bonelessly down, her head held above water by Connor's strong arms.

Effortlessly, he turned her until she was straddling his hips, the tip of his erection probing her vibrating flesh.

"What do I win?" His hot breath fluttered the damp hair by her ear as he pushed into her, immediately setting the pace.

"How about a deal on this house?" She was only half kidding but laughed along with him, enjoying the pleasant warmth filling her with each thrust of his hips.

Too bad the house was unfurnished. She must be getting old. She could really use a nap.

Remarkably, she felt revived after their bath. So much so, in fact, she managed multiple orgasms in the rest of the rooms of the beach house. A few times were even with Connor. Good grief, was she experiencing hormone surges? She truly couldn't remember being so horny, so responsive. Ever. Well, certainly not in the last few years, for sure.

Was it her partner, or would any penis have done the trick?

She bit back a smile as she watched him bury their condoms in the flower bed by the pool. Such a gentleman. It was very sweet of him to be concerned about her reputation. Her breath caught as she watched him rinse his hands in the pool and dry them on the legs of his cargo shorts. Remembering how his hands had felt as they'd explored every inch of her body, she clamped her thighs together in an effort to staunch the moisture.

No, she was pretty sure only Connor O'Brian could elicit

the kind of mind-blowing orgasms she'd experienced. The kind she wanted to continue experiencing for as long as possible.

Because of that, it was difficult to be disappointed by his lack of decision about a house.

Her nipples tingled at the prospect of future orgasms as she continued showing him property.

Hey, it was only fair. She deserved something for her time. Why not enjoy whatever she could get?

"Are you ready to look at another house?" Damn, her voice sounded eager.

He shook his head, and she tamped down her disappointment, schooling her features.

"No, it's getting too dark. Unless the other places have lights?"

"No, they're all empty. Unless you'd like to see an older listing, not on the waterway?"

"Now, Andrea, I told you how I feel about that." He slipped his arm around her shoulders and guided her back into the house, giving her shoulders a quick squeeze. "Besides, I'm hungry. How about room service back at my hotel?"

Ordinarily, she'd hesitate. After all, she'd stepped out of the parameter of propriety. She shouldn't compound it by going back to his hotel room with him.

Then again, she wanted to spend more time with him. She wanted more sex with him.

She wanted to make a sale.

She wanted it bad.

# 13

Connor glanced at the clock by the sofa in his hotel room and frowned. The room service he'd ordered would be there any minute. Where was Andrea?

Although she'd hesitated, she hadn't seemed reluctant at the idea of spending more time with him. He'd assumed that would include more sex.

He couldn't wipe off the smile the thought elicited. He loved having sex with Andrea. The possibility of having it without the specter of house hunting attached could only be a plus. Enjoying harmless foreplay and the inevitable sex in the privacy of his hotel suite made the idea that much sweeter.

"C'mon, Andrea, where are you?" He checked his watch against the clock. The time was identical.

Andrea ignored the flush of sexual excitement as she folded the barely-there nightgown and tucked it into the bottom of her briefcase, along with her toothbrush and panties.

She didn't plan to spend the night with Connor, but if the opportunity presented itself, she wouldn't turn him down.

Besides, it would give her more time to get his signature on the contracts she'd had made up and also tucked into her brief-case. He'd seen several properties, along with two distinct pos-sibilities. If he decided he wanted to make an offer, she wasn't about to be unprepared.

Pressing the TALK button on her phone, she said, "I'm ready. Bring the car around." Maybe taking the limo to the hotel was presumptuous, but it made more sense than worrying about where to park her car, should she end up spending the night.

Spending the night.

The thought gave her pause. She'd never stooped to having sex with a client to get a sale but found it had been quite easy.

After all they'd shared, sharing a bed for the night would be the logical chain of events in a normal dating type situation.

But they weren't dating.

And, because they weren't dating, weren't really involved, except sexually, it made perfect sense to take the contracts along with her.

It never hurt to be prepared.

And speaking of being prepared . . . She glanced at the bag of sex toys Lisa shoved into her hand that morning. Did she dare take them to the hotel? What would Connor think?

Then again, maybe it would sweeten the deal.

She tamped down the niggling guilt. Men could copulate and conquer. They were heroes for it, while women who did it were entirely different.

But she'd always enjoyed being different. While other little girls were playing house, she played office. While they dreamed of a family and white-picket fences, she'd dreamed of corner offices and limousines. She had more than a corner office now. She had two limousines. Yet the burning desire to excel re-mained. Like something was missing.

Shoving the bag into her now-bulging briefcase, she strode

to the door to meet the waiting limo, determined to stop thinking and just do and enjoy.

Andrea swept into Connor's hotel room like she was storming a boardroom, briefcase in hand.

"You brought your briefcase?" He tried not to sound disappointed, but damn! The woman had spread her legs for him just hours ago and helped him christen every room of the house he'd seen. "I thought we were going to have dinner and relax, not do business."

With a secret smile, she strolled back to him, pushing the open door shut. The pink dress she wore was sexy as hell. Reminding him of cotton candy, it made his mouth water. His whole body reacted to her nearness.

She sidled up to him, backing him against the closed door. "Hi," she whispered, taking his glasses and laying them on the built-in entertainment center, then covered his mouth with her glossed lips.

Even her lip gloss tasted sweet, he thought, returning her kiss. His tongue swept her mouth.

Her body became pliant, melting against him, while she sucked his tongue. Her leg hitched over his, pulling her up and closer against his arousal, aligning their bodies.

Panting, she broke the kiss, leaning back in his arms. "Did you order dinner?"

"Yeah. It will be delivered in about an hour." Good thing he'd called and changed delivery times.

Grinning, she tugged on his waistband, pulling him with her as she walked to her briefcase. "I brought entertainment."

"That's not necessary. I can get Pay-Per-View or—"

"Hush." Her hand over his mouth stopped him. "Not that kind of entertainment, Junior." She dug around in a paper bag, then stuck something in the pocket of her dress. She pulled out three little jars and two paintbrushes. "For dessert," she explained. He must have looked as confused as he felt, because she laughed and said, "It's edible body frosting."

His cock tented his shorts, evidently liking the idea.

"What else do you have in that bag?" He leaned over her shoulder, discreetly inhaling her flowery fragrance.

"Flavored lubricants," she said with a smile, "and a small assortment of, um, personal vibrators." She shrugged. "And a few other things I have no idea what they are or how to use them. Maybe we could figure them out together?"

He growled and pushed her hand against his erection. "I don't think you'll be needing any more personal vibrators than the one I have right here."

Laughing, she gave a light squeeze. "Oh, really, big boy? Bring it on."

With that, she dipped her hand into his pants, closing her fist around his eager cock, her thumb grazing back and forth over its head. Her other hand shoved his shorts and boxers to his ankles.

While he stood with his family jewels hanging out, she laughed again and straightened. She untied the sheer pink shoulder straps, letting her dress fall to her waist. She wasn't wearing a bra, which thrilled little Connor. Big Connor was pretty pleasantly surprised as well.

Wiggling, she pushed her dress over her hips and stepped out, laying it on the arm of the sofa. "I don't want to get any frosting on it," she explained.

"Oh, well, then, you should probably take off your panties, too." He pulled his shirt over his head and grinned when he saw she'd already divested herself of her underwear.

Shaking a small can, she advanced on him. Her warm mouth kissed his lips, his throat, his chest. She dropped to her knees, working her way down his body with light, teasing kisses.

His breath caught when she ran the tip of her tongue over the head of his penis.

Eyes bright, she grinned up at him, then liberally squirted a pink-whipped-cream-looking substance from the base of his penis to its head and then proceeded to lick it off.

He locked his knees to remain upright, his eyes glued to the erotic scene of the sexiest woman on Earth on her knees pleasuring him with her mouth.

"Mmm," she said as she licked the last remnants from his erection. "More." She squirted again, covering the head of his penis, then swirling it around and over her nipples, spreading the sweet-smelling goo.

Muscles vibrating, he thrust his slick cock between her breasts, reveling in the feel of slippery skin against slippery skin. Just as his tempo increased, the muscles in the backs of his legs tightening, she stopped and stood up.

"Your turn." She made elaborate flowerettes of the whipped stuff on each breast before offering them up to his nearly drooling mouth.

Cherries. The stuff tasted like silky cherries, warming his lips as they closed over her breast. While he sucked and licked every bit of the fluffy concoction from her, she moaned, leaning into him, rubbing her moisture against his thigh.

Suddenly, cool air surrounded him.

Andrea walked back to her bag of tricks and pulled out a little vial. It looked a little like perfume when she tilted it and dripped a few drops onto her fingers.

The smell of pineapple filled the sitting area.

Her hand skimmed down her body, leaving an oily trail, before she palmed her folds, slicking them with the scented oil.

Not waiting for an invitation, he dropped to his knees in front of her, burying his face between her legs, inhaling the sweet scent as his tongue delved into her folds for a taste.

Her thigh muscles vibrated against his ears. She moaned when he smoothed his hand around her slick cheeks, probing her with his fingers until she tilted her hips for greater access.

Her excitement filled his mouth, sweetening the pineapple flavor of the oil. She stumbled back but he caught her, laying her against the sofa cushions, her legs spread wide, her feet resting against the legs of the coffee table while he continued to feast.

She whimpered as more moisture surged and tried to shove him away. He easily pushed her hands away, delving deep with his tongue to drink the last of her nectar.

Their labored breathing echoed from the walls. He sat back on his heels, unable to look away from the glistening folds.

Slowly, as though waking from a sated dream, she sat up and smiled.

At that moment, realization hit him squarely between the eyes. He loved her.

# 14

---

"What's wrong?" Her smile slid from her face. "Connor? Are you okay?"

"Hmm? Oh, yeah." He dragged his finger along her moist folds, eliciting another moan from Andrea. "Just thinking that was a hell of an appetizer."

Grinning, she slid from the couch to kneel between his spread legs, gripping his still rock-hard erection. "How about a second helping?" She drew the head of his penis around and up and down her slickness, causing his hips to buck, seeking more.

Getting her feet under her, she raised herself until she was able to tease his tip with her hot opening, going around and around, dipping just barely into her wet heat, then withdrawing.

When he began to flex again, pulling her closer, her hand against his abdomen held him away from fully entering her.

"Hold that thought. We need a condom."

*Knock. Knock. Knock.* "Room service."

Connor closed his eyes and took a deep breath.

When he reopened them, Andrea was on her knees, facing him and smiling. She gripped his penis, outlining her opening with its head, then stood up and grabbed her dress. "More later, Junior. Grab your shorts and answer the door while I make myself presentable."

Connor never realized how difficult it was to don a pair of shorts with a monster hard-on. He kicked his boxers under the couch and headed for the door, pulling his shirt on along the way.

By the time the bellman set up their dinner and left, Andrea strolled back into the room.

"Yum! Crab. Love it." She looked back down at her dress. "But, again, I'd hate to ruin my dress. . . ."

Connor nodded, unable to keep the smile from his face. "Yeah, it would be a shame to get butter on it. Guess you're just going to have to eat naked." Sighing, he untied the shoulder straps, baring her to the waist before tugging the dress down her legs. He met her wide-eyed gaze and winked. "Good thing you didn't bother putting your underwear back on."

After slaking their hunger for crab, they slaked a different hunger, dipping bits of crab into the drawn butter and painting each other, then licking it off.

Surprised to find the crab gone and more than a little turned on, Connor grinned at Andrea. "We're a mess." He swung her slippery, naked body into his arms. "Let's take a shower—or would you prefer another whirlpool bath?"

Her head lolled against his shoulder. "I'm not sure I have the strength for either."

"Don't worry. I'll handle it." He waggled his eyebrows as he balanced her on his hip to turn on the water to fill the two-person tub.

It took some doing, being so slippery from the oils and butter, but they finally were immersed in the tub. Connor pushed the button to start the jets and reached for a little bottle of bath gel.

He squinted at the label. "It's kind of hard to read without my glasses, but I think it says this is energizing. Citrus and something else." He shrugged and dumped a glob into his hand.

Rubbing his hands together, he gave what he hoped was an evil-seducer laugh. "C'mon over here, sweet thing. Let me make it all better."

If it got any better, she thought, she'd faint dead away. Still, she rallied, feeling a little glimmer of interest when his soap-slicked hands covered her suddenly aching breasts and began massaging them.

Head against the edge of the tub, she closed her eyes, savoring the feel of his hands on her needy body. If their time was drawing to a close, she wanted to bask in every touch, every moment she had left.

Connor's touch became more intimate, his fingers gliding into her while he petted her clitoris beneath the hot, churning water.

A smile curved her lips as she opened one eye.

He smiled back and shrugged, causing water to slosh over her breasts in an interesting manner.

Her climax took her by surprise, washing over her, leaving her wrung out and ready for a nap.

But Connor was having none of that. His hands gripped her beneath the arms and lifted her until she straddled his hips.

The tip of his penis probed her opening. She sighed, allowing him to lower her a millimeter at a time. Just when she'd have taken him completely into her body, she stiffened her arms, raising up until only the very tip of his erection stayed inside.

His thumbs massaged her puckered nipples. He leaned forward to nibble the edge of her lips.

"C-ondom," she finally managed to choke out around the lump of arousal caught in her throat.

"Taken care of," he said against her mouth. "While you had your eyes closed."

Somehow she knew he wouldn't lie to her. But she checked, anyway.

He told the truth.

Relaxing against his shoulder, she rode him, allowing him total control. She'd come more times in one night than she'd done in the past year. She could afford to let him get off any way he wanted. And it wasn't unpleasant, the feel of warm water and warmer male flesh surging in and out of her sated body.

In fact, she could get used to it.

Her eyes flew open. What was she thinking? Sex was great, especially with Connor, and she'd always be grateful to him for awakening her hormones—even if it was their swan song. But to think about doing this on a regular basis was nuts.

Especially the idea of doing it with anyone other than Connor O'Brian.

Intent on her thoughts, she didn't notice the telltale quickening of her pulse, the inner clampings, until they were upon her. Her back arched as all her internal muscles contracted. The wave washed over her, nearly drowning her in her pleasure.

Connor came in the next heartbeat, clutching her limp body to him as he roared his completion.

When their breathing had settled somewhere near normal, Connor lifted her from the tub and gently dried her. He carried her to the bed, where he stroked lotion over every inch of her limp body. She didn't care if it was the same energizing fragrance as the bath gel. Her body couldn't rally from the last orgasm yet.

He pulled the sheet over her naked body. The rumble of his voice told her he spoke, but her brain was already so sleep-fogged she couldn't make out the words.

Equally naked, he crawled into bed and pulled her close to his heat as he settled the covers over them.

The sexy nightgown in her briefcase crossed her mind, but

she didn't have the strength to get up and put it on. She'd just rest for a little while, then go get the gown and contracts and seduce Connor until he signed one of them.

She frowned and snuggled closer, breathing in his scent. She wasn't being deceitful. She was being a shrewd businesswoman.

After she'd had a little rest, she'd feel less guilty, less vulnerable.

Less like believing the terrifying possibility she might be falling in love.

# 15

Connor woke alone. The warmth of the sheets next to him said Andrea must have just gotten up. He squinted at the digital clock. Four o'clock. Surely she wasn't thinking about going home at this hour. "Andrea?"

The bathroom door opened, framing her in the light. He felt around on the nightstand for his glasses, blinking as the sexy vision came into focus.

She stood with one leg cocked, her arm outstretched on the door frame. Light from the bathroom spilled through her ultra-sheer, next-to-nothing nightgown. It was so short that he thought maybe it was the top to a pair of pajamas. Very sheer, very sexy pajamas, of course.

The light went out, and it took a second for his eyes to adjust.

The mattress dipped. He immediately reached for her, getting his hands caught in the sheer fabric surrounding the body he craved.

"Very pretty," he said against her lips. "Take it off."

Immediately, she rose to her knees to draw the sheer fabric from her body and toss it aside.

He ran his hand up her leg to her hip. "Get rid of the panties, too."

"Can't," she whispered.

"What do you mean you can't?" He tugged them down a fraction.

She pulled away, pulling them back into place. "They're your dessert."

"My what?"

Cool air flowed around him as she flipped back the covers. She lay spread eagle on the white sheets, naked except for a very small thong.

"Your dessert. Remember? I told you I brought dessert. Go ahead. They're edible."

Instantly aroused, he crawled between her legs and gave her crotch a test swipe of his tongue. "Strawberries. And . . . something else."

"The package said strawberry shortcake with whipped cream." She giggled when he took a nip, pulling the crotch out.

The flavor exploded in his mouth, then immediately dissolved. He swallowed, then took another bite of the side strap.

Andrea shivered, not sure if she was chilled or turned on. Or both.

Connor chose that time to place his hot hand over her pubis, cupping his fingers between her legs until he could probe while he finished off the panties.

Her breath caught. Her heart thundered, threatening to break out of her chest. She wanted . . . more. She tried to squirm in order to position herself for better access, but his heavy arm prevented much lateral movement.

His mouth covered hers in a deep kiss that tasted like fake strawberries.

"Not bad," he said against her lips, "but I'm still hungry."

He slid down her body, pushing her legs up until her knees framed her face.

The warm velvet of his tongue licked her folds, arching her up on the mattress.

She wanted to spread her legs wider. She wanted to grab his head and push him closer. She wanted . . . him. But the way he had her positioned on the firm mattress had her pretty well pinned in place. Helpless to do much of anything but watch as he licked and sucked her into one screaming climax after another.

Weak and sweating, shaking from her last orgasm, she couldn't do more than make a weak grunt when, still holding her in a compromising position, he slid into her aching folds, the tip of his erection causing a faint ache deep within.

Numb, her mind was numb, as was her body. It wasn't unpleasant.

She looked down, watching in fascination as his colorfully sheathed penis slid in and out of her receptive body. A sated smile curved her lips as she stretched. The action drove Connor deeper. He picked up the pace, pumping into her with fierce abandonment.

A tiny tickle, deep within, grew exponentially until it became a driving force, spurring her on, her hips meeting each thrust eagerly. The rhythmic slapping of flesh filled the darkened hotel room.

Afterward, she lay in the dark, waiting for her breathing to regulate.

She wanted to laugh. She wanted to cry.

She wanted to do it again.

Beside her, Connor's breathing slowed down, signaling his slide toward dreamland.

She had to act fast.

Tamping down her renewed feeling of tawdriness, she padded into the living room and pulled the contracts from her briefcase.

Sliding naked back into bed, she rubbed against Connor.

He grunted and pulled her close.

Wiggling, she pulled him until his mouth closed over her aching breast.

Against her leg, she felt his penis stir with renewed interest. She smiled and offered her other breast.

Within seconds, Connor was humping her thigh, ready for action. She was wet, too, but determined.

As soon as he signed on the dotted line, she'd fuck his brains out.

But not until he made a decision.

# 16

---

"Wait." She gripped Connor's wrist, preventing him from reaching for another condom.

Their gazes met, and even in the dark she could see his confusion. She didn't blame him.

But, damn it, she needed a sale.

Swallowing nervous nausea, she stretched to turn on the light. "This is important, Connor." She sat up and reached for the stack of contracts and her gold pen. "I've taken the liberty of drawing up contracts on the last three homes you saw." She tapped her pen on the first page. "You'll note the price on each one, here."

Avoiding eye contact, she spread the contracts on the bed, swallowing her shame at what she was about to do.

"If you'd like to read them over, I'll be over there in the chair. Let me know if you have any questions."

On wobbly legs, she padded to the oversized upholstered chair and picked up the purple vibrator on her way.

Dipping a brush in a pot of lemon-flavored oil, she brushed

the head of the dildo, then licked it off before meeting Connor's heated gaze.

"Go on," he said in a hoarse whisper, his back rigid. She'd love to know if his penis was in a similar state—it would make things so much easier—but it was impossible to tell with the way the sheet was bunched around his hips.

After oiling the bulbous head again, she flipped the switch on the base. A muffled hum filled the room.

Bracing the soles of her feet on the cushion, she let her knees drop, exposing herself to Connor's rapt attention.

Slowly, she circled her opening with the vibrating oiled tip, wishing it was Connor's warm penis probing her instead of the cool plastic. The thought brought silly tears to her eyes, and she blinked furiously to bring him back into focus. Maybe if she concentrated on him hard enough, she could trick her body into believing it was him between her spread legs. And maybe, just maybe, if she put on a convincing enough show, he would sign anything she put in front of him.

As a reward—for both of them—she would let him do anything he wanted. And she'd love it.

Rock still, Connor watched Andrea pleasure herself. Part of him was fascinated by the sight. Another part was repulsed, yet still he couldn't tear his gaze from her well-loved pussy. With all his heart, he wanted it to be his cock pleasuring her.

But maybe he needed to see this.

Maybe Bill was right about Andrea Redd.

Andrea wished Connor would at least look at the contracts. Maybe if he read them, she wouldn't feel so cheap and dirty for doing what she planned.

Instead, he watched intently while she pushed the vibrating phallus into her dryness. Biting back a wince, she applied more lubricant, closing her eyes and envisioning Connor poised above her.

Immediately her muscles relaxed, her knees parted, her natural moisture returned. Yes . . .

The slick head of the vibrator worked its magic on her clit, her vulva. Aching, she imagined Connor's erection filling her, vibrating his need deep within her.

With a cry, she came, her back arching, nipples aching as waves of ecstasy washed over her again and again.

Spent and weak, she opened her eyes to find Connor standing in front of her, his cargo shorts riding low on his lean hips, his erection painfully obvious by the way the fly tented.

He held the contracts and pen in his shaking hand.

She licked her lips and tried to smile. "So, which property did you choose?"

"None." He dropped the pile of papers into her lap, the sharp edges slicing into her sex. "Do you need a cab?"

"Excuse me?"

"You heard me. Oh, I'm sorry." He stalked into the other room and came back with his wallet. "How much?"

She continued staring at him, willing away the tears that threatened.

"How much do you usually charge for fucking and a sex show? Huh? Because that's what it was, wasn't it?"

"That's not how I do business!" She jumped up and grabbed her nightgown for at least some kind of coverage. "I told you I'd never done this kind of thing before." She swiped at a tear and looked frantically around for something more substantial to put on.

It was apparent she was in imminent danger of being thrown out of his suite.

He stalked from the room, then came back to toss her clothes at her. "Send me a bill."

"B-but you . . . I mean . . . are you saying you don't want to buy a beach house now?"

"Oh, no, I will still buy one. Just not from you."

"But . . . please, Connor. Please, hear me out." She sniffed and stepped into her dress, her hands shaking while she tied the straps. "I understand why you may be angry with me. I obviously misunderstood our, um, situation. But don't take it out on Redd Hot Properties! We're the best agency on the island. Please, give us a chance. If you don't want to work with me, I can assign another agent or—"

"No." His nostrils flared. Behind the lenses of his glasses, his green eyes flashed. "I am going to buy a beach house. And I'll continue to use Redd Hot Properties. On one condition." He leaned close. Close enough to kiss, but she wasn't stupid enough to try. "I will only work with the owner."

"You do know that's me, right?" She kept looking at him while she stuffed her belongings into her briefcase.

"I'm aware of that. It will be strictly business from now on. Understand? No sex in the limousine, not even foreplay. And no sex at any of the properties."

"I can do that," she whispered, and let herself out of the suite.

Connor dropped to the sofa, gripping his head in his hands.

"I'm not sure I can."

# 17

"Ugh!" Andrea crossed her deck and flopped down in a chaise next to Lisa. "Thanks for bringing dinner, not to mention the blender of strawberry daiquiris you mixed." She hefted her glass in a silent salute to her friend and took a sip. "Yum! I can never get mine to turn out like this." Leaning her head back, she closed her eyes and sighed. "I can't tell you how great this is, after the day from hell I had."

"I take it Connor O'Brian isn't cooperating on the house hunt?"

"Hah! That's an understatement." She turned to face Lisa. "You know what's the kicker? I think I was closer to getting the deal before I slept with him." She flopped back onto the chair. "And seeing him all day with this new hands-off policy in place is killing me."

"Maybe you need to institute a new *hands-on* policy. I've seen him, Drea, and I think he's as miserable with this situation as you are. Why don't you be the adult here and end it?"

"You seem to forget—I am the adult. Which is probably a good reason to not start anything again."

"Who are you trying to convince?" Lisa pushed her sunglasses on top of her blond hair and narrowed her eyes. "Drea, admit it. Connor O'Brian was more than a client, a potential sale. Much more." She held up her hand, stopping Andrea's protest. "And we both also know he was more than a POA or even a casual sex partner. As I said before, I know you can be ruthless, but I also know you'd never barter sex for a sale. And you also aren't into the whole casual-sex thing, IMHO." She took a sip of her drink. "So . . . what are you going to do about it? I mean, it's beyond torture to keep showing him houses. You know what I think?"

"No, but I'm sure you'll tell me." The cool strawberry drink slid down her throat, numbing it. She wished she could numb her heart just as easily.

"I think Connor isn't planning to buy a house. Think about it, Drea. We still haven't received his preapproval. I know, I know, he said he'd get it when and if he found a house he wanted. But I think it's not the preapproval that's holding him back. I think he doesn't want to commit to a house, because it would spell the end of this stupid game he's playing with you. IOW, he has it bad for you, too, and just doesn't want to admit it. By continuing to show him property, you're just prolonging the agony."

"Maybe you're right." What a depressing thought.

"There is an alternative, you know."

"And what would that be?"

"Your place. Think about it, it's perfect. Exactly what he's been looking for. You'd both win. He'd get a great house, you'd make a major sale."

"But there's just one flaw with your plan, Lisa. My house is not for sale." She loved the beach and her custom-built home and pool. And she wasn't selling it to anyone, not even Connor.

Especially not Connor.

"There has to be another way. I'm not selling my home.

Besides, you love this place, too. Where would we hang out and walk on the beach and drink?"

"True. There is that." Lisa perked up. "OMG! Why didn't I think about this before? Ask him to move in! You wouldn't make a sale, but you wouldn't lose one, either. And think of all the hot sex you'd have." She waved her hand in front of her face. "Then, too, we wouldn't have to bother with his dumb old preapproval letter."

"Tempting as that thought sounds, you're forgetting he doesn't want to date me, much less have sex with me. There is no way he'd move in here!"

But after Lisa left, Andrea lay in bed thinking about how she might convince Connor to resume their relationship—not that it really was an actual relationship, but she'd like to at least see where it might lead.

Rolling to the side of the bed, she lay with her hand on the phone.

What if he turned her down?

Better to wait until morning. She was showing him the last available house. If he still seemed disinclined to making an offer, she'd have a decision to make.

The fact that she might have feelings for Connor terrified her. As for being in love, as Lisa maintained, it was absurd.

But living together might be the best solution. They could spend time together, having hot sex whenever and wherever they chose, yet maintain their individual identity.

She was a modern woman, she decided as she dressed the next morning. Why shouldn't she enjoy Connor for whatever time they had together? So what if he's younger? So what if he's unemployed? She made enough money to support them both. Somehow she had to convince him it was okay to let her take care of him. Assuming he'd be willing to make even that much of a commitment to her. Not that she'd really want more, anyway.

After picking Connor up at his hotel, she found herself going through the motions of showing him the house. As beach houses go, it was okay. Not one she'd ever consider, but for the right person, it was doable. Connor was not the right person for the house. Even she could see that.

"Is there a problem, Ms. Redd?" Connor asked as he walked up to where she stood by the patio door, looking out over the murky water of the shallow inlet. "You don't seem very enthusiastic. Is there a problem with the house?"

"No, it's fine . . . if you like this kind of house, which I know from experience you don't." Shoulders slumped, she sighed and met his gaze. "If you must know, I miss you." At his raised eyebrow, she hurried on. "Us. Together. I'm so sorry I messed things up." She sniffed and wiped at a tear. "I know I'm older than you and I—"

"Will you stop acting like you're a child molester? I saw your license. You're not that much older than me." He stepped closer. "And you and I both know that's not the reason we had to end our relationship." He put his palm over her mouth. "And, yes, it was a relationship. At least for me." His brows drew together. "But I refuse to let sex influence a sale."

"I know." She moved in closer, until their chests touched. "And I promise to never connect the two again."

"I can't sleep with my Realtor. It's unethical and we already found out it just doesn't work."

"I can have someone else in the office show you properties."

He drew her into his embrace. "I guess I could live with that." He ground against her. "So, what do you say? Once more for old time's sake?"

\* \* \*

Andrea paused in her kitchen, suddenly nervous. The sex that afternoon had been fabulous, everything she remembered and more. Why the feeling of disquiet?

They had incredible chemistry. She had a big house. If he didn't want to live in her bedroom with her, he could have his pick of five others. Surely they could reach an amicable understanding.

"Here we go," she said with more cheerfulness than she felt as she walked out onto the patio with a sweating pitcher of margaritas. "The housekeeper is a fabulous cook, and she left dinner warming for us. If you're hungry, we could eat now."

In answer, he ran his hand up under her skirt as he took a glass from the tray. "I can wait," he said with a smile as he poured their drinks.

"Good," she said, taking a quick sip as she sat next to him on the patio sofa. "Because I have a proposition for you."

His eyebrows rose. "Really? I thought you already propositioned me this afternoon."

She laughed and set her glass on the coffee table before taking his hands in hers. "I love being with you again."

He looked down at their joined hands before meeting her gaze. "And I love being with you again, too. What's this all about?"

"I don't like sleeping apart. This is a big house. Too big for one person. There's no reason why you couldn't just move in here. With me." She held up her hand. "Hear me out. It's okay if you don't have a job. I make enough money for both of us. All you'd have to do is be here for me when I get home and—"

"What would I do while you're gone?"

"That's the thing. You could do anything you wanted. Or nothing. Work on your tan." She gestured toward the beach, just outside her yard. "Run on the beach, surf. Whatever."

"So, just to be clear, I'd be . . . what? A gigolo? Your boy toy?"

"No, you don't understand—"

"Oh, I understand just fine, Ms. Redd." He leaned closer. "Not interested but thanks, anyway." He tugged his hands from hers and strode to the gate. "I'll let myself out. Is this the servants' entrance? I wouldn't want anyone to see me leaving by the front door."

Andrea sat in stunned silence, long after Connor's exit. He'd be back. For some reason, he craved her body as much as she did his. She'd be a fool to turn him away. She was no fool. Such a talented lover, even as a temporary sex partner, was something she could not refuse.

Connor was young, despite his chronological age, she reasoned. He still thought with his little head. All the ways he'd *thought* played through her mind, causing her to smile. Oh, yeah, she'd take whatever he was willing to give for as long as he was willing to give it.

Thank goodness she hadn't done something stupid and told him she'd fallen in love with him.

Despite sleeping next to her phone, it did not ring all night.

Groggy and generally sad, she made her way to her office the next morning, relieved when Lisa was not at her desk.

Slow steps took her to her desk, where she collapsed into the chair, wondering how long she could wait before breaking her vow and calling Connor.

Lisa's unmistakable footfall sounded on the tile hallway seconds before she screeched to a halt in the doorway of Andrea's office, waving a piece of paper.

"It came! It's here! OMG! UR not going to believe it!" She nearly skipped to the desk and pressed the paper into Andrea's hands. "Connor is worth a fortune, if that confirmation letter is any indication!"

"Oh, no!" Andrea closed her eyes, waiting for death. "I'm such a fool. No wonder he was offended by my offer!"

"Offer?"

Andrea nodded. "Yes. I basically offered to make him a kept man." She dropped her head to her hands and moaned, then banged her head against her desk. "Stupid, stupid, stupid."

"You could say that. The guy could buy most of the town." She shoved the phone toward her boss. "Call him."

Andrea looked up. "And say what? Sorry I'm an idiot and, oh, by the way, how about looking at more houses?" She blinked back tears and reached for a tissue. "It's over, Lisa."

Connor pressed 1 to replay his messages. Four from Andrea, all varying forms of apology, and one from Bill saying, basically, I told you so. He deleted Bill's message and replayed Andrea's again. And again. Just to hear her voice.

He sighed and sank to the sofa, then pressed 1 again. Did she sound sad? Was that a hint of tears in her voice? Did he want there to be?

Dropping the phone to the cushions, he rubbed his eyes. He hadn't slept worth a damn.

Until he decided what to do about the Andrea situation, he probably would never sleep again.

After another restless night, Andrea dragged herself to the office. Lisa wasn't in yet, so she made coffee, then trudged to her office.

The message light on the phone console blinked at her.

Afraid to hope, she stood, staring at it.

"Hey, sorry I'm late!" Lisa's voice came from the outer office. "Oh, great, you made coffee! Thanks. Did you remember to actually put coffee into the little basket this time?"

Her bright head appeared in the open doorway. "Drea? What's wrong? Hey, there's a message. Push the button."

When Andrea still stood, staring, Lisa sighed and walked over. She punched the flashing button.

"Hey. It's Connor. Connor O'Brian. The guy who's been looking at vacation beach houses." Andrea and Lisa looked at each other and rolled their eyes. "Anyway, I'm calling—it's about, um, two in the morning, by the way. Sorry to call so late. Or early. Anyway . . . I wanted . . . I mean this message is for Andrea. Redd. Andrea Redd. I'm sorry, I really hate talking to a machine. I'll call back later." *Click.*

"Interesting." Lisa sang the word with a smile.

"Don't get your hopes up. He was probably calling to tell me to go to hell—again."

"Aren't you going to return his call?"

Andrea thought for a second, then shook her head. "No point in prolonging things."

"Well, I'll call him, then!"

"Go for it." Andrea purposely shut her door behind Lisa. She opened the armoire and turned on the TV. She wasn't interested in watching anything, but she also didn't want to hear Lisa's call.

The light on the phone went out, to be followed immediately by Lisa's scream.

The door swung open. Lisa danced around Andrea's office, pumping her fist in the air. "Yea!" She stopped, fists on bony hips, and glared. "Aren't you even curious?"

"Okay, tell me. I know you're dying to, anyway." Had Connor changed his mind about her proposition? Beneath her silk blouse, her heart hammered.

"He said he's decided on a beach house and wants you to come to his hotel room with a contract! How cool is that?"

"Did he happen to say which property he'd chosen?" *Be happy*, she chided, *be happy.* It's the sale she wanted. The sale she needed. She should be dancing with joy along with Lisa.

"Nope. I tried to pin him down. He wants you to bring a blank contract."

"What? I don't want to take a blank contract. I don't do blank contracts." So what if Connor had money? It gave him no right to call all the shots.

"I know!" Lisa ran to the cabinet and began opening drawers. "We'll make up a contract for every house you showed him. Cover all the bases."

"What if he's found a house without us?" Not that she wouldn't be grateful to still get the sale, but it would be somewhat of a slap.

"Take a blank contract, too, just in case," Lisa advised, flipping on the printer.

Andrea put a hand on her nervous stomach as she exited the elevator. Connor had no idea how difficult it was for her to come back to the scene of the crime. Not to mention riding all the way up to the penthouse in an elevator. He'd better be appreciative.

She blinked back tears, telling herself they were just from nerves. But she knew better. Whoever said it was better to have loved and lost than to have never loved at all was full of crap.

In her heart, she'd known parting ways with Connor was bound to happen. She just wished their fling had lasted longer.

But it was past time to do the honorable thing. If he wouldn't be her "boy toy," she at least owed him an honorable ending.

Gathering her courage, she checked her appearance and then knocked on the door to his suite.

Connor opened the door before she could lower her hand. "C'mon in."

He closed the door, looking oddly nervous. Of course, she thought, he's probably just as uneasy as she about the contract.

She walked to the desk and opened her briefcase. "Since you

didn't tell Lisa which property you chose, I took the liberty of bringing a contract for each of them."

"But I—"

"I have to tell you something first, though; then you can decide. The property I first showed you, on the lake, really isn't one you want. Besides being on a lake, it's not very well constructed. And the rooms are small. It's also—"

"I don't want the lake property. I already told you that, remember?" He stepped closer. Close enough for her to smell his aftershave.

It made her mouth water.

"Great. Well, alternatively, the last couple of homes would work for you. I have contracts for them as well as the house with the infinity pool and spa." She averted her eyes, knowing they would give away her feelings about that particular property. It would always hold a special place in her heart, and the idea of him living there was difficult.

After a minute of total silence, she peeked through her lashes.

Connor was shaking his head. And smiling. "I've found a different property. Better than any you showed me, but thanks, anyway. I've kind of got my heart set on it."

"Oh. Were you working with another Realtor? If you give me their name, I'd be happy to contact—"

"No, there's no other Realtor. You're my Realtor." He stepped closer until he had her pinned against the desk, then told her the address of the property he wanted to make an offer on.

She blinked.

It was her address.

"That property is not for sale," she said when she found her voice. True, she needed a sale, but not that badly.

"Sure it is," he said, kissing her neck, short-circuiting her defenses. "Everything is negotiable, if you know what you're doing."

"Then obviously you don't know what you're doing." Strong. She had to be strong when all she really wanted to do was grab him and never let go.

"You don't understand." When she tried to walk away, he tightened his arms. "Stop running. Fill out the contract. I'll pay whatever you want, but I want you to be the co-owner."

She stopped struggling. "That's out of the question."

"You haven't heard my contingency clause yet."

"It doesn't matter, because the house is not for sale. I told you I—" Her words were stopped by his kiss.

"The contingency," he said when he broke the kiss, "is that you give us a chance. We have to trust each other. Moving in together is the first step. I love you and will only go into this if you admit you love me, too."

She slid her arms around his neck and smiled for the first time in days. "I can live with that."

# JUST RIGHT

# 1

---

Ashley Clark took another sip of her margarita, then wiped at the remaining tears clinging to her eyelashes. She sniffed and looked across the table at her best friend, her rock, the only man who understood her and defended her unconditionally.

She chewed on her lower lip. Did she have the nerve to ask?

She watched Daryl Garrett slouch in the booth as he took a leisurely swig from his longneck, secretly admiring the way his throat rippled with each swallow.

She had to ask.

"Daryl," she began, setting her glass on the table between them. "Have you ever wondered why we never hooked up?"

He immediately choked, sputtering and spraying beer across the table.

Ashley jumped back, avoiding most of the mist. Frowning, she swiped at her arm with a cocktail napkin. Maybe that was the reason.

Daryl narrowed his eyes while he tried to inhale much-needed air. He'd been right. The one night they'd spent together was so insignificant in Ashley's mind that she'd totally forgotten.

Too bad every second of their encounter was indelibly etched on his cerebellum for eternity.

"Never mind," she grumbled in typical Ashley fashion when he didn't answer right away. "I shouldn't have asked. It was a stupid question. Forget it, okay?"

Taking a deep breath, he set his bottle on the table and looked at the woman he'd loved since third grade. "If you really thought it was stupid, you wouldn't have asked."

"Stop analyzing me, Daryl. It's annoying." She blinked back fresh tears. "You're supposed to be my friend. That's why I called you tonight." She blew her nose. "I really need you," she said in a small voice.

*You have no idea how true that statement is, Ash.* But what could he do about it? Ashley made her own decisions, and time after time, she continually made the wrong ones.

"Hey, you've got me." He raised his hand to signal for another round. "And, if you really want an answer to your question, I'll give you one." He took her cold hands in his and hoped he would find the right words.

"I just wondered, that's all." She shrugged. "Aren't you a little curious? We've been friends forever."

"Which is exactly why we never hooked up," he lied. "That, and the fact you were involved with my best friends for the last four years or so."

"Thanks so much for reminding me," she said in a watery voice as she swiped at more tears.

"You lived with Andre for almost two years," he continued. "Then, not long after you broke up with him, you started dating Collin." He shook his head, then met her red-rimmed, blue-eyed gaze. "As I recall, I tried to discourage you at the time. Not only did you not listen to me or any voice of wisdom, but you also ended up engaged to Collin before you'd dated more than a couple of months."

"That's so not true! We dated for, well, a lot longer than that."

"Ah, yes, and we see how well that turned out." He handed the cocktail waitress his credit card, then grasped Ashley's hands again. "Ash, we talked about this before—"

"We did not! We've never talked about why we haven't hooked up." She pulled her hands from his and crossed her arms, putting the ample breasts he'd been doing so admirably at ignoring front and center of his attention. "I'd have remembered that," she mumbled, drawing his attention back to her red-blotched face.

"I didn't mean your question; I meant we talked about your track record with men—more specifically, your relationships."

"That's why I asked." She reached for her raincoat and purse. "Through every mess I've made in my life, you were the one constant. I always tell my clients to trust the one they turn to first. The one they run to. With me, that would be you. Yet, we've never . . . well, you know."

Yeah, he knew. And it was killing him that she didn't.

# 2

---

Ashley stood and shrugged into her raincoat, then picked up her purse again. "I should get going." She walked to his side of the booth and leaned down, brushing a chaste kiss on his cheek. "Thanks for the drink." Her scent enveloped him when she pulled him into an impromptu hug, the soft pillows of flesh lurking just beneath the thin fabric of her fitted white shirt pressed enticingly against his cheeks.

It made him instantly hard.

"Wait." He grabbed her hand as she turned to leave. "I've thought about it," he blurted out.

Thought about it? Hell, he'd obsessed over it for more years than he cared to remember. And their one encounter, at the Halloween party the night before she'd moved in with Andre, did nothing but fuel the fire of the torch he carried for her.

"About why we never hooked up?" She sank back into her seat. "Please don't tell me it's because I'm so undesirable the thought never crossed your mind. I'm not sure my fragile ego could take it at this point."

"Don't even kid about that, Ash." Reaching across the table, he squeezed her shoulders. "You are easily one of the hottest women I've ever met. But you're also one of my best friends. Did you ever think I never hit on you because I didn't want to ruin our friendship?" *Say it. Tell me you at least remember our time together. Call me on my lie.* He gave a little fake growl that brought a smile to her tear-stained face, then gave her blond hair a playful tug. "Besides, Goldilocks, what red-blooded bear wouldn't want you in his bed?"

"Obviously you," she groused, but with a little smile still lurking. "Okay, if you don't want to talk about why you aren't compelled to jump my bones, why did you want me to wait?"

"I'd say for the pleasure of your company, but I have to tell you, Ash, you've been kind of a downer the last day or two." He grinned and took another swig of beer. "Naw, I just had an idea. Sort of an experiment." But did he have the balls to follow through? On some level, it felt wrong, deceitful. But all was fair in love and war, so why not?

Ashley looked reticent. "I don't know. It doesn't involve drugs or monkey sex again, does it?"

"Would you stop bringing that up? We were in college, and I was only joking. After all the time we've known each other, I'd have thought you'd realize that." He glared at her, then slid his hands down to hers, covertly checking her pulse rate. He'd discovered a person's pulse often was a truer indicator of their feelings than their words. "So, no, it doesn't. This is different. I'd have to call it more of an, um, intervention than a true experiment."

"An intervention? Whose intervention?" She leaned forward, her breasts so close to his hands that his fingers itched. By the widened eyes and color on her cheeks, he knew he had her hooked.

Now all he needed to do was reel her in.

"Daryl? Whose intervention?"

"Now, don't take this the wrong way—"

"What? Are you saying you want to do an intervention on me?" Her heightened color didn't bode well. Neither did the spike of her pulse.

"Just hear me out, Ash. Let's look at this in a clinical, non-threatening way." He squeezed her hands with each point. "One, out of the blue, you moved in with my roommate." Worse, she did it the day after having mind-blowing sex with Daryl. But for some reason, she refused to acknowledge it had happened. "Two, after investing in that relationship for way too long than was comfortable for anyone—and be honest, you know it's the truth—he finally had the balls to dump you. What did you do when that happened?"

"Fell into a million pieces you had to pick up and put back together again," she mumbled.

"Well, yes, but my point was you came to me to cuss and discuss as well as to dissect what went wrong." *And, in reality, what was wrong was you were sleeping with the wrong guy.* But she needed to figure that out on her own. Which is why he had to convince her of what he was about to propose. "Almost immediately, you hopped into a relationship with Collin, which leads us to point three, which is your choice in partners. I love you, Ashley." At her widened eyes, he hurried to qualify his statement. "As a friend, of course. Which is why I'm telling you this now."

She took a deep breath, her cleavage momentarily distracting him.

"What?"

"Hmm?" He tore his gaze from her assets. "What?"

"That's what I said. What are you telling me, Daryl? Because, so far, you haven't told me anything we didn't both already know."

"Oh. Right. What I'm suggesting is—and don't shoot it down until you at least give it some thought—a sex-only relationship."

She blinked. But she didn't laugh in his face. Or slap him.

That had to mean something. But with Ashley, you never knew.

"With anybody in particular?" Her glossed lips twitched as though she was holding in a laugh.

"Don't be obtuse." He glared and gripped her hands tighter. "We've seen how well you do with picking partners. No, this time, I get to choose. Hell, it couldn't be any worse."

"Have you already picked someone out?" All laughter was gone.

"Ah, well, I mean . . . how about me?" At her stunned expression, he knew he had only a few seconds, at best, to plead his case. "Think about it. We've known each other for years. We've been through pretty much everything a couple can go through . . . except intimacy, of course."

"Of course."

"I know you're familiar with the term *friends with benefits.*"

"I believe they're called *fuck buddies,* Daryl." Her eyes narrowed. "What's all this really about? Are you just horny and think I'd be an easy victim because I'm lonely and desperate? So desperate I'd accept pity sex?"

This wasn't going well.

"No! My point is you have no success with relationships that involve emotions *and* sex. Remember your training? To see the problem, you have to first be able to isolate and identify it. By entering into a sex-only relationship with, um, well, me, we could better understand your needs, both physically and psychologically. From that analysis, we would be able to develop a strategy that would, ultimately, lead to a successful long-term relationship."

"Okay."

"Okay, what?" He knew her—if he didn't make her spell out what she was agreeing to, she could back out.

"Okay to what you said."

"You'll have a sex-only relationship with me?" Could it really have been that easy? He took a deep breath, telling his body to stop doing a possibly premature happy dance.

"No, I will think about being fuck buddies." She laughed and stood again. "Call me tomorrow." After brushing a kiss on his forehead, she strolled out of the bar.

Fuck buddies? What a dismal, depressing thought. The only good thing was the fuck part of it. Ashley had become his obsession, emotional and sexual. Fuck buddies? Oh, they'd be more, much more, than that by the time their experiment was over.

He hoped.

# 3

---

Ashley shoved the sheet down her sweating, naked body with the soles of her feet as she writhed on the damp sheet.

Close. She was so close.

Damn Daryl Garrett. It was his fault she was so restless, so needy. So horny.

Of course, she'd been pretty free and easy about throwing the f-word around, so she couldn't totally blame Daryl. And saying it made her think about doing it. And thinking about doing it with Daryl, of all people, inhibited her. That had to be it.

Not that she hadn't thought about it, fantasized about it, on more than one occasion since puberty. But the timing had never been right. Then there was the whole best-friend thing they had going on.

She flipped the switch on her vibrator, increasing the speed, and held it firmly against her aching clitoris. Eyes squeezed shut, she tried to envision the one magical night of sexual bliss she'd had almost five years ago . . .

The Halloween party had been packed, everyone in costume. When the guy dressed as the phantom asked her to dance, she'd been willing—after all, even in costume, it was obvious he had a killer body. Within seconds, she'd been practically rubbing her needy body against his clearly excited one. She'd followed willingly into the storage closet, where he'd blown every sexual fantasy she'd had out of the water. She'd fallen instantly in love, having to force herself to allow him to leave her side. When he reappeared to drive her home and she finally took off his mask, she was thrilled to discover it was Andre, one of the guys who had been persistently asking her out. She'd pushed past her natural reticence and moved in with him and his roommates the following day. She wasn't about to let him get away.

But the sex was never the same, and he became angry when she asked him to put on the costume again. . . .

A frustrated moan escaped her. Dang it, all she could see was Daryl's face.

How could she even consider having sex with Daryl, of all people? Especially when even thinking about him made her trusty vibrator dysfunctional?

She paused, remembering the sexy way his hair looked, as though he'd just rolled out of bed—a bed where a thoroughly sated woman had been running her fingers through his hair.

Why couldn't she be the woman raking her hands through his thick brown hair? It wasn't as though he was unattractive.

The thought sent tingles to her nether regions. Or the vibrator was finally doing its thing. Could be either.

Regardless, within seconds of relaxing and anticipating having sex with Daryl, her back arched off the mattress as waves of satisfaction washed over her.

Enjoying the breeze from the ceiling fan above her bed, she waited for her breathing to return to normal while she applied lubricant to the vibrator, idly rubbing the excess oil into her aching nipples.

When her lust rose again, she had no problem envisioning Daryl's face, Daryl's hard body, rubbing against her excited flesh, his erection sliding forcefully into her eager body. One thrust later, she climaxed again. Then again.

Maybe fuck buddies was a good idea after all.

Daryl rolled over and looked at the glowing numbers on his clock radio. Four-fifteen in the morning was probably too early to call Ashley and ask if she'd made a decision yet.

He rolled to his stomach. Rather, he tried to roll but found it uncomfortable with the hard-on he'd maintained pretty much since seeing Ashley in the bar the night before.

Flopping onto his back, he huffed out a sigh. He needed sleep. He had four patients to see in less than five hours.

His hand slid beneath his boxer briefs. Trying to imagine it was Ashley's hand didn't work. The calluses on his hand from his tennis racket interfered with his normally vivid imagination. The pad of his thumb brushed over the sensitive tip, eliciting a drop of moisture. He rubbed it in, wishing Ashley were the one touching him so intimately. Would she take him into her mouth?

His hips bucked.

Hand dipping lower, he caressed his testicles. Maybe he should do his monthly lump check, since he was already touching that area . . .

With a groan, he pulled his hand out of his boxers and rolled over, punching the pillow for good measure.

Maybe he was an idiot. An oversexed, sleep-deprived idiot.

An annoying buzz intruded on Ashley's x-rated dream. Sunlight spilled in through the partially opened shutters.

She slapped at the alarm clock a few times. When the buzzing did not relent, she cracked open one eye just in time to see her cell buzz itself clear off the nightstand, hitting the hardwood floor with a crack.

*Buzz.*

Whoever was calling was persistent at . . . Crap, was it already almost ten o'clock?

Hanging off the side of the tall mattress, she grabbed her phone and flipped it open. "Hel—" She cleared her throat. "Hello?"

"Did I wake you up? Don't you have to be at work soon?"

"Hi, Daryl." She smiled and rolled to her back, absently rubbing her bare chest. Her nipples responded to the cooler air, immediately puckering. She plucked at them, wondering if Daryl would like to play with her breasts.

The thought made her squirm with renewed moisture. Sighing, she rolled back to her stomach, allowing her aching folds to rub on the sheet while she talked. "No, I don't have any clients this morning." She arched her back, stretching, luxuriating in the feel of cotton against her hard nipples and swollen clit. "Don't have to be at the office until after lunch, in fact." Was he calling to continue their discussion about a sex-only relationship? The thought made her wet.

Maybe he wanted to come over to get started on it—on her—now.

That thought gave her pause.

Was that what she wanted? What if having sex ruined their friendship?

"What are you wearing?" Hey, she'd had plenty of guys ask her that. Why shouldn't she ask? Funny, she'd always thought it was a stupid thing to ask but found she suddenly really wanted to know. Just out of idle curiosity, of course.

"Huh? Ah, pants, a shirt, a tie. You know, the usual Monday shrink uniform."

She smiled. Poor Daryl. He sounded distinctly uncomfortable. The idea he had daily outfits he wore each week was suddenly endearing.

"No suit today?" Rolling to her back, she plucked at her nipples, bringing them to even stiffer peaks.

"No, I went casual, remember? I stopped wearing suits and sport coats a few years ago. But why are you asking?"

"Just curious." Her hand slid between her legs. "I mean, if we become, um, more than friends, I need to know what you wear." She lowered her voice to what she hoped was a sultry whisper. "Day and night."

Daryl cleared his throat. "Ah, okay . . . What are you wearing?"

"A smile." She flipped the phone shut and reached for her vibrator.

This time when she came, she knew exactly why.

Daryl stared at the phone, then hung up. Thanks to Ashley, he had to wait a few minutes for his boner to dissipate before seeing his next patient.

"Your next appointment is here," the voice of his receptionist, Tiffany, sang through his intercom.

He stood and made an adjustment, then pushed the button. "Send her in."

Maybe Mrs. Jetton would take his mind off Ashley for a while.

She was lying on the couch when he walked into the inner office, her legs crossed, her eyes shut, like some sacrificial lamb.

With her looks and come-hither voice, not to mention her sex addiction, it was out of the question to call her a sacrificial virgin.

Daryl bit back a smile. He'd told her many times it wasn't necessary to lie on the couch, that sitting in the guest chair or on the couch was fine. But she'd insisted. In her early sixties, Mrs. Jetton wasn't really a sex addict; she just liked to think she was. But he hoped she didn't verbalize her latest prurient fantasies today. His already excited libido may not survive.

"How are you today, Mrs. Jetton?" He took his seat and picked up his recorder as he pushed the RECORD button.

"Horny." She opened one eye. "Looks like you are, too, Doc. Want to swap fantasies?"

It was going to be a long day.

* * *

Ashley trudged into her apartment and tossed her keys into the basket by the door. Her briefcase slid into its spot beneath the entry table.

What a bitch of a day.

Couples counseling seemed to get more difficult with each session. But she'd signed the contract with C.I. Industries, so she was just going to have to put up with it. Rubbing her temples, she kicked off her shoes and padded into the kitchen.

Food. She'd been too stressed about the possibility of having sex with her best friend to be able to swallow a bite of breakfast or lunch. Now she felt as though she could polish off an entire buffet.

Slinging open her French-door refrigerator, she hoped the food fairy had visited since the day before.

She hadn't. Ashley scanned the contents: a container of black olives with a curious-looking whitish fuzz growing on top, a partial package of cream cheese with a coordinating green fuzz, and a half loaf of bread.

"Crap." She let the doors swing shut as she flipped through her takeout menus.

The phone rang, startling her.

"Speak," she said after pushing the speaker phone button.

"Did you get them? Did you get the reservations?" Her associate at the clinic, Amy, sounded excited. "Did you call and make your counter offer?"

Ashley gritted her teeth. She should have kept her big mouth shut today at work. But Amy had been her friend since college. She knew Daryl. Ashley had hoped Amy would tell her all the reasons why doing the deed with Daryl would not be a bright idea.

Instead, Amy had jumped on the Daryl bandwagon and practically twisted her arm about accepting. She'd even talked Ashley into footing the bill for a romantic getaway.

"Yes," she told Amy, "I made the reservations. Do you think

it would be tacky to ask Daryl to pay for half?" She could afford it, but Daryl made way more money.

"What part of *go for it* didn't you understand? How can you go for it when you ask your boy toy to foot half the bill? Besides, I know you. If it doesn't work out, you will feel guilty for asking him to invest and stay with him out of guilt. That's your MO."

"It is not!" She tossed the menus back into the basket and wondered if Daryl would be interested in splitting a pizza.

"It certainly is, too. Remember what happened with Andre? After you had such hot sex at the Halloween party, you were practically willing to have his baby. In the blink of an eye, you moved in with him and poor Daryl. Be honest. The next time you had sex with Andre again, you were disappointed. Majorly. Am I right?"

"Yes, okay, you're right. But that doesn't prove anything. We all know hot sex cools over time."

"Not by the second time, girlfriend! Wake up and smell the coffee." Amy sounded like she was eating something. Probably something delicious. "And what did you do? You hung in there for almost two whole years. And why? Because you were so committed after that one multiorgasmic time that you felt guilty that he couldn't make you come again. As if that was your fault! Like I said, it's what you do. And don't try to deny it."

Ashley leaned against the granite counter and rubbed her temples. "So you're saying I shouldn't take Daryl up on his proposition? Or that I shouldn't whisk him away?"

"Girlfriend, haven't you listened to a word I said all day? Heck, no, I'm not saying those things! Do not pass go; do not collect two hundred dollars. Grab that hunk and lock him in your hotel room. Then I want you to promise me something."

"What?"

"Don't scrutinize it; don't analyze it. Make me proud. Screw his brains out."

# 4

Daryl glanced down at his cell and ignored its ring. Ashley. He wanted to answer. He was afraid to answer. He was afraid he knew what her answer was going to be.

"Aren't you going to get that?" Collin, Ashley's now-ex-fiancé and one of Daryl's best friends, leaned back in the booth, wiping the remnants of their shared hot wings from his hands with a Wet-Nap.

"Tell me again why you dumped Ashley?"

Collin threw his wipe on the table and heaved a sigh. "Bottom line? We were incompatible." He shrugged. "End of story. I woke up one day and realized some things." He ticked off his points on his fingers. "We were engaged. Engaged meant we would marry. I realized I had no intention of marrying someone I obviously couldn't satisfy, if you know what I mean. I'd have a miserable life. So would she, for that matter." He picked up his draft beer and took a swig.

"Sexually incompatible, right? But you loved her."

That question earned another shrug from Collin's broad shoulders. If rumors were true, Collin was a stud, a god among studs, even. And yet, he couldn't sexually satisfy Ashley. How could Daryl compete?

Just as he thought Collin wasn't going to answer, he mumbled, "There was that, too." He leveled a look. "I guess, on some level, I knew I didn't love her. Not the way I should have. I watched her with Andre, wanting her. She had a smoking-hot body. Still does, but . . . Did you ever hear them going at it at night when we all lived together?" He shook his head, his long black hair swinging. "I walked around with a boner for two years. I admit, I wanted some of that. And I wanted it bad."

Which was exactly why Daryl had opted to move out.

"So," Daryl began, half holding his breath at what the answer might be. "I take it you have no lingering feelings for Ashley? You wouldn't be, well, jealous, if someone else went out with her?"

Collin cuffed Daryl's arm, causing him to wince.

"You have my blessing, my man." He lifted his mug and grinned. "Along with my sincere sympathies." He leaned closer and lowered his voice. "Ashley is frigid." He nodded vigorously. "It's true. Ask Andre."

"But we heard them—"

Collin snickered. "Yeah, from what I hear, it was all her, trying to get in the mood. Never did. My advice, bro, is if you're looking to dip your wick, you need to look elsewhere. Ashley Clark will make your nuts shrivel."

Daryl paused outside Ashley's apartment door and took a deep breath.

Collin and Andre were wrong. Ashley was a hot, responsive lover. He knew. He also knew she'd climaxed, multiple times, the one time they'd been together. Sure, women faked that stuff all the time, but she'd been so wet it had been hard to stay inside. And he'd held her wrist. Pulses don't lie.

Ashley Clark may be frigid with everyone else, but he knew, deep in his heart, she was anything but that with him.

Now he just needed to convince her.

Ashley threw open the door at his knock, temporarily short-circuiting his thought processes with the Hawaiian-print strapless number she probably considered a casual sundress. To him, it was a primal signal for sex. Of course, Ash probably wouldn't agree. He took a step back.

"Oh!" Her slender hand fluttered by her throat like a nervous hummingbird, the brilliant blue stone of the ring on her middle finger flashing with each movement. "Hi." She smiled up at him, taking his breath away. "I thought you were the pizza guy."

He looked beyond her bare shoulder into her empty apartment. The relief he felt at finding her alone was disproportionate to the situation, but he couldn't help it. "Mind if I join you? I had a few wings earlier, but I'm starving."

Without waiting for an invitation—after all, they'd been friends forever, and it would seem sort of weird for him to politely stand in the hallway, waiting to be invited in—he pushed past her and walked into her kitchen. "What kind did you order? There's enough for me, right?"

She sighed and closed the door but was smiling when she turned to face him. He decided that was a good sign.

"Hand-tossed stuffed crust, bacon, black olives, pepperoni, ham, mushrooms, green pepper, and double cheese." She grinned and shrugged. "You know, the usual health food. I think we should be able to eek by with the extra-large."

Her flowery perfume wrapped around him as she brushed past to open a cabinet over the dishwasher. "Get the napkins, will you?" Rising on tiptoes, she stretched for the plates.

"Here, let me get those for you." He lurched behind her, reaching over her head as he pinned her against the counter.

Against his belly, he felt her turn, the soft pillows of her breasts squishing against his thundering heart.

Obviously Ashley had neglected to put on a bra.

He had no complaints.

They stood, plastered against each other, mouths inches apart, breath mingling.

Daryl could think of a few other things he wouldn't mind mingling.

"Daryl," she whispered.

"Ashley," he said at the same time.

He stepped back, pleased when she didn't immediately take advantage of the space. "Ladies first."

"I've been, um, thinking about your idea." She licked her lips, and he wished she'd just shut up and kiss him. "And I'm—"

"Not sure it's a good idea, right?" He nodded sagely, schooling his expression. "Perfectly understandable. But before you make your decision, you really need to weigh all the pros and cons."

Her eyebrow arched, and she crossed her arms, pushing up her already-impressive cleavage. "Really?"

He swallowed audibly and had to force his gaze to meet hers. "Absolutely. It's the only way to make an informed, educated decision."

Ashley bit her lip to stop the giggle that threatened to erupt. Even if sex with Daryl was a dismal failure, it would be fun. She really could use some fun. A glance at the clock on the microwave told her they had at least another twenty minutes before their pizza would arrive.

Between her on-and-off attraction to Daryl for most of her life and Amy's pep talk that afternoon, she'd already decided to take him up on his offer.

But it might be fun to tease him a little.

"I'm sure you've talked to Andre. Maybe even Collin." He

nodded, a wary look on his face. "Then you know their opinions about me, where sex is concerned?"

He nodded again. "But I've never seen any indication of anhedonia, despite their claims. After all, no experiment uses only two test subjects and—"

"Anhedonia? That's a crock! I can, too, absolutely experience pleasure."

"I know." He looked down. "I mean, I'm sure you can, especially given the right stimuli."

She stepped close, close enough to feel her nipples pushing against the elasticized bodice of her sundress where her breasts touched Daryl's firm chest. She'd show him stimuli. Was that a shudder she felt ripple through him?

"Do you like my sundress? I picked it up today on my way home from work." She normally wore things she could wear a bra with, but the upcoming sex-only vacation with Daryl made the sundress a perfect choice.

Daryl swallowed again. "It's, um, very nice. It will probably be nice and cool this summer."

Nice was not the look she was going for when she bought the dang dress. Pouting, she forced a sigh. "Thanks. But I have one problem. If I take a deep breath and do this." To demonstrate, she extended her arms above her head with the same results she'd had in the fitting room: her bodice flipped, rolling to her waist, leaving her breasts totally exposed.

Daryl immediately turned, averting his eyes. But not before she noted the telltale tent on the front of his khaki slacks.

Biting back a smile, she waited a few seconds. When he remained rooted to the tile, she said, "How do you expect us to have a sex-only relationship experiment if you can't even stand to look at my breasts?" Pause. "Do you think I need a boob job? Would that make me more appealing to you?"

"What! No! You're fine. They're fine." His shoulders slumped. "They're perfect," he said in a rough whisper.

"Then turn around and look at them, Daryl. Please. If we're going to go through with this, I have to not feel uncomfortable with you."

Slowly he turned, his gaze zooming in on her nipples, which immediately puckered. "They really are, um spectacular, just the way they are, Ash."

He stretched his arm, finger extended, until it grazed the tip of her right nipple.

Electric awareness zipped from the tip of her nipple directly into her aching core.

Her breath caught. It took all her strength to not fling herself into his arms and beg. But she wasn't sure what she would beg for, so she locked her knees. "More," she whispered as their eyes met.

He stepped closer, his warm palms enveloping each breast, breasts that grew noticeably heavier within seconds.

His thumbs brushed back and forth across her nipples, the action causing a distinct wetness between her legs.

He licked his lips. "Pretty," he said in a reverent whisper.

*Suck them,* she wanted to shout. But speech evaded her. Instead, she slid her hands up his arms until she gripped each side of his head. In slow motion, she drew him down until she felt his hot breath against her puckered nipple.

Rising on the tips of her toes, she arched her back, the action causing her nipple to brush the seam of his mouth.

Daryl had always been smart, a quick learner. He immediately latched on to her aching nipple, suckling greedily, his arms crushing her close to him.

Each strong pull of his mouth created an answering ache deep within her. Almost light-headed with relief to find they were attracted to each other, she rubbed shamelessly against him, practically riding his leg.

One of his arms dropped lower as he bunched her skirt

higher and higher until his hand was on the trembling cheek of her excited bottom, revealed by her new thong.

Wild for him now, she writhed against him in an attempt to climb his body and appease the ache growing to monster proportions deep within.

His hand flexed, squeezing her cheek, before sliding down to dip between her legs, his fingertips tracing the wet satin crotch of her thong.

His mouth switched to her other breast. A growl sounded deep in his throat. Wait, maybe that came from her. Regardless, it was thrilling.

His shaking hand shoved the string of fabric aside, immediately petting her wetness.

Their labored breathing filled the small kitchen.

Good grief, she couldn't remember ever wanting anyone the way she wanted Daryl at that moment. She tried reaching for his zipper but found her arms weren't quite long enough.

She wanted him. She wanted all of him, and she wanted him now. Right there, in the kitchen of her apartment, on the granite counters she'd just polished that morning. Heck, she didn't care if they did it on the tile floor. She just knew she had to feel him, naked and ready against her own nudity. Had to feel the hardness pressed against her without the hamper of fabric. Had to . . .

*Ding-dong.*

# 5

---

Daryl immediately released her. Cool air bathed her wet nipples.

She stared at him.

He stared at her breasts.

*Ding-dong.*

"P-pizza's here." Fumbling with her bodice, she finally managed to pull it back into place.

"Wait. Here." He pulled a wad of cash from his pocket, grabbed her wrist, and pushed the bills into her hand. "You paid last time; this one's on me."

Numb, she could only nod.

*Ding-dong.*

On wobbly legs, she made her way to the door. Instead of her usual delivery boy, a man old enough to be her father stood in the hall, an unzipped insulated bag in his outstretched arm.

An awkward silence filled the space, during which his bifocaled gaze skimmed her from her bare feet to her head.

Pizza Guy smiled, revealing a split between his front teeth.

"Extra-large, hand-tossed stuffed crust, double cheese, black olives, ham, pepperoni, green peppers, and bacon?"

"Light sauce?" He nodded and she handed him the money. "That's me. Thanks!"

After passing her the pizza, he glanced at the money in his hand. "Change?" When she shook her head, he flashed another smile and winked. "Thanks. Have a great evening!"

Leaning against the closed door, Ashley shivered as Daryl took the pizza out of her hand.

"Ash?" He put the pizza box on the entry table. "You okay?"

"He knew. Did you see the way he looked at me? He knew!"

"Knew what?" Gently, he pulled her away from the door, into the living room.

"That I, that we . . . you know. I could tell by the way he looked at me. He knew."

Daryl led her to the leather sofa and waited until she was sitting before retrieving the pizza box and taking his place next to her. "Here," he said, handing her a piece of pizza, melted cheese practically dripping from its pointed end. "Eat. It will make you feel better. You always overreact when you're hungry."

He was right, of course. Dang his hide, he was always right. But that didn't mean she had to like it.

"Can we talk about what just happened?" she asked when he returned from the kitchen with plates and napkins.

Wordlessly, he handed her another piece of pizza as he nodded.

She wanted to tell him she'd changed her mind, but she hadn't. She wanted to tell him he wasn't her type. But, she'd just realized, he was. She wanted to tell him he was wrong, that she wasn't hungry, but since she was already reaching for her third piece of pizza, he'd know she was lying.

Maybe having a sexual relationship with a psychiatrist wasn't one of her brighter ideas.

But now that the idea was planted in her brain, she couldn't bring the words to her mouth to end it before it began.

"Why are you smiling?" She didn't trust a smiling Daryl, especially not after what he—they—had just done before the pizza arrived. Well, almost done.

He reached for another slice. "'Cause I love stuffed crusts. I always forget to order it that way."

"Glad I made you happy."

He stopped chewing and glanced down at her bodice. His swallow echoed in the quiet living room. "Ash, you have no idea."

"Listen," she began, turning and tucking one foot beneath her leg. "While I agree we have some chemistry going for us." At his arched brow, she amended her words. "Okay, we have a lot of chemistry. But I don't think a sexual relationship between us would work. I mean, think of the awkwardness. What would we do when we didn't have sex scheduled? I don't want to be a burden to you, make you feel you had to perform whenever we were together. Face it, Daryl, we're together a lot. If we tried to have sex every time we were together, we'd be worn out in no time. See what I mean?"

"I do and I don't agree." He wiped his mouth and sat back. "Got any beer?"

"Yeah, in the fridge. I'll get it." She stood and picked up their plates.

Daryl thought she was calling the whole thing off. Was that what she was trying to do? If she was smart, that's exactly what she'd do.

Unfortunately, she'd never been smart when it came to men. Why start now? Then again, what better time?

But the ache from the episode in the kitchen remained, tainting her judgment. At least that was the excuse she used. Besides, she really loved spending time with Daryl. Even if they agreed to never have sex, she knew they would have a great getaway.

When she returned with his beer, she said, "Since we agree a sexual relationship would probably not work, I have a counter proposition." When he paused with the bottle poised at his lips, she hurried on. "I thought maybe a sex-only vacation would work better for us, especially since it would be a finite time. Easier and less messy than an actual sexual relationship would be. So . . . that's why I rented a beach house in Corpus Christi. I also made plane reservations, so it's too late to back out," she finished in a rush. Holding her breath, she chewed on her lower lip.

"We could drive to Corpus, save some money."

Releasing the air, she nodded. "But it's cheap and the flight is less than an hour. It will give us more time at the beach house. Plus, like I said, it's nonrefundable."

He frowned. "Let me reimburse you."

"No. It was my idea; I'll pay."

"Then let me at least pay half. I know how much beach houses cost to rent."

She sighed. If she allowed him to pay half, she would be giving up control. Then again, if she didn't allow him to pay, she might max out her credit card.

"Okay, I'll tell you what. I'll pay for the house and flight, you pay for everything else. Food, entertainment, whatever." Condoms. She just realized she hoped lots of condoms would be needed.

"Okay." His nod was reluctant. "But if you discover you need me to toss in any more money, just say the word."

"So you agree? We can go on a sex-only vacation? No strings, no commitment?" She wouldn't be totally disappointed if he backed out. In fact, it would probably be for the best, she told herself in an effort to stave off the fear of impending rejection.

"When do we leave?"

# 6

Daryl glanced at Ashley as he maneuvered their rental SUV through the afternoon congestion on Ocean Boulevard and forced thoughts of canceled appointments and potentially disappointed or irate patients from his mind. He was right where he needed to be. But he wondered about Ashley.

Nervous. That was the only way to describe how she looked, huddled against the passenger door, gnawing on her lower lip.

He'd wanted a sexual relationship with her for more years than he'd care to admit. But not because of the sex. Because he knew, deep down, if she would give him a chance sexually, he could get past her defenses and make her see how right they were for each other.

He hoped. That was the grand plan, anyway. And now they wouldn't even have that, just a sex-only vacation. Could he convince her to take a chance on him in such a short time frame?

"Does it bother you," Ashley broke the silence at last, "that I lived with Andre and Collin—your two best friends—and now I'm going to be having sex with you?"

He glanced over at her. "Not unless you're planning to do a play-by-play comparison." It was a blatant lie, but he'd already decided he'd take her any way he could get her. "Why? Does it bother you?"

She took a sip from her bottle of water and set it back in the cup holder before answering. "Trust me, no."

"All together, you invested almost four years with Andre and Collin." He shrugged. "There's bound to be at least a little apprehension, if not comparison. It's human nature."

"Daryl Garrett, if you're going to start analyzing everything I say or do, you can turn this car around and take me right back to the airport!" She swiped at her eyes. "I don't need any more stress."

"Sorry." He focused on the road in front of him, clenching his jaw. "I don't want to mix stress into our relationship any more than you do." Hell, he had so much riding on their time to-gether; he had enough stress of his own.

"I'm sorry," she whispered, placing a warm hand on his knee, practically burning a hole in his jeans. "Do you think we added to the tension by not finishing what we started last night before the pizza came?"

If the ice-cold shower he'd taken after leaving her was any indication, then yes.

Instead, he managed a credible laugh. "Naw, we were both tired. Besides, you had a point when you said it will add to the pleasure when we get to the beach house." He tugged on her ponytail. "I'm counting on it."

"Counting on what?"

"Adding to the pleasure." Taking a deep breath, he shifted in the bucket seat. "But if you don't move your hand back down to my knee, I may have to change my plan and pull over so we can start our vacation on the side of the road."

"Oh!" Ashley drew her hand back as though it had touched a hot burner. "Sorry. I didn't realize . . . I mean, I wasn't paying attention . . . just drive, okay?"

"Ash?" He glanced over a few minutes later to see her worrying her lower lip and felt his cock stir. "I'm only human. If you kept stroking my leg like that, going higher and higher, I'd have no choice but to pull over and let you have your way with me. Not that I'd mind. And, trust me, once we get to the beach house, you can touch me anywhere your heart desires." He gave an exaggerated eyebrow wiggle. "As long as I get the same privilege."

She clutched her hands together in her lap and looked out the window, making him wish he hadn't stopped her. He missed the warmth of her hand on his leg. And higher.

Time enough for that once they reached the beach house.

Ashley fought the urge to sit on her hands. What was wrong with her? She'd never been the type to fondle dates. Then again, was this really a date? Sex. They were going to a beach house for a week of sex. And to play. Sex play. Sex and sex play with easily the best friend she'd ever had. Would their friendship survive? But if she called it off right now, would she survive?

Ashley and Daryl had met in the third grade, when he'd rescued her from being beaten up by some fourth-grade boys who loved to pick on little girls. She'd stood up to them, exhibiting false bravado, trading taunts. When the first boy, Richard, her first crush, had punched her, she'd experienced her first heartbreak. It was instantly compounded when another boy had grabbed her arms, pinning them behind her back while an unrepentant Richard had continued to punch her in the stomach until she'd been afraid she was going to embarrass herself further by losing her lunch.

Suddenly, Richard had stopped punching her, and the boy holding her arms relaxed his grasp. Richard turned away from her, only to immediately be knocked to the ground, blood spurting from his nose. Above him, a skinny kid with glasses stood, fists raised. Daryl.

The bullies had run away, crying. Daryl had walked over and helped Ashley up from where she'd collapsed into a puddle of pain and tears. He had offered her a shredded tissue from his pocket and helped her pick up her books.

He'd been her knight, her protector, her best friend ever since that day.

Off and on, she'd been romantically attracted to him. But when they got older, whenever she'd felt those feelings, he'd had a girlfriend. Then she'd have a boyfriend, and the urge to explore her attraction had been relegated to the back burner.

Now it would be on the front burner. The thought both excited and terrified her.

She hoped the resulting heat didn't burn them up.

"Wow," Daryl said a few minutes later as he pulled the rental into a shallow circular drive in front of a weathered-siding-covered house on six-foot stilts. "You actually paid for this?"

"Shut up. The Internet ad had gorgeous pictures. The owner said it was being renovated. That's why it was such a good deal, I guess." She smiled. "Don't judge a book by its cover, Daryl. At least reserve your judgment until we see the inside." Reaching for her door handle, she looked back at him. "You bring the suitcases while I unlock the door."

"I'm not holding my breath. Any place that has you take your own bedding, including the mattress, doesn't strike me as a five-star place to stay."

"Don't be such a party pooper. Oh, that reminds me, the box with the air mattress is in the trunk, too."

Scampering up the stairs, she wondered if Daryl would want to have sex immediately. She was sort of hungry. Hey, it was her vacation, too. She had a say in whether they had sex or went out for an early dinner. How could she feel romantic with a growling stomach?

Daryl frowned as he watched Ashley practically run up the wooden stairs to the wraparound deck. In the distance, seagulls called as waves lapped the beach. A calm washed over him, relaxing him.

He loved the beach. Almost as much as he loved Ashley. Hefting the suitcases from the trunk, he grabbed the mattress-in-a-box, beeped the locks, and trudged toward the steps. He needed a vacation. A sex vacation was even better. But the fact was, sex or no sex, any time he spent with Ashley would be a good time.

Pausing at the top of the worn stairs, he looked out over the bay, squinting at the golden reflection of the sun on the water. Between the house and the water stretched an expanse of white sand, begging for him to sink his toes in and stay a while.

Tension eased from his muscles, leaving him with the almost overpowering urge to lie down and take a nap in the sun.

He made his way to the open door, which faced the water. "Ash?"

"In here," she called from somewhere inside. "Daryl, come take a look at the view from our bedroom window!"

Smiling at her phrasing—*our bedroom*—he followed the sound of her voice.

The door to the bedroom was just to the right of the front entrance. Eager to check out the bedroom—and the bed—he hurried into the room.

Ashley stood by a skinny set of French doors. More like windows masquerading as doors, their wood frame was so warped he doubted they could sufficiently close. He glanced around. No wonder the wood floors were so dull. Every scrap of varnish had probably been sandblasted off due to improper seals on the windows and doors.

Reaching out, he grasped the chipped, painted iron headboard and gave an experimental shake. It creaked, the entire frame twisting in an unstable way. "Ash, I'm not sure we'll be able to sleep on this."

"Oh, stop being such a grump." She waved a dismissive hand. "I'm sure it will be fine once we get the mattress blown up and on it."

He wasn't so sure, but since it appeared to be the only place he could sleep with Ashley, he was game. "You want me to blow it up now?"

Ashley shifted, averting her gaze. "Um, I'm kind of hungry. How about you? I was thinking we might go see if we can find a restaurant or deli before we start unpacking."

"I could eat. But, Ashley, look at me." He gripped her shoulders, turning her to face him. "It's okay. I'm not going to attack you." He grinned. "Not right now, anyway." Her arms were thinner than he remembered where he rubbed his hands up and down them. "Why don't we get the bed set up and made, then go find somewhere to eat dinner before we come back and finish unpacking?"

"You don't mind?"

He crushed her to him for a quick hug. "I didn't say that. But I've waited this long to be with you; what's another couple of hours? Thought maybe we'd check out the crab shack. Then, afterward, we can move on to the reason we're here."

The thought didn't seem to put her any more at ease than it did him.

His brain sorted through every article he'd ever read regarding foreplay while he unboxed their mattress.

Ashley glanced up from the instruction sheet. "It says to screw the little hose into that hole on the side, plug the cord in, and push the green button."

He followed her instructions. A low hum filled the room. Within minutes, the mattress sprang to life, eliciting a squeak of surprise from Ashley.

"What size mattress did you buy?" When he picked it up, it scraped the low ceiling. Struggling, he wrestled it to the bed, where it hung over on each side as well as over the footboard. "Ashley, this doesn't fit."

"Sure it does." As if to demonstrate, she sat down on one side. And immediately fell to the floor when the mattress flipped over her head. "Ow."

Rushing to her side, he helped her up and righted the mattress. "Are you okay?"

She nodded. "I guess we'll just have to sleep toward the middle."

The thought of sleeping anywhere with Ashley haunted him all the way down the beach to Pirate's Booty, the crab shack they'd seen advertised on their drive toward the bay.

Ashley grinned at him over the table as their pirate-costumed waiter walked away. "I didn't think about it being a themed restaurant."

Arms folded on the table, he smiled back. "Me neither. I hope they don't try to be too authentic. I'd hate to get parrot poop in my food—you know, from the pirate guy having one on his shoulder while he cooked our food?" At the look of alarm on her face, he hurried on, "It's a joke, Ash. Relax. Besides, stuff like that would get their permits yanked."

Nodding, she looked around the small, darkened dining area. Probably on the lookout for parrots. He should have kept his big mouth shut and not tried to be funny.

Say something. "Are you going to the mental health conference next month?" Great. Real smooth. Nothing kills the mood faster than shoptalk.

Although, he suspected, the mood he strove for was in its death throes.

"No. Life coaches aren't considered mental health professionals."

Ouch.

A comment was not necessary as their pirate brought their drinks and appetizers to the table.

Over the sampler platter, he wondered if anyone would notice if he stripped Ashley and ate his appetizers from her bare skin.

"Stop looking at me like that," Ashley warned. "You'll ruin my appetite. I'm nervous enough."

"True, and we both know how cranky you get when you're hungry."

A hush puppy hit him squarely between the eyes.

A moist breeze off the ocean caressed their faces as they walked, hand in hand, back to the beach house. With each step, Daryl felt Ashley get a little more tense.

"I had an idea back there, when we were eating." He stepped aside, indicating she should go up first.

"Oh?" She looked back over her shoulder as she climbed the stairs. "What?"

Stepping onto the porch, he drew her into his arms. "Have you ever tried role-playing?" He hadn't, but if it would make Ashley more at ease, he was willing to try.

She shook her head, the action causing some of her hair to cascade over her cheek.

With gentle reverence, he tucked it behind her ear, then brushed a kiss across her lips.

Relief disproportionate to the situation rushed through him when she noticeably relaxed, leaning her lush body into him.

Swaying with her in his arms, he prayed he would come up with the right words.

"Want to play pirate?" Grinning, he held his breath.

Cocking her head, she smiled up at him. "You mean like a sexy pirate?"

"Oh, yeah," he said, rubbing his erection against her with each sway of his hips.

Her shrug brushed her breasts against his chest, further inflaming his senses.

"What did you have in mind?" Backing toward the door, she pulled him along.

Other than getting her naked and horizontal? Not a damn thing.

"Stop." His hand covered hers when she reached for the light switch. "Pirates didn't have electricity."

"Maybe modern ones do," she suggested.

In answer, he shook his head and walked her backward toward the bedroom.

Spying a yardstick by the bedroom door, he grabbed it, holding her at bay with it. "I didn't make you walk the plank, my comely wench, so now you will be my slave, to do as I command."

"Are you serious, Daryl?"

"Argh! The name's not Daryl. It's . . . No Beard."

"No Beard the pirate?" She giggled. "You've got to be kidding."

"Don't laugh, wench!" Shrugging, he struggled to hide his grin. "Hey, it's the best I can come up with."

"Pretty lame, if you ask me."

"No one asked you! Now obey my command. Strip!"

Dropping a slight curtsy, she said, "Yes, my lord."

"Ash? Pirates weren't royalty. *Sir* is fine."

"Yes, sir." Eyes locked with his, she untied the bows at her shoulders. Her sundress would have fallen like the one she'd worn at her apartment, but it stuck on the swells of her breasts.

Did he help by tugging it down? Role-playing was a lot harder than he'd assumed.

A slight breeze drifted through their open window, cooling his face as it wrapped him in her seductive scent along with the sultry smell of the ocean.

It made him impossibly harder.

The yardstick dropped to the plank floor.

His palms itched with the need to feel her bare skin.

He took a step closer, looking down at the dress clinging to her curves.

With each breath she took, the top of the dress slipped a little farther down the slope of her breasts.

Unable to stand the suspense, he gripped the soft cotton on each side of her ribs and gave a little tug.

The bodice fell to her waist.

His breath seized in his lungs. Unable to swallow, he felt as though he may drown in his physical reaction to her.

His hand shook as he traced the edge of one breast with his fingertip.

Her little gasp echoed in the quiet room.

His cock stirred at the sight of her nipples drawing into tight buds.

Sliding his arm around the smooth skin of her bare back, he pulled her close, thoughts of pirates and role-playing leaving his mind. His only thought was of getting intimate with Ashley.

Her hands bunched up the fabric of his polo shirt, shoving it up into his armpits. On tiptoe, she tugged and pulled in her effort to remove it.

He jerked it over his head, tossing it toward the corner. His breath caught at the feel of her nipples on his bare skin. Electricity raced across his skin to his extremities.

Willing his hand to stop shaking, he traced the edge of her breast with his free hand while he trailed kisses up the side of her neck.

Beneath his lips, her pulse fluttered.

"Ash, it's me. I'd never hurt you. You know that, don't you?" She gave a faint nod. "Relax, darlin', it's going to be all right. Better than all right," he quickly corrected, "phenomenal."

A series of tugs shoved her dress over her hips. It slid down to puddle around her feet. Hands cupping her breasts, he urged her to step out of it, then walked her backward to the edge of the mattress.

"My turn," she whispered, reaching for the button on his jeans. The sound of waves washing to shore counterbalanced the sound of his zipper releasing tooth by tooth.

Just as he thought he would howl his frustration, she slipped her hands beneath the denim. Warmth seared his hips as she slid her hands around to palm his butt. They swayed back and forth, his fabric-covered erection dragging across her abdomen.

After an eternity, she pushed on his jeans until they slid down his legs, the change in his pocket making a chinking sound against the plank flooring.

She continued swaying, rubbing the hardened tips of her breasts against him.

He clenched his teeth, tamping down the urge to rip the scrap of fabric from her delectable body and plunge into the wet heat he'd craved for so many years.

But he didn't want to scare her. If she needed time, he could afford to give it to her. After all, he was in it for the long haul.

Lost in his thoughts, he almost yelped when her mouth closed over one of his nipples.

Her delicate tongue toyed with the rapidly puckering tip, her hot breath ratcheting up his already-monstrous desire for her.

Their gazes met.

Ashley dropped to her knees, pushing on the waistband of his tighty-whities, her jaw set in determination.

He grabbed her hands, stopping the downward progression of his underwear.

If she took him into her mouth, it would be over before it began. And that would be just one of the problems. He needed more time.

At her puzzled look, he shrugged, hoping she wouldn't misunderstand. "Later," he managed to choke out. "I want to see you. All of you," he said, pulling her to her feet and reaching for the sides of her thong. "We've waited so long."

In answer, she pushed her panties down and stepped out to stand before him, the setting sun gilding her toned body.

Overwhelmed, he was speechless as his eyes caressed her.

"No Beard? Ah, Daryl?" Her cheeks darkened while she attempted to cover her nudity with her hands. "Did I do something wrong? Am I moving too fast?" Tears swam in her eyes. "I knew this was not a good idea."

"Shh." He kissed her eyes closed, trailed kisses down to her mouth, and then brushed his lips across her trembling ones. "It's perfect. You're perfect. I was just admiring the view. And I don't mean the ocean. Did anyone ever tell you you're gorgeous?"

She shook her head, toying with the elastic of his waistband. "Then why are you still wearing these?"

It felt as though his whole body smiled. "Good question." He stepped out of his underwear, making sure his hands were strategically located.

"C'mon," she whispered in a seductive voice as she backed away to sit on the edge of the mattress.

Her shriek immediately followed when she hit the floor with a resounding thud, the mattress flipping over her head.

"Ashley!" Daryl shoved the mattress aside and helped her up. "Are you okay?"

"No," she mumbled, dragging the cotton thermal blanket off the flipped mattress to cover her nudity. "I'm embarrassed." She looked up into his concerned eyes. "And I'm afraid, Daryl," she whispered. "What if we're making a terrible mistake?"

Her eyes didn't obey her mental command to stop ogling her best friend. Who knew Daryl was so built? More importantly, how could she have not noticed over the years?

"If it's a mistake," Daryl said in what sounded like carefully enunciated words, "*terrible* isn't the word I'd use. Even as a mistake, it would qualify as pretty damn great, in my book." He pulled her to him, blanket and all. "Ashley, we don't have to have sex to enjoy being together, you know. We—"

"I knew it!" Struggling with the yards of blanket tangling her arms, she tried to move with at least a modicum of dignity. *Don't cry,* her mind screamed. *It was your stupid idea to have a sex-only vacation with Daryl, of all people. He either just was not all that interested in you or obviously knew it would be a disaster and was just too polite to turn you down.*

Still, it stung to know he didn't find her doable. Oh, sure, he had an erection. But it had been her experience that pretty much any guy would get a hard-on at the sight of a naked woman. Any naked woman.

She wanted to be special.

# 8

---

"I understand."

Daryl's voice broke into her internal pity party.

"You understand what?" She paused in her fight with the blanket.

"It's a big step for us, Ash." His warm hands cupped her shoulders.

She had to lock her knees to prevent leaning into his solid warmth.

"It's understandable to have, well, reservations, after everything you've been through romantically for the past several years. But I hope you know I'd never hurt you. Not intentionally, anyway."

"But I can't even get into role-playing." Blinking back tears, she stared at their bare feet. Feet that looked amazingly erotic for some reason. "I'm just a big fat loser," she choked out.

Daryl had the nerve to laugh.

She'd have socked him, but he pulled her into a quick hug, pinning her arms beneath the blanket at her sides.

"You're not big, you're definitely not fat, and no way are

you a loser." His finger beneath her chin tilted her face up to his. "You're my best friend. Always have been, always will be, regardless of what takes place in this beach house. Or doesn't take place. Got that?"

Nodding, she sniffed. "Now what?"

He scooped her up in his arms, holding her tight when she squealed and tried to wiggle from his grasp. "Hold still! I don't want to drop you. Now we're going to check out the rest of the house." He flipped the wall switch with his elbow, illuminating the shabby living room. "I think it looked better in the dark."

Arching her neck, she saw what he meant. The sage-green sofa, while fairly contemporary in style, had definitely seen better days. Or a lot of action. The thought heated her cheeks.

Oblivious, Daryl strode past the scarred end tables to a door on the far side of the room, elbowing another light switch. "Ah, a kitchen. Sort of." Smiling, he rubbed noses with her. "Good thing we enjoy eating out."

"It's not so bad," she said, sliding out of his arms to stand on the cool tiled floor while she tugged at her blanket, his arms around her from behind feeling secure. Feeling right. "Maybe we can go buy some food tomorrow morning. Nothing fancy. Maybe some bread and stuff for sandwiches, some bagels, butter." She shrugged. "The toaster looks clean and fairly new. Look, there's a coffeemaker, too."

"What's wrong with Starbucks?"

Good old Daryl. He was so predictable.

"Nothing," she said, peering into the first empty cabinet. "But I didn't see any close by. Did you? Hey, we're roughing it. We can make our own coffee."

"We can?" He stood directly behind her, the warmth of his hands branding her hips through the layers of blanket. "I don't know, Ash. I sort of like my amenities."

"Oh? Like what?" Sure, the beach house looked nothing like the ad, but it wasn't that bad. She stepped back.

"Well, take, for instance, the last pizza we had delivered. Remember that?" She nodded and he continued, stalking her until he had her backed against the sink. "After I left your place, I couldn't stop thinking about all the opportunities I missed with that pizza. Those kind of opportunities come with amenities."

"Opportunities?" Her heartbeat echoed in her ears.

He nodded, pressing closer to her suddenly eager body.

His hands slid beneath her arms as he lifted her to sit on the counter next to the sink. "Missed opportunities, Ash. Think about it." He tugged the blanket until it parted, baring her breasts. "For instance, I could have taken a piece of pizza and stroked you like this." He dragged his fingertips over her breasts, causing her nipples to jump to attention.

"Th-that might have been, um, a little messy," she managed to say around her shallow breaths.

"Which is another missed opportunity. An opportunity to do this." Bending slightly, he covered her nipple with his mouth, surrounding her in his heat, and sucked, the action causing her hips to lift off the counter. "And this." He repeated the action on the other breast, then licked both breasts until they were thoroughly wet and aching.

"Then what?" she whispered.

The smile he shot her made her wet.

He nudged between her legs, spreading the blanket out to the sides. "Then I'd have laid you down and given my famous pepperoni massage."

She couldn't stop the giggle the thought evoked. "Really. Pepperoni massage?" She tsked. "Daryl, I thought you could come up with something better than that."

"Ah, but you would be wrong, because you have no knowledge of my many sensual talents, Goldilocks." He waggled his eyebrows. "And I see you're a natural blond."

She smacked his arm and tried to pull the blanket back

around to at least partially cover her nudity. "I didn't have time to wax before we left. Thanks so much for pointing that out, by the way."

He chuckled and pulled the blanket from her grasp. "Cut it out. I'm still telling you what you missed last night. Where was I? Oh, yeah, my pepperoni massage. First, I'd have taken a couple of pieces off the pizza; then I would have stroked them all the way down your body, like this." He demonstrated by stroking her sensitized flesh with just the tips of his fingers, outlining the bottom of her breasts, then going ever so slowly down until he reached the juncture of her thighs. "At this point, I'd lay you back and do this." Her bare back met the cool countertop. He lifted her legs until she lay flat.

Excited beyond reason, she closed her eyes, trying to forget her best friend was seeing her totally naked.

He nudged her inner thighs, urging her to spread her legs. She eagerly complied, somewhat surprised to feel the warmth of his palm against her cleft.

"Down here, I'd move the pepperoni around, mixing it with your juices," he whispered, his breath hot against her ear as he ground his palm into her aching flesh.

She whimpered, doing her dangdest to not writhe against his hand, begging for more. Her ache was palpable when he moved on to massage her legs and feet. Still, she waited.

The wait was short. She felt his mouth begin its tortuous journey back up the inside of her calves, then the inside of each thigh, each time stopping short of the place weeping for his touch.

Just when she thought she could stand no more teasing, his breath fanned her swollen folds. "Of course, then I'd have to make sure I removed all the pepperoni oils."

"Of course," she squeaked, her breath coming in rapid pants as his hot mouth covered her, his tongue flicking her distended nub, driving her higher and higher.

Then his tongue speared her, taking her over the edge as wave after wave of pleasure washed over her while his tongue lapped at her.

She tried in vain to clamp her legs together, sure she would die from pleasure if she didn't stop right that moment.

Daryl wouldn't allow it.

Using his forearms, he pried her legs apart, his fingers and thumbs busily massaging every erogenous inch of her.

She was on sexual overload. Did anyone die of bliss? Just her luck, she'd be the first victim. Her mother would be mortified.

Normally, thoughts of her mother during sex would have the immediate effect of a wet blanket.

Not this time, for some odd reason.

"Wait," Daryl said, his voice vibrating her labia, "there's more." His tongue swiped her engorged folds. "Much more," he said, his breath poker hot.

The sensation that followed had her gasping, struggling to raise her head enough to see what the heck he was doing to her pliable body.

Braced on his elbows, forearms holding her legs splayed, he cupped her outer lips with the outer three fingers of each hand, pushing with his thumbs until her distended labia formed a shiny purplish pink mound, while his index fingers massaged and probed her clitoris. The effect, along with the pressure it caused on her vagina, brought her to screaming climax within seconds.

Panting, she collapsed back on the drainboard, wondering if she'd spoken in tongues. She couldn't remember ever coming so forcefully. Well, maybe once before . . .

Daryl chose that moment to interrupt her afterglow by placing her feet on his shoulders and closing his mouth over her again.

His tongue swirled around and around her swollen clit before sucking it deeply into his mouth.

She screamed and arched her back, not sure if she was wanting him to stop or wanting more.

He continued to suck her excited nubbin as he slid his finger into her eager body, revolving his fingertip deep within her.

Her back arched. The third climax roared through her like a tsunami, dragging her in its undertow, robbing her of breath or even coherent thought.

She wasn't entirely sure, but she may have lost consciousness.

# 9

Daryl's muscles vibrated, head to toe and everywhere in between, as he reined in his lust. His erection thumped against the cabinet with each move he made. Instead of cooling his ardor, it excited him even more.

He rubbed his face against Ashley's soft blond stubble, inhaling her unique scent, willing his heart to slow down. At that point, he could easily ravage her with very little provocation.

He didn't want to do that. He wanted their lovemaking to be mutually satisfying.

He also wanted to make love to her for the first time in a bed. Where the hell was a damn bed when you needed one?

Ashley's hand reached out to stroke his bare hip, causing his penis to jerk as his hard-on intensified.

"Daryl?" Her voice was soft in the quiet kitchen. "I think I'd like to go to bed now. Please," she added, her hand dipping to give his cock an encouraging squeeze.

He required no further encouragement.

Scooping her into his arms, he headed for the bedroom,

stumbling and tripping on the long tail of the blanket in his haste.

He paused at the doorway of their bedroom and took a deep breath. Suddenly the room didn't look at all weather-beaten and drab.

The chipped bed frame glowed with the moonlight spilling through the open French doors, the ocean's ebb and flow making erotic background music.

Ashley's sigh drew his attention. "Aren't you glad we rented this house now?" she whispered.

He wanted to tell her yes. He wanted to qualify it by adding any place they were together was heaven to him. But the lump in his throat prevented him from doing anything other than nod and flip the light switch.

He walked toward the bed with his precious cargo, gazes locked.

"Daryl?" He looked down at her and had the urge to tell her how the moonlight intensified her beauty. "Turn out the light, okay?" She shrugged. "Without curtains, lights would make us a peep show for anyone walking by."

He cleared his throat. "Good point. But wouldn't you like the breeze from the fan? I know the ocean breeze will make it cooler later on, but right now it's a little muggy."

"Okay. I think I see a little piece of string. If you lift me higher, I can pull it. I bet it will turn off the light portion." Her shriek echoed from the walls. "Careful! A little higher, I almost have it."

*Click.* The room plunged into moonlit darkness.

Slowly, he lowered Ashley until their breaths mingled.

His toes tangled in the dangling corner of Ashley's blanket.

Try as he might, he couldn't recover his balance. Clutching her tightly, he braced for impact.

Instead, they bounced and rolled on the air mattress Ashley had toppled earlier. Their laughter drowned out the surf.

"Daryl!" Ashley's voice was muffled. "I can barely breathe with you squeezing me so tightly." She giggled when he released his grip, smiling up at him. "You really know how to get a girl in the mood, goofball." She tweaked his ear.

Crushing her against his still-partially-excited body, he growled, "Given the opportunity, I can do better than that."

Instead of melting from his sexual heat, she had the audacity to laugh. Again.

"Much as I enjoyed what went on in the kitchen, I'm really tired." She inhaled deeply and smiled at him. "Being at the beach is always so relaxing." She patted his shoulder, drawing her hand down his chest, across his nipples. "I would worry someone was trying to tell us something, but I loved the foreplay in the kitchen too much to listen." Another pat, this time in the general vicinity of his sternum. "Rain check?" She leaned close, brushing her lips across his surprised mouth. "I'll make it up to you tomorrow, I promise," she whispered.

Make it up to him? She didn't owe him a damn thing. Did she think he was keeping score?

Say something.

"Ash, don't look so worried. I don't care if we never have sex," he lied. "I just want to spend some time with you. And, of course, if we do end up sleeping together, I'd like to explore that as well—oof!" Ashley's elbow connected with his unsuspecting abs.

"You're such a weirdo!" she said, and laughed. But then she grabbed his arm when he began to move away from her. "And do not even think about getting dressed again." At his questioning look, she hurried on. "I meant it, Daryl, about having a sex vacation with you. Really. Don't laugh. Why can't we stay naked and just cuddle tonight?"

Why can't they just cuddle? Naked? He could probably come

up with about a hundred reasons, just off the top of his head. But he wasn't about to rock the boat.

Instead, he lay down beside her on the felled mattress and pulled her close as he pulled up the blanket. "Sounds like a plan. Good night, Ash." He kissed her ear, then whispered, "Wake me up if you decide you want to have your way with me."

"Don't you want to put the mattress back on the bed?"

"Nope. Too much effort; plus it would probably just dump us back on the floor sometime during the night. This way, we just eliminate a step." He kissed her neck. "Much more efficient."

Besides, by staying on the floor, she wouldn't see his monster hard-on.

Dawn's first blush lit the bedroom of the beach house in a warm glow. Ashley opened her eyes and stretched, a smile curving her lips. Beside her, Daryl slept in all his magnificent nudity.

She did a leisurely perusal. Yes, no doubt about it, her best friend had a smoking-hot body. How could she have not noticed it for so many years?

Fists clenched to avoid the temptation of touching him, she began her closer inspection, finding the shadow of his morning beard adorable and sexy. Her lips itched to kiss his Adam's apple. Broad shoulders reminded her how far removed he was from the skinny kid he'd been when they'd first met.

She visually caressed his chest, then frowned at the corner of the blanket that protected his modesty but blocked her view.

Did she dare raise it for a peek?

Moving slowly, she tugged at the offending piece of cotton thermal material until his hips were bare.

Licking her lips, she looked down.

Her laughter erupted, jerking Daryl awake.

# 10

Daryl jerked awake from what was easily the most X-rated dream of Ashley to date.

Funny, in all the years he'd dreamed of waking up naked with her at his side, he'd never once dreamed she'd be pointing at his package and laughing.

His hands hurried to belatedly cover the object of her hilarity. "Hey, my boys were sleeping. They were hunkered down for the night."

Sobered, she blinked at him. Then her eyes crinkled and her laughter sprang forth again to echo from the ceiling.

"Okay, Ash, I get it. You can stop laughing now, before you hurt my feelings." Scooting to the edge of the mattress, he wedged his hip against the bed frame. "Cut it out. There's a fine line between humor and hostility. And you're walking that line."

Smiling, she wiped a tear from her eye. "Oh, don't be like that. I wasn't laughing at your, um, privates. Really." A snicker escaped. "When did you get a tattoo?"

Shit. And he'd been careful to cover it last night. He sighed, eyes closed. "I don't want to talk about it."

"Oh, come on!" She scooted closer, her soft, naked breasts pressed intimately against his thundering heart. "It's so cute."

"Cute is not the look I was going for, Ash."

"Honestly, Daryl, what were you thinking?"

"I said I don't want to talk about it!" He'd get up, but she was lying on the blanket, and he wasn't about to flaunt the stupid tattoo. Or anything else, for that matter. At least, not now.

Morning sunlight bounced off her golden curls when she shook her head. "You know I'm just going to keep after you until you tell me."

She ignored his warning glare.

"Seriously, Daryl. 'The South Shall Rise Again' with a little Confederate flag?" Her giggle just added to his humiliation. "Move your hands. I want to get a closer look. I still can't believe you did it."

"I was drunk. It was spring break. Enough said."

"Move your hands." She rolled to straddle him, batting his hands away, then holding them at his sides while she inspected the artwork adorning his lower abdomen with such an intense look on her face, he felt a blush burning his face and neck.

Their eyes met. "Did you have to shave for them to get it that far down?"

*This conversation cannot be happening.* He swallowed and cleared his throat. "I don't remember."

"Sure you do."

He closed his eyes for a second before meeting her earnest gaze. "No. I was, um, less hairy in college." He shrugged. "Like I said, I was drunk. It seemed like a good idea at the time." His abs jerked at the feel of her fingertip tracing the tiny flag. "Wh-what are you doing?"

"Just looking. Did it hurt?"

"Not as I recall. But, then, I'd had plenty of anesthetic."

Before he could take another breath, Ashley bent down and brushed a kiss over the flag tattoo, then traced it again, this time with the tip of her tongue.

He tried to think of baseball.

Her sexy smile and twinkling eyes greeted him when she raised her head. "I think the South has risen," she whispered, scooting up until she lay on top of his excited body. "Let's celebrate," she said, rubbing her damp folds against his renewed erection.

"I . . . but . . . condoms . . ." he stammered. He'd longed for just such a situation, dreamed of it, since he'd found out about sex. The yearning had only intensified after their one night together. Now that it appeared to actually be about to happen, the idea excited him beyond human reason.

And it also scared the shit out of him.

What if they were not as terrific in the sack as his memory insisted they were? What if being intimate did not make her fall in love with him? Was it worth risking their friendship to find out?

Maybe agreeing to a sex-only vacation wasn't the brilliant idea he'd thought. Maybe he should just stick with his memory of that one perfect encounter.

Ashley chose that moment to suck on his earlobe while rubbing her breasts suggestively against his chest.

Then again, maybe he was an idiot to even hesitate. After all, sex had been his idea. Sure, he'd meant a sexual relationship. Which he'd hoped would lead to more. Like opening her eyes to see the guy she should have been with all along. But he'd readily agreed to a sex vacation. And now he wanted to wait. Wait for what? For Ashley to get discouraged and go sleep with yet another wrong guy? Not damn likely.

His fingertips stroked her perfect, smooth skin from her buttocks, up her ribs, to finally cup her breasts. "Grab my shorts, would you? They're by your left foot."

She slowly shook her head. "Don't even think about getting dressed, Stud."

Stud. No one had ever called him Stud. He brushed a strand

of silky hair from her face, tucking it behind her ear, and then kissed the tip of her nose. "I have condoms in the pockets." He grinned. "Lots of condoms."

"Ooh." She smiled and did a little shimmy that went straight to his groin. "I love a confident man."

Love.

He planned to do his damndest to make that a literal statement.

But, for now, he would take it slow and easy. Rubbing her nipples into stiff peaks between his forefingers and thumbs, he grinned back and said, "I prefer to think of it as being prepared."

"Like a Boy Scout?" Ripping open a packet, she sheathed him in record time before climbing back to her previous position.

He chose not to think about how many times she may have performed such a service for her previous lovers.

Because, if things went as planned, he would be her last lover.

Poised above him, her heat scorched the tip of his penis. He gritted his teeth to prevent eagerly flexing his hips and filling her. It had been so long.

On some level, he knew it was important to allow her to take the lead. At least once.

Knees clutching his hips, she arched her back, her breasts jutting out, begging him to play.

He didn't believe in making her beg.

Caressing her knees, he inched his hands up the smooth, firm flesh of her thighs. His fingers silently counted her ribs. He palmed her breasts, enjoying the heaviness in his palms, the smooth warmth of her skin, the little hitch in her breath when he rubbed the pads of his thumbs across her puckered nipples. "You like that?"

She raised her head, her gaze locked with his, and nodded

slowly. "But I can't wait anymore." Leaning closer, she stretched until her nipples brushed his lips.

Gently pulling her closer, he squeezed her firm flesh, pushing her nipple deep into his hungry mouth.

Ashley squirmed with excitement as Daryl's satiny tongue circled her nipple, then drew it deep within the heat of his mouth. Had anything ever felt so good, so right?

She arched her back, pushing deeper into his voracious mouth, rubbing shamelessly against his abdomen, reveling in the feel of his skin against her most intimate part.

While he sucked her, his hands kneaded her breasts, firing her excitement to the boiling point.

She whimpered when his hands left her, not at all pleased with the cool air bathing her heated skin. Thankfully, the heat of his hands returned as they skimmed down her body, paused to circle her belly button, then continued their path to her excited core.

Another whimper escaped when he stopped, his thumbs teasing her, rubbing the sensitized skin just shy of the spot yearning for his touch. Having already experienced world-shattering orgasms by those hands, she knew their capabilities and eagerly anticipated a replay. What was he waiting for?

Adjusting, she widened her stance, nudging his wrists with her thighs to tell him what she wanted. What she needed.

But instead of moving downward, his maddening hands moved up. They cupped her breasts, flexing and squeezing them until she decided it wouldn't be terrible if he sucked them again.

No sooner had that thought crossed her mind than his hands were on the move again until they gripped her beneath the arms and lifted. Lifted until she hung suspended over his head. Before she could form a question, he lowered her, his tongue circling her opening, licking her swollen folds, sucking her clitoris deeply into his talented mouth.

She'd scarcely settled into the rhythm of his tongue when

her climax was upon her. Reflexively, her knees gripped his head while she rode out the orgasm, his breath hot on her sex, her muscles twitching.

Before she caught her breath, he was moving her, pushing her shoulders downward until the tip of his erection kissed her swollen labia.

He murmured something, setting off vibrations in her chest. Did she actually hear the word *love*? Love what? Love her? Impossible. Love sex with her? Much more probable. And a sentiment she shared.

Air whooshed from Daryl's lungs as he flexed his hips, plunging deep into her eager flesh.

He paused, the only sound their labored breathing mingled with the surf.

"Open your eyes, Ashley," he said in a low, rough voice. "I want you to know who's inside you, loving you."

She lifted heavy lids to meet his green gaze. "I know," she whispered, then moved her hips for a better, deeper alignment.

Hard hands gripped her hip bones, lifting her slightly away from the warmth of his body. "Look, Ash. Look at us. Watch me filling you. Watch your gorgeous pussy stretch to accommodate my cock. It feels even more amazing when you watch what we're doing."

Fascinated, she could only nod, watching the veined erection, shiny with her fluid, disappear deep into her body, then reappear again. It took her breath away and puckered her nipples. Every nerve ending was on alert, feeling every millimeter as Daryl went in and out of her excited body.

She'd never watched the actual act of intercourse before and found it fascinating, alluring, intoxicating. And exciting as all get-out.

A renewed gush made Daryl's skin slick against her inner thighs. She was forced to slow the thrusts of her pelvis or risk having his penis pop out of her slick folds. It was agony, torture, when all she really wanted to do was grip his lean hips tighter between her thighs and ride him hard. Harder. Until they both were exhausted.

Then she wanted to do it again. And again.

She hadn't felt this way in years. Five to be exact. Her movements slowed. If she didn't know better, she'd think it had been Daryl that night in the storage closet. But that was ridiculous.

Wasn't it?

Daryl slid his hand between their bodies, derailing her thought, pushing her higher on his shaft. "Keep watching," he said in a gruff voice.

His hand slid lower, pushing her labia together. The purple pearl of her clitoris peeked through, shiny with moisture. He massaged it with the pad of his thumb, bringing her to an instant, breath-stealing, heart-racing climax.

When she would have collapsed on his solid warmth, he held her hips in a viselike grip as he increased the speed and power of his thrusts.

It was pleasant, she thought, a smile tugging at her tired lips as she enjoyed the delicious friction of each forceful thrust.

She'd had her orgasm; she'd just go along for the ride while she waited for his completion. Her eyes opened wide as another wave of sensation washed over her, almost drowning her in her release.

Inner shock waves were just beginning to subside when he flipped her to her stomach and entered her again, pulling her up to her hands and knees as his hips pistoned into her.

Her excitement built again, wetting her inner thighs, when he reached around to play with her aching nipples.

"Again!" His breath was hot against her neck when he bent over her back, grinding a little harder and deeper with each thrust. "I want you to come for me again, Ash." He pinched her nipples, eliciting a cry of release from her as he pounded into her receptive flesh for a second and third time before shuddering with his own climax.

Pulling her tightly against him, he lowered her, rolled with her until they were once again lying on the mattress, front to back, with his arms securely wrapped around her.

His hand stroked her damp hair from her face. "Good morning."

She giggled and reached back to pat his bare hip. "Good morning to you, too."

"What a way to start the day," he said against her ear.

"Mmmm." Smiling, she tilted her head, baring her neck for his kisses. Speaking required too much effort at the moment.

Besides, she didn't want whatever they had going on to end. At least not yet. And if they started talking, it just might.

No, she wanted to bask in the afterglow for at least a few more minutes.

"Ash? Are you okay?"

She sighed. Apparently Daryl was done with his basking.

"Ashley?"

"What?"

"Are you mad? I thought you . . . I mean, I know we . . . Where are you going?"

Tugging the blanket until it was out from under Daryl's weight, she refused to look at him. When she had the blanket secured around her, she headed for the door. "I'm going to go take a quick shower, then go to the Quickie Mart for something to make for breakfast. If you want to go with me, I can call you when I get out of the shower."

Feeling vulnerable, Daryl grabbed a pillow to cover his assets. Ashley had made it clear she was showering alone. Fine with him. At least this time. "Sounds like a plan," he said, avoiding eye contact.

He refused to look up until he heard the bathroom door close.

Being a sex object was turning out to be a lot harder than he'd anticipated.

# 11

Ashley stood beneath the stinging spray of the shower and wished she hadn't locked the bathroom door. Would Daryl have joined her behind the cheerful rubber-duck-print shower curtain? Would she have welcomed him?

Heck, yes.

Instead, she'd made it clear she planned to shower alone.

Dumb, she thought, really dumb. Water slicked her skin. Bubbles from her shampoo slid over her shoulders to caress her still-sensitive nipples, making her wish it were Daryl.

With a growl of frustration, she grabbed her body wash and finished her shower in record time.

Wrapped in one of her beach towels, she opened the door, allowing the steam to escape from the little bathroom.

Daryl stood just outside the bathroom door, leaning casually against the wall, a venti cup of coffee in each hand. "I thought you might like a cup of coffee before we leave."

"Where . . . ?" Even in her confusion, she reached for a cup.

He shrugged. "I remembered seeing a Starbucks in the little strip mall down the road on our way in. I knew I had plenty of time to get dressed and make the coffee run." His teeth flashed white when he grinned. "I notice you still take marathon showers."

Nodding, she savored the taste of her latte, barely managing to refrain from moaning her appreciation. After her first swallow, she opened her eyes to find him staring at her. "Leave it to you to spot a Starbucks in any direction while driving eighty."

"It's a gift." He tossed his cup into the dented metal waste basket by the kitchen door. "Let me grab a quick shower, then I'll drive you to get groceries. I thought maybe we could have a late breakfast somewhere, then hit the beach after we put everything away."

"Oh, ick," Ashley grumbled when she turned over on the blanket next to Daryl. "I have sand in my teeth."

"I told you not to eat that last chip," he said, his eyes closed to the bright afternoon sun.

"Yeah, but you didn't tell me it was sandy." She made a combination gagging-spitting sound that made him smile. "Don't laugh at me, Daryl Garrett. I'm warning you."

Since he was easily a half a foot taller and fifty pounds heavier, the warning was laughable.

In hindsight, he probably should not have laughed, he realized, when she pulled his bathing suit open and poured a handful of sand into his crotch.

Howling, he jumped to his feet, immediately shaking the waistband in an effort to dislodge the sand clinging to his sweating abs and farther down. "You're playing with fire, Clark."

He lunged, but she got away, shrieking as she ran across the hot sand toward the waves, with him in hot pursuit.

At the edge of the water, he caught her, his arm grabbing her around the waist, and lifted her off her feet.

"Put me down!"

"Stop kicking! You may hit something vital. Ash, cut it

out!" He'd meant a playful toss. Instead, he was surprised to see her fly through the air to land several yards out into the Gulf of Mexico with a *splat*.

"Ash!" He waded toward the spot where she'd gone under. "Ashley! Are you okay?"

Her head broke the surface a scarce foot in front of him. Coughing and sputtering, she shoved wet hair from her face. "That was mean."

But she was smiling. Upon closer inspection, he saw it was a somewhat evil smile, so he began backing away.

"I don't trust that smile, Ash." She stood facing him and reached for the waistband of his trunks. "What are you doing?"

"Just helping you get the sand out." She jerked, pulling him until he stood abdomen to abdomen with her. "What are you doing?"

"Returning the favor," he said, tugging on the tie strings holding her bikini bottom together.

"Daryl, I don't have any sand in my suit."

"Maybe we should check."

"Oh, yeah, well, maybe we should check yours first." She thrust her hand deep, smiling up at him when she felt his erection. "We need to get all this gritty old sand off." Dipping lower, she made a production of brushing the sand from his testicles, swishing water around them.

"Ash-ley." His jaw ached from gritting his teeth, but he really didn't want to get hot and bothered in the water. On a public beach. He closed his hand over her arm, pulling her hand out of his pants before he embarrassed both of them.

She giggled.

He pulled her into his arms and reveled in the feel of her against him as they swayed with the incoming waves.

"Thanks," he said, his voice husky with the emotions racing through him.

"For what?"

They watched her breasts rub against his chest with each wave breaking against them.

"For inviting me," he finally answered. "It was a great idea." In more ways than one.

"About this morning . . ."

"Yeah? What about it?" Beneath his suit, his cock perked up again at the thought of sex with Ashley.

"It was . . . Will you stop untying my bottoms? I could lose them."

Waggling his eyebrows, he said, "That's what I'm hoping."

"Well, I'm not! How would I get back to the house bottom-less?"

"But think of how much fun we could have here in the water without them." The flutter-smooth touch inside his suit made him grow impossibly harder. "If you're not interested, why are your hands in my pants?"

"My hands aren't in your pants."

# 12

"What do you mean your hands aren't in my pants?" He knew what he felt.

To demonstrate, she held up both hands.

Strange. The caressing sensation continued.

Horrifying reality dawned.

Hopping around, he tore at his waistband. "What the hell is in my pants?"

Ashley grinned and started to make a smart-ass comeback, then realized he wasn't joking. Something really was in Daryl's pants. Something besides Daryl.

He continued to flail around, hopping and jumping, his hand buried to the elbow in his swimsuit.

"Oh, my!" She began hopping along with him. "What if it's a snake? Do they have snakes in the Gulf? Can water moccasins live in salt water?"

Daryl glared at her. "Thanks a lot. I wasn't worried until you opened your mouth." Did poisonous snakes live in salt water? He suddenly wished he'd paid more attention in his science classes.

His hand finally touched something besides his own terri-fied body. Something cool and slick. When he closed his fingers around it, it began a fast shimmy. Retaining his grip, he pulled it from his trunks.

Light reflected off silvery gold scales a second before the fish slipped from his grasp and reentered the water with a splash.

Ashley sagged against him. "Not a snake. Thank the Lord! What was that, a sunfish?"

"Looked like it. Doesn't matter. I'm just glad it's out."

"Do you have a valid fishing license?" Ashley sputtered at her wit. "I know you have the pole." Her laughter carried across the water.

"Ha. Ha. You're a riot, Ash." He took her hand, recalling his plans of a few minutes ago. "Let's go back to the house and take a nap."

"Um, Daryl?" Sobered, she glanced around.

"Hmm?"

"We have, um, a problem."

He stopped tugging on her hand and cocked his eyebrow. "What's that?"

"I seem to have lost the bottom of my bikini."

Under normal circumstances, especially since becoming her lover, Daryl would have been pleased at the idea of a bottom-less Ashley. Easy access.

And, although the idea still had certain merits as well as a tit-illating possibility, the reality was a mood breaker.

Even if they could ignore protocol and have raunchy sex in the buoyant salt water, there was the problem of getting Ashley back to the beach house afterward without, well, exposure. Not to mention the very real possibility of her being turned off by the entire prospect.

He couldn't blame her. And giving her his suit wouldn't help the situation.

"Plan B. Stay here and I'll go get the beach blanket. You can wrap up in it, and then we'll go back to the house."

"So we can have sex? That's what you're thinking, isn't it?" Hands on hips, she glared at him.

Yep, definitely a mood breaker.

Breath whooshed out. "No," he insisted. "Well, okay, it crossed my mind. Don't give me that look. I'm a guy. We always think about sex. It's in our DNA. But I didn't mean go back to the house to have sex. Not now, anyway. I thought you might want to go parasailing." They'd discussed it earlier. He kissed the tip of her nose. "And, while I wouldn't mind, other people might be offended if you went bottomless."

Her shoulders slumped. "That was embarrassing. I'm such a loser. Forget I said anything, okay?"

"Which time?"

"Shut up and go get the blanket."

"I think I'm permanently deaf in my right ear." Daryl dropped onto the sagging sofa in the beach house living room. "Anyone ever tell you your voice could break glass?"

"I was scared. A lot of people scream when they're scared. Even when they're having fun, like on a roller coaster." She bent to sweep away their sandy footprints with the damp beach towel.

"So you're saying you were screaming because you were having fun?"

"No, I was terrified." She smiled. "But I'm glad we went. One more thing to check off my to-do list."

"Of things to do before you die?"

She shuddered. "Don't mention death and parasailing, please. No, I meant cross off of our list of things to do while we're on vacation."

"You actually made a list?"

The damp towel hit his face.

"Forget the dang list, Daryl. There is no list. Geez, you're so literal. I'm going to grab a quick shower." .

"'Kay," he mumbled, eyes closed.

Was he that worn out? She reached for the straps of her maillot and peeled it down her legs.

"Daryl? Are you asleep?" She walked toward him on her way to the bathroom. "Want to take a shower together?"

His eyes popped open, then widened at her nudity.

"Oh, yeah."

By the time the water was hot, Daryl was naked and kissing her in the way that always curled her toes. Though she was turned on, a part of her mind couldn't help comparing his kisses to Andre's that first night they were together at the Halloween party. Maybe time had dulled her memories. Daryl's kisses were every bit as potent as Andre's had been that night, maybe even more.

After the obligatory shower sex to take the edge off, they leisurely soaped up.

Ashley had to lock her knees as she enjoyed Daryl's sensuous massage in order to keep from dissolving into a puddle on the bottom of the old tub. She loved the roughness of his palms where they slid around her breasts, his thumbs flicking her nipples, causing them to pucker.

He turned her to face the spray and rinsed her off, making sure every trace of soap was gone from her aching folds.

A squeak escaped her lips when he lifted her to stand on the edge of the tub, her feet slipping precariously on the slick enamel surface.

"Spread you legs for me, darlin'." His voice echoed in the steam of their shower.

Eager to comply, she slid her right foot to the side. Unfortunately, her left foot wanted to follow, and the next horrifying second, cool air engulfed her as she felt herself falling.

With a shriek, she simultaneously grabbed for Daryl and the shower curtain in her attempt to regain her balance.

It didn't work.

Ashley peered from behind her magazine at Daryl, who was holding a frozen corn dog on his eye. "Do you think we'll have to pay for the shower curtain?"

He grunted.

"How's your eye?"

Another grunt, then he lowered the corn dog and glared through the swollen flesh surrounding his right eye. "Do I have a black eye?"

"Not yet. It's swollen and still sort of, um, colorful."

He growled and took a vicious bite off the end of the corn dog, then stuck the blunt end against his injured eye while chewing vigorously.

"Isn't that still frozen? I can cook it for you, if you're hungry."

He swallowed. "I bit off the end to get to the colder part. But thanks, anyway," he added.

She peeked through her lashes at him. Even with a swollen eye, he was still cute. And sexy. She'd always known he was those things but thought his sexiness more of an illusion brought on by the assumption she would never have firsthand knowledge. Sort of like lusting after something or someone unattainable.

Was he still unattainable?

Their sex vacation could have the potential for morphing into something more, couldn't it?

"Daryl?"

"Hmm?"

"I had a good time today. I know we always have a good time together, but I meant, um, sexually. You were probably the best time I've ever had, in fact."

He slowly lowered the corn dog. "Probably?"

"Okay, the best." She hurried on. "The only reason I said *probably* was because the first time Andre and I—"

Daryl held up his hand. "Stop. I don't want to hear about it."

"Well, it's not like it's a big secret. I lived with him for almost two years. You lived there, too, for most of that time. You had to know we—"

"I said stop!" Tossing the corn dog in the general vicinity of the trash, he strode toward the door.

"Where are you going?" Hurrying across the room, she slammed her hand against the closed door. "Don't leave. Please. If it bothers you to hear about other stuff, well, I just won't talk about it. Okay?" Pulling on the front of his T-shirt, she tugged him closer. "I don't want to fight." Her lips brushed his.

"What do you want to do?" His arms pulled her closer still.

She rubbed against his obvious erection. "I don't know. I thought maybe we could go in the bedroom and, um, see what comes up."

"Oh, yeah? I was thinking maybe we could go out on the porch and watch the sunset . . . and see what comes up."

She smiled up at him, her fingers toying with the curls at the nape of his neck. "I like that idea. We could make margaritas with the mix we bought."

"Sounds like a plan." He turned her toward the kitchen, lightly tapping her butt. "I'll help this time."

"That was not my fault this afternoon! I think it must be a defective blender."

"And I maintain it's operator error. Let's check it out."

Plunking the big bottle of tequila on the counter next to the blender, she narrowed her eyes. "Okay, you do it this time. The measuring cup is behind you. I'll get the ice and glasses."

"Did we bring extra blankets?" Daryl measured the tequila, then the liquid mixer and dumped them in the blender, following up with the bowl of ice. "It would be more comfortable to sit on than the old wooden deck chairs."

"You're probably right. That way, too, if it gets cool, we'll have something to wrap up in. Ready?"

Nodding, he pushed the button, filling the room with so much noise, talking would be impossible. The last chunk of ice made the blender vibrate and dance toward the edge of the scarred yellow counter.

"Catch it!" Her voice was barely audible above the growling whir of the blender.

Daryl's hands closed around the base just before the top blew off, greenish yellow slush spewing up and over both of them.

Ashley jumped back but not before a stream of sticky, cold margaritas-in-progress hit her face, streaming down into the neck of the clean pink knit shirt she'd just put on. Groaning, she stepped back. Coldness seared the bottom of her bare foot as it slid out from under her. Slipping and sliding in the mess, she lost her footing for the second time that day.

Flailing her arms to regain her balance, she knocked the blender out of Daryl's hands, sending the rest of the mixture flowing down on them.

Eyes closed, she took a deep breath, thankful she hadn't fallen again. And that she hadn't dragged Daryl down along with her. He certainly didn't need another black eye.

Daryl's laughter filled the little kitchen.

Opening her eyes, she glared at him. "It's not funny. It's like we're jinxed." Tightening her lips to keep from joining in on the laughter, she added, "And I really wanted a margarita."

"We can try again. Or, if you're really thirsty, we can always clean up and walk down to the crab shack. Theirs are pretty good."

Sighing, she looked around at the recent devastation. "You don't understand. I wanted our margaritas. I wanted to sit on the porch and drink them, enjoying the ambience of being at a beach house. Enjoying spending time with you. And if you laugh at me, I swear I'm going to clock you."

He pulled her to him, ignoring her wince when their sticky wet skin and clothing touched. "I'm not laughing. I was looking forward to that stuff, too." Without warning, he licked the side of her face. "Mmm. I may have discovered a better way to enjoy my margaritas." His tongue outlined her ear with an exaggerated slurping sound. "We can lick it off of each other," he whispered in her ear, setting off a flash fire of goose bumps.

# 13

Ashley sighed and rolled to her side, her skin slightly sticking to Daryl's despite the vigorous tongue bath they'd both recently enjoyed.

He pressed his lips to her temple, a feeling of such contentment and satisfaction threatening to overwhelm him that he wished he could freeze-frame their time together.

"I'm glad we decided to take a chance on this," Ashley said, her arm securely across his belly.

He grunted in reply. *Glad* was such a tame word for what he was feeling. But he knew he had to take it slow with Ashley, even if it killed him. She'd jumped into her last two relationships. It wouldn't be unusual for her to fear making another mistake. Of course, she didn't realize it was because she'd chosen the wrong guy the last two times. Unfortunately, it was something she would have to discover for herself.

He could wait for her to come to the realization they belonged together.

Their breathing slowly became normal again.

"Why couldn't we have done this years ago?" she persisted.

He kissed her nose and nuzzled her neck before saying, "Timing." He toyed with her nipple, hoping to distract her from the conversation she seemed intent on developing.

"I suppose," she said, tilting her head to give him better access to kiss her neck. "Lord knows my timing hasn't been great. Take Andre, for instance. He'd asked me out literally dozens of times before we got together. I suppose, even though I thought he was moderately attractive, the timing just wasn't right for us then, either."

"Ancient history. In the past. You don't have to talk about it, Ash."

"But why do you suppose it worked out like it did? The sex, that first time, was beyond orgasmic. Then I moved in with him, and it was like I was sleeping with a stranger."

"Ash, really, you don't have to talk about it." Please. It still smarted to realize she'd had mind-blowing sex with him and his roommate on the same evening. To add insult to injury, to know she'd chosen Andre over him.

"Then, crazy as it seems, I found myself attracted to Connor at odd moments. I don't know, maybe it was the way he looked at me all the time. Did you ever notice that?"

Yeah, he'd noticed it, and frankly, it creeped him out. Not to mention it made him jealous as hell. He certainly did not need to hear she had been looking back.

"And what did I do?" Ashley was clearly on a streak and had no intention of taking his subtle hints. "I fell right into bed with Connor. It was okay, but not nearly what I'd expected. Especially after everything I'd heard over the years about his, well, prowess. But did I let that deter me? Heck, no. I kept pushing and pushing until I found myself engaged to the guy." She climbed up to straddle his naked hips. "I'm fortunate he realized we were making a huge mistake, because otherwise we would have been married by now."

Obviously Ash was not taking hints. "Could we not talk about other guys while we're naked in bed together, Ash?"

She dropped down for a quick hug. "Sorry. I guess it's just because we've known each other for so long and you're such a good listener. I feel like I can tell you anything." Her chuckle jiggled her breasts against his chest in a disconcerting way. "Of course, that is your job, isn't it?"

He flipped her to her back, taking his weight on his elbows. "Yes, and, in case you hadn't noticed, I'm not working right now."

"What exactly are you doing?" Smiling, she wiggled against his erection.

"If you have to ask, I must not be doing it right." Grinding himself against her softness, he breathed a sigh of relief that he'd been able to distract her from her conversational track.

"Um, Daryl? Didn't we use the last condom this afternoon?"

"Just the first box." He pushed her into a sitting position and cupped her breasts. "I love your breasts."

*I love you.* Her eyes widened. That couldn't be right. She'd known Daryl Garrett practically all her life. If she was going to fall in love with him, she'd have done it long before now.

It had to be proximity. Face it, she had the annoying habit of falling for whomever she became involved with sexually, and it always turned out badly.

Could Daryl break her streak? Did she want him to?

"Ash? Grab a condom from the pile on the nightstand. Now."

Her eyes widened again at the size of the pile of condoms. "Big plans for tonight?"

"Just optimistic."

"I'd call it being an overachiever."

As she stretched to reach for the condom, he took her nipple into his mouth, drawing it deeply, sucking in time to the bucking of his hips against hers.

The pull on her breast temporarily short-circuited her thought process. Head back, she lolled against the pillow, enjoying the sensations streaking through her body.

Making love with Daryl—and though she would never call it anything but sex to him, in her heart and mind she'd been making love—had quickly become a habit. Like an addict, she craved his body and the things he could do with it.

Cool air wafted across her wet nipple. Idly she watched him roll on the condom. Even that was a turn-on.

What was it about Daryl that had flipped her hedonistic switch?

Sitting cross-legged on the bed, he pulled her to sit on his lap, arranging her legs around his lean hips before entering her with a powerful thrust.

Against her breast, his heart thundered. The muscles in his arms constricted around her.

They paused, enjoying the sensation of him filling her for a few seconds before he began moving his hips, pushing deeper, nudging her uterus, pushing an internal button that sent heat streaking to her extremities. Every nerve ending stood on alert as a wildfire of sensation swept through her.

He held her tightly against his sweat-slicked chest, continuing to move in tight circles deep within her as she slowly came down from her pinnacle.

Before she caught her breath, he began moving again, this time thrusting harder, pushing her higher.

He rolled her over until the sheet touched her back, never breaking their connection, while he, on his hands and knees, continued to pound into her.

She admired the fierce determination on his handsome face. She wanted to stroke the grim set of his lips, caress his cheek, but her hands and arms refused to obey her command. Relaxed and sated, she watched him, reveling in the feel of his firm flesh deep within, the faint scrape of his whiskers on the side of her face. Her nostrils flared at their combined scent.

The scent of sex.

Daryl rose, still embedded deep within her, dragging her to the edge of the mattress, where he resumed thrusting. Sliding his hands down her legs, he grasped her calves and placed her feet on his shoulders, deepening his already impossibly deep penetration.

Each thrust pushed her a little along the sheets, his firm grasp on her shoulders preventing her from sliding too far. Leaning forward, he swiped the tips of her breast with his tongue.

Instant awareness zinged through her, waking the erogenous zones she'd been sure were asleep for the night. Her breath caught. A fresh wave of completion washed over her, causing her to bite her lip to keep from screaming her satisfaction.

Still Daryl continued, picking up her limp body and holding her close while he continued his now-rapid-fire thrusts.

Cool plaster walls met her back as Daryl slammed into her once, twice, three times before tensing and releasing a hedonistic roar of completion.

He squeezed what little air remained in her lungs as he hugged her to him, trailing kisses along her hairline, whispering words her roaring blood drowned out.

Whatever they had going on between them, Ashley knew one thing for certain:

She didn't want it to end.

# 14

---

"What if someone sees us?" Ashley tugged at her bathing suit while Daryl did his best to remove it.

The morning sun sparkled on the Gulf. Granted, the beach was currently deserted, but she knew it could change soon.

"You said you'd never tanned in the nude, Ash. I'm just trying to help you out. Broaden your horizons."

She swatted at his busy hands. "There are a lot of things I've never tried, but that doesn't mean I plan to, either."

He slid a suntan-oiled finger beneath the cup of her bikini top and stroked her traitorous nipple. "Don't you like to feel my hands on you?"

"You know danged well I do. I may like it too much." She couldn't prevent the little shiver his touch ignited. "Which is what has me worried. What if we get carried away and forget we're on a public beach?"

"We have a blanket," he countered. "We could always hide what we're doing with that. Not that we'd necessarily be doing anything. I'm just saying, just in case." He rubbed oil from her hips to her breast, slipping his fingers beneath the loose-fitting bikini cups. "C'mon, Ash, cut loose and live a little. What have you got to lose?"

"My dignity? My privacy? My bathing suit? This is my last one. If I lose it, our vacation fun in the sun is finished."

"We only have one more day here, anyway. And it's not like there are no stores around. We can always buy more suits." His well-oiled fingers slid the spaghetti straps from her shoulders. "And it's not like we're in the water. Where would it disappear to? I'll keep it right here, and the second you begin to feel uncomfortable, or if we have unexpected company, I'll give it back. What do you say? Wouldn't a hot-oil massage feel good?"

Her eyes darted around the deserted beach while he stripped the top from her and immediately began a sensuous massage she'd bet was probably illegal in some states.

"Relax," he whispered against her ear as he laid her back on the blanket and brushed the bottom of her suit away as though it were an annoying gnat. "So pretty." He propped his big body on one arm, shielding her from potential eyes while he slicked oil from her sternum to her pubis, swirling his oiled finger across her labia, occasionally dipping in to rub her already-aching clitoris. "Relax. No one can see us. Doesn't that feel good?"

No, it felt fabulous. The combination of Daryl's languid strokes, the warmth of the sun, and the oil on her skin worked its magic. Muscles relaxed. Inhibitions floated away with the tide.

When he slipped his finger into her, she was aching and ready. Beside her, his naked body slipped up and down on the oil he'd applied, his erection gently thumping her hip in time with the waves hitting the shore.

Hot. All she felt was heat, inside and out. The relentless South Texas sun bathed her in its heat, wrapped her in the sensuality of Texas summer humidity. Within, Daryl's fingers continued to work their magic as climaxes broke free to wash over her in wave after wave of orgasmic sensation.

It was sensory overload.

She wanted more.

"Let's go back to the beach house. Now!" She gasped as another sensation towed her under.

"I don't think I could make the trek in my current condition." Daryl's breath huffed against her ear with each word, his excitement palpable.

"Then here," she said in what sounded suspiciously like a whine. "Take me here. Right here, right now. You brought condoms, right?"

She felt more than saw him nod.

"In the beach bag," he said, breathing heavily.

"Well, crap, Daryl, roll it on!" Wiggling closer, she could feel another climax cresting, her nipple drawn into aching buds of sensation.

"You said no sex in public," he reminded her, but she noticed he was reaching for the bag.

"You're already flashing your lily-white behind to God and everybody. What's the difference if it's moving up and down?"

"True. But I was trying to protect your modesty."

"Hah! I'd say my modesty is pretty much a thing of the past when I'm around you." Her breath caught. "Hurry. A little to the left. Agh!"

Darkness enshrouded her as fine grains of sand rained down on her head.

Spitting sand, she barely made out Daryl's face above her. His chest slipped smoothly over the oil, creating a delicious friction.

His sheathed erection slid home.

They sighed.

"Hang on," Daryl whispered. "We're covered by the blanket. Well, pretty much, I think, anyway."

"Don't you think people will still know what we're doing?" She tried, in vain, to flex her hips, to get him to pump faster.

"Maybe not. Not if we do it slow and easy." He kissed the tip of her nose. "And if you can keep from screaming."

"I only did that once. Well, okay, maybe twice. And you had something to do with that, too, mister."

"Ash?"

"Hmm?"

"Shut up and fuck me."

The feel of oil-slicked skin on oil-slicked skin was pleasant. Ashley had more than met her orgasm quotient. She lay there, enjoying the sounds of the waves and the seagulls, the feel of Daryl sliding on her oiled skin, the solid feel of him within her.

That had to be the reason her climax snuck up on her.

One moment she was relaxed, enjoying her personal internal massage.

And the next moment she came to a screaming release, clamping Daryl to her in an attempt to pull him deeper into her body.

Daryl was right behind her, his body bowing as every muscle tightened in preparation for his release. It came quickly, signaled by the low growl in his throat that vibrated her chest, setting off more contractions deep within her sex.

When her heart stopped trying to escape through her chest, she chuckled. "Wow. I think we set a new personal best."

A growl sounded next to her ear. Daryl was on the other side just a second ago. She turned and met a pair of black eyes. They were set above a long, black, furry snout.

She screamed again, but this time not in a good way, and struggled to topple Daryl.

He hung on.

"Shit!" Daryl lunged, but since they were still connected, he didn't go far.

Sand flew up, stinging their faces.

"What was that? A bear?"

"No," Daryl said, disengaging and sliding to her side, keeping their blanket securely over them. "A dog. That's the good news."

"But it's gone now, right? What's the bad news?"

"He took your suit."

# 15

Ashley trudged up the stairs to the beach house, the blanket trailing behind her like a royal cape.

"Aren't you going to wait for me?" Daryl readjusted the weight of their cooler and beach bag as he followed her.

She shot him a glare. "What are you complaining about? You still have a bathing suit. I've lost both of mine."

"Well, technically, you still have half of one of them," he pointed out.

That earned another glare.

The screen door whacked the siding, and she entered the house.

Dropping the gear inside the door, he hurried to catch up to her before she shut the bathroom door. "Ash, don't be mad. In the grand scheme of things, it's really not a big deal."

"Cut the psychobabble. I'm not in the mood." She tried to slip from his grasp, but he tightened his fingers.

He moved his hands to her neck, allowing the blanket to fall to the plank floor, ordering his eyes to maintain eye contact instead of traveling down her sun-kissed nude body. He moved his hands down, but only to her shoulders. He needed something to hang on to in order to keep his hands off her breasts.

"What are you in the mood for, Ash? It's our last night here. We can do anything you want." He rubbed the skin over her collar bones with his thumbs.

"I need a bath. I have sand stuck in all that oil." She looked down and shrugged. "I guess it would be okay if you took one with me." Her gaze met his. "Just to save time and water."

Right. "I could do that."

"But I'm hungry, so no funny stuff. As soon as we bathe, I want either a steak or lobster. Or both."

"I saw a steak house on our way into town. Or we could go back to the crab shack."

"Let's go to the crab shack since it's our last night, and we can walk." She turned on the faucets and reached for towels from the stack on the vanity. "I can't believe it's our last night here already."

"Me neither." It still thrilled and amazed him how quickly Ashley had acclimated to walking around naked with him. "I'm sorry we didn't get to stay the whole week. Maybe next time."

"It wasn't your fault the owner contracted for the remodeling to start before our time ended."

Next time. She hadn't even acknowledged it. Would there be a next time? He waited for Ashley to call him on his innuendo. Instead, she dumped some girly smelling bubbles into the tub.

"That stuff isn't going to make me smell like a girl, is it?" He paused with his hands on the waistband of his bathing suit.

"No, it's just moisturizing. Doesn't really leave a scent on your skin." Without a backward glance, she stepped into the tub, sighing once she was submerged.

Shucking his trunks in record time, he stepped into the surprisingly hot water, then settled behind her, his knees framing hers.

"Geez, Ash, do you think the water's hot enough? Are you trying to boil my boys?"

"Stop whining. If my girls can take it, so can your boys." Sighing, she relaxed, using his chest as a cushion.

He didn't mind.

"This feels so good. . . ."

He silently ordered his interested cock to behave. "Ah, yeah, it does. But we probably shouldn't hang around in here too long. Want to beat the dinner crowd."

Ashley snickered, her eyes closed. "Yeah, right. I think there were less than twenty people in the place last time. Don't worry." She patted his knee with a touch he felt in his groin. "There's plenty of time."

They must have dozed off for a while, because the next time Daryl roused, the water was considerably cooler.

"Ash?" He touched her shoulder, biting back a smile when she mumbled and turned to snuggle closer against his chest. "Ash? We need to finish washing the sand off and get going."

Dinner was good, if not great. Crab was the special, so they each had a huge platter with all the sides, then split a cheesecake for dessert.

By the time their waiter brought the check, the band was warming up.

"I forgot they have live music on the weekends." He reached for Ashley's hand. "Want to dance before we leave?"

After gazing at the band with a look that could only be described as longing, she shook her head. "I'd rather take a walk on the beach before we head back."

"We can do that." After he signed for their meal, he led her out of the restaurant, down the wooden steps to the beach.

"Listen," he said. "We can hear the band down here. Let's dance."

She didn't resist when he pulled her into his arms, following as flawlessly as though they'd danced together their entire lives. If he had his way, they would be dancing together for the rest of their lives.

Ashley sighed when the song ended, not resisting when he slung his arm over her shoulder, drawing her close to his side as they began the walk back to the beach house.

There was so much he wanted to say to her. He wanted to tell her how much their time at the beach had meant to him. He wanted to tell her he'd lusted after her since the first time they'd made love, at the Halloween party, how devastated he'd been to find her gone when he returned with their drinks. That feeling had only intensified when she'd moved in with his friend the very next day.

But he didn't want to cast blame, even if it stung to know she'd had sex with him and then spent the night with one of his best friends.

And it had about killed him when she and Andre broke up, and immediately she and Connor were engaged.

He wanted to tell her he wanted to keep seeing her, keep sleeping with her, after they returned to Houston.

He wanted to tell her he loved her.

But he didn't think she was ready to hear any declarations of love yet. He just hoped she was ready to continue with whatever it was they had, once they were home.

He couldn't imagine going back to being pals. Just friends. Not even fuck buddies. He wanted more.

Not to say he wouldn't take fuck buddies if that's all she was willing to give at this point.

"You're awfully quiet." Ashley smiled up at him. "I feel like I'm walking alone."

He hugged her to him, planting a smacking kiss on the top of her head. "Never alone, Ash. As long as I'm around, you'll never be alone."

Instead of responding, she did one of her vague nods and started climbing the stairs to the house.

"I want to dance with you again," Ashley announced when they walked into the moonlit bedroom. "One more time, here at the beach."

He'd planned on making love until they collapsed, but if she wanted to dance, they'd dance. "Sure. Do you want to go back to the crab shack?" She shook her head. "You want to dance on the beach? We may be able to hear the music from here."

She shook her head and walked to stand before him. With a secretive smile, she reached for the lone shoulder strap on her sundress and released the red flower-shaped button. The bodice fell to her waist. She immediately stepped out of the dress, tossing it to the open suitcase by the window.

Daryl's mouth went dry, his heart pounding so hard it threatened to burst from his chest. He swallowed. "I must have missed the fact that you didn't put on any underwear."

She stepped forward and tugged his shirt out of his pants, then began unbuttoning it.

He found his voice again when she shoved his shirt off his shoulders, down his arms, and off. "I thought you wanted to dance."

"I do," she insisted, shoving his unbuckled pants and boxers down. Stroking his excited body, she whispered, "I want to dance naked."

Naked. She wanted to dance naked. If this was a dream, he didn't want to wake up.

She moved into his arms, her breasts rubbing his abdomen, and they began swaying to silent music, shuffling to a secret beat.

Dancing naked in the moonlight.

# 16

Ashley stretched on tiptoe and brushed a kiss on Daryl's swollen, discolored eye. "Looks like you'll be taking back a souvenir from our trip."

He chuckled and trailed tiny kisses up her neck. "I don't mind. It was worth it."

"We did have a good time, didn't we?"

"No, we had a great time." He continued to take nibbling kisses, closer and closer to her mouth, his obvious erection bumping her abdomen.

"No regrets?" Her lips against his, she could feel his breath, could practically taste him.

He outlined her lips with the tip of his tongue, then breathed, "None," into her mouth before settling in for a soul-deep kiss.

Desire, never far from the surface since she began her sex vacation with Daryl, boiled to the surface. Deepening a kiss she would have sworn could not be deepened, she all but climbed his fit body, her legs circling his narrow hips as she rubbed shamelessly against his hard length.

Daryl made a guttural sound and lifted her higher, groaning when she wiggled, aligning him with her opening.

He tore his mouth from hers. "Condoms." He gasped the word, lurching for the stash on the nightstand, his arm firmly around her, holding her high on his excited body.

Within seconds, he was sheathed and plunging into her aching body. She was so primed for him, so ready, so wet, he had a difficult time staying in.

They groaned their frustration.

Gripping her tighter, he wedged her against the cool wall as he slammed into her body, the sound of their skin meeting echoing gentle slapping sounds in the room.

Wild for him, she held on to his shoulders, her legs gripping him closer as she rode him, meeting each thrust with carnal abandon.

Her orgasm came forcefully, ripping a primal sound from her throat as her body contracted violently around Daryl. Gasping, she arched and would have fallen had he not had a firm grip as he found his release.

Sweating and panting, he staggered to the bed, where he sat and rolled, still joined, to lay with her cocooned in his arms.

As she struggled to regain her breath, she fought the urge to drift off. It was their last night at the beach. She wanted to talk and make love all night—not necessarily in that order.

Smiling, she turned and placed a string of kisses along his collar bone, then up the side of his neck.

He patted her shoulder with a heavy hand. "Give me a few minutes, babe."

She rolled him to his back, then hugged him, resting her head on his shoulder.

"So . . . what are your plans when you get back to Houston?" Maybe, since they technically still had two days left of their vacation, he might want to spend it with her. In bed would be good. Either at her place or his. She was flexible.

She just knew she wasn't ready for their time to end. Why had she insisted on a sex vacation instead of a real relationship? Even a sexual relationship implied a possibility of a future. What did a sex-only vacation imply? Not a heck of a lot, she realized with a frown.

"I have some patients I need to contact," he said, interrupting her inner turmoil. "I feel badly to have canceled their appointments on short notice. I need to check in with them, possibly schedule makeup sessions. And, of course, do laundry. I think everything I own needs washing. My cleaning lady comes on Monday, so I have to get everything picked up before then. How about you?"

"I don't have a cleaning lady. My laundry, what there is of it, is pretty much done, especially since I lost both bathing suits and spent most of the rest of the time naked. Not that I'm complaining," she added, stroking his chest.

"No makeup sessions at work?"

"Nope. Unlike you big-bucks guys, I work for someone. When I'm not there, they have someone to fill in. Amy took most of my sessions this week. No one probably even noticed I was gone." She watched him walk to the bathroom to dispose of the condom, wishing he'd tell her something, anything, to let her know he wanted more than a few days of hot sex with her.

She frowned. But maybe that's exactly what he wanted. Maybe a few days of fun in the sun was all it took to satisfy his curiosity about how it would be with her.

What a dismal thought.

The mattress dipped precariously when he climbed back in bed. Instead of immediately pulling her into his arms, as she'd come to expect, he stretched out on his back, hands behind his head.

Determined, she plastered herself against his side, stroking his chest. She placed a gentle kiss on his shoulder.

No response.

"What are you thinking about?" There, she'd initiated a conversation.

"Nothing."

"Nothing? Since when? I've known you since we were eight and know for a fact you're always thinking about something."

His shoulder lifted, bobbing her head. "That's not true. There are plenty of times I'm not thinking about anything in particular. But tonight, as much as I hate to admit it, you're right. Ow! Don't pinch."

"Were you thinking about when we get back to Houston?" She was determined to talk it out, even if she had to drag everything out of him.

His arm moved, its warmth encircling her shoulder. "Yeah," he finally answered. "I have a lot of stuff to take care of once I get back. Patients, calls, dental checkup, you know, all the mundane stuff."

"What about the unmundane stuff?" Like me. Like us. "You don't have a girlfriend hidden somewhere, do you?" Although she'd love to hear he considered her his girlfriend, she had to know if there was competition. It was possible, in her misery, she hadn't heard if he was involved with someone. What she would do or feel if he answered in the affirmative, she had no idea, but it was always good to know where one stood. "If you do, how did you explain us going away this week?" The thought made her physically ill, but she had to know.

"I just told her I was going on a fuck buddy getaway; she understood. Ow! Cut it out! I was kidding!" He gave her shoulder a squeeze. "You've known me most of my life. Do you really think I would do the things I've done with you if I was involved with someone else? Do you?"

"No, I guess not." She sighed. "I know I've occupied a big chunk of your time with all my, er, domestic issues. I guess I was just so inwardly focused, I didn't stop to think I may be taking up your time. Time you may want to spend with someone else." *Your turn. Tell me there is no one else.* She knew she shouldn't be like that. There had been many someone elses in her life over the years.

But she did care. A lot.

"Naw, I'd have told you." He stretched. "I'm currently between girlfriends, so you're timing was impeccable, Goldilocks," he said, tugging on her hair in the same way he'd done since elementary school.

"But what if you're missing an opportunity to find Ms. Right while you've been holding my hand?"

"I've been holding more than your hand, lately. Ouch! When did you develop a violent streak? I'm going to be black and blue to match my eye."

"I'm trying to have a serious conversation here, and you keep cracking jokes."

"Sorry. Serious, huh? Okay, sure, I'd like to meet someone and settle down. I know there's someone out there who will be just right for me. Someone who likes all the things I like, who enjoys spending time with me as much as I enjoy being with her. Someone to laugh and cry with me. You know, in short, someone who is perfect for me."

*Someone who is not me.* A knot of misery fisted in her stomach. She'd waited too late to discover all the wonderful things about Daryl, spent too many years being just friends.

"Ash? You awake?"

Forcing regulated breathing, she kept her eyes closed and didn't answer.

She couldn't answer. Talking to him now would hurt too much.

He pulled her close and settled down. In a few minutes, his deep breathing told her he slept.

Brushing stupid tears away, she lay listening to him breathing, enjoying the tactile pleasure of his skin against hers for the last time.

Summoning her strength, she eased from his grasp and picked up her suitcase. In the bathroom, she used her cell to call a cab to take her to the airport, then hurried and got dressed.

With a final look at Daryl, sleeping peacefully, she slipped out the door to go wait for the cab.

# 17

---

Daryl knew, before he opened his eyes, that Ashley was gone. So it was no surprise to find her suitcase missing, her toiletries no longer littering the bathroom counter.

He should have known when he'd droned on about finding Ms. Right to Ashley's utter silence that she didn't feel what he felt. But he'd kept hoping she would interrupt him, tell him she didn't want to be with anyone else and didn't want him to be with anyone but her.

Didn't happen.

He'd gambled and lost. Pretty much the story of his life since meeting Ashley. That first gamble had paid off, though, when he'd defended her in third grade. He'd earned a friend for life.

Maybe that's all they were meant to be. Maybe by wishing and hoping for more, he'd indeed missed opportunities to meet other women. Obsessed with his love for Ashley, he'd had on blinders when it came to women, wanting to remain free if Ashley needed him.

Maybe it was time to grow up and face the fact he and Ashley were never meant to be more than friends.

Even being fuck buddies hadn't worked out for them. He just hoped it hadn't ruined their friendship.

Who was he kidding? Of course it ruined it. How could he ever spend time with her again without remembering what it was like to make love to her, to hold her in his arms as a lot more than a friend?

It was best to just make a clean break so they could both get on with their lives, he thought, throwing the last of his belongings into his duffel bag.

With one last look around the beach house, he locked the door, knowing he was locking away his past.

He had no choice.

"I can see by your less-than-cheerful face that he still hasn't called," Amy observed as she poured coffee into her travel mug. She walked over and took a chair opposite Ashley at the round table in the company break room. "And you haven't called him, either, have you?"

"What's the point?" Ashley sniffed and dabbed at her nose with a tissue, blinking back the waterworks that had plagued her for the last two weeks since leaving the beach. "He pretty much said it all during our last conversation. He's looking for his soul mate, and obviously I'm not her. There's no point in prolonging the misery." She took a sip of her cold coffee and gagged.

Amy stretched to peer into Ashley's cup. "You did it again. Forgot to pour coffee in. That's pure creamer. Ashley, why don't you call Daryl? Maybe he's just as miserable. You always said he was your best friend. Best friends talk to each other."

"I think, after our beach experiment, our friendship is a thing of the past, Amy." The thought caused an ache in the pit of her stomach. How would she get through the rest of her life without Daryl? "It was so stupid! Stupid, stupid, stupid," she finished in a choked voice, swiping at fresh tears. "Now, not only have I lost the best lover I ever had, but I also lost my best friend." She sighed. "I'd seriously consider becoming a lesbian, except I'm not really attracted to women."

"I'm sure lesbians around the world appreciate that," Amy said in a droll voice. "Seriously, you need to talk to Daryl. Tell him how you feel. How do you feel, by the way?"

"Confused. Abandoned. Lonely. Incomplete," she finished on a sob.

"Sounds to me, girlfriend, like you fell in love with your best friend."

Love? "No, I don't think so. It's too soon. Isn't it?"

"Too soon? Didn't you tell me you two met when you were eight years old? That's over twenty years! How much time do you need?" Amy bit into a doughnut she'd plucked from the open box on the table, closing her eyes while she chewed appreciatively. After swallowing, she opened her eyes, a faint dusting of powdered sugar frosting the cocoa-colored skin around her mouth, and glared at Ashley. "You're no earthly good to anyone right now, and I'm betting Daryl is the same. Whether it's love or lust, don't you think you deserve to find out? You can't just leave things like this hanging, unfinished. It's bad karma. At the very least, you need closure. Closure is very important; take it from me," she said, reaching for another doughnut. "I know these things," she said around a mouthful of pastry.

"I know what you're saying, but the phone works both ways, Amy. Daryl has made no move to contact me." Her shoulders slumped. "I miss him. And not even sexually," she said at Amy's raised eyebrow. "We saw each other at least two or three times a week before . . . well, you know. I should never have agreed to that stupid sex experiment!"

Amy swallowed and took a sip of her coffee. "Hey, I hate to

remind you, but the sex-only vacation was your brilliant idea. Okay, maybe I had a tad to do with it, but mainly it was yours. What I'm saying is you can't lay all the blame on Daryl. He just planted the seed." She took another sip of coffee. "And speaking of planting seeds, you two practiced birth control, right? You didn't get caught up in the passion of the moment, did you? I'm too young to be an aunt!"

Ashley chuckled, wiping away another tear. "Don't worry. We used protection."

"Great. Enough info. So, since you're free, why don't you go clubbing with us tonight?"

Ashley shook her head. "No, I don't think—"

"That's right. Don't think, girlfriend. It's not like I'm asking you to join in on an orgy. Just a few drinks with a bunch of women. No pressure, no commitment. Who knows, maybe you'll meet someone."

Maybe she already did.

Ashley sat alone at a darkened table in the crowded bar, taking timid sips of her first drink while she watched Amy and several girls from the office dance, their inhibitions numbed by several drinks.

On the floor, Amy was gyrating and hopping. Ashley grinned. What Amy lacked in ability, she made up for in enthusiasm.

Amy's face lost its smile. Ashley craned her neck to see what her friend was looking at, but too many people blocked her view. Amy said something to her partner and headed for the table, a grim look on her usually cheerful face.

"Let's go," Amy said, grabbing her purse. "I'm bored."

"You didn't look bored out there. What happened?" Despite her words, Ashley picked up her purse, scooting back her chair as she spoke. "But if you want to leave, I'll—" Her words stuck in her throat as she followed Amy's nervous glance.

Daryl Garret sat at the bar. And he wasn't alone.

Sure, she could try to fool herself by saying maybe he just happened to be sitting next to a gorgeous brunette, but the proprietary hand the woman placed on Daryl's arm blew that theory out of the water.

Swallowing the bile rising in her throat, she choked out, "Let's go. I've seen enough." Turning on her heel, she made her way to the door, determined not to look back.

She looked back.

Daryl was looking right at her, ignoring whatever his date was saying to him. Expressionless, he continued to stare until Ashley broke eye contact and left.

"Daryl?" Rhonda, his next-door neighbor's sister, placed her hand on his arm again. Hadn't the woman ever heard of not invading personal space? "Daryl? Did you hear what I said?"

Trying not to recoil from her long-nailed touch, he blinked her back into focus. "Sorry. I just saw, um, a patient I need to speak to. She shouldn't have been in a bar."

Rhonda nodded sagely. "Ah, an alcoholic?"

His first inclination was to agree, anything to get rid of her; then he remembered his training. "I'm not really at liberty to discuss it. Patient confidentiality. You understand, right?"

She nodded again and picked up the little satin thing she'd placed on the bar. "Of course. I'll be in town all week. Maybe we can do this again."

He nodded in what he hoped was a noncommittal way as he ushered her toward the door.

After dropping Rhonda at her brother's condo, he went home.

Pacing for the next hour brought him no closer to a conclusion as to what his next move should be.

His cell phone vibrated, threatening to fall from the table he'd dropped it on when he'd walked in the door. Ashley? Would she be calling to ask who his date had been? Would she be calling to tell him she missed him and wanted to see him again?

He anxiously glanced at the caller ID. Andre.

"Hey, stranger," Andre's voice boomed above the background noise. "What the hell you doing answering your phone on a Friday night?"

*Why did you call if you didn't expect me to answer?* "Not much, just answering a drunk dipshit's call, evidently."

Andre's laughter boomed though the phone, making Daryl wince. "Good one. Hey, we're at the Lair. Get the fuck over here! We need to party!" He hung up before Daryl could decline.

He didn't feel like partying. He glanced at the phone. Then again, he really didn't have anything better to do. He slipped the phone in his pocket and headed for the door. If Ashley did call, he would feel his phone vibrate.

And if she didn't? Well, he'd be better off drowning his sorrow than hanging around waiting.

The Lair, originally a corner pub in the last century, was tiny, dark, and loud. Because of the bar's size, Daryl had no problem finding Andre and several other friends.

After greeting everyone, he ordered a beer and sat back, listening to the drunken revelry, missing Ashley so much his teeth hurt.

Andre slid onto the barstool next to him, motioning to the bartender to bring two more beers as he slapped Daryl on the shoulder. "Where you been, dude? I haven't seen you in a while." He shoved money across the bar and raised his frosted mug. "Since you're alone and here, I can only assume you saw the light with the ice maiden. Way to go!" He raised his mug and chugged several swallows, then wiped his mouth on the back of his hand and laughed. "We tried to warn you, bro. That bitch is a ball breaker."

"Who?" He knew who but wanted Andre to clarify before he broke his nose.

"Who?" Andre broke into another peal of laughter. "Ashley the ice queen, who else? Don't look at me like that. We all knew you had a major boner for her for years." He slapped Daryl's shoulder again, sloshing beer on his hand. "And here you are. You were just a faster learner than old Connor and me!"

Daryl looked at their reflection in the mirror behind the bar, taken aback by what he saw. They'd always been mistaken for brothers, but until tonight, he'd never seen the resemblance.

Beside him, Andre rambled on. "Just about fucked my brains out when I drove her home from the party—"

"What party?"

"You don't remember? You know, that stupid costume party what's-his-name and his wife threw that Halloween. What was it? Had to be at least four or five years ago. Anyway, I came late. Ashley was alone on the freaking patio, looking so doable I almost came in my pants. Since you weren't the only one with a boner for her in those days, and I'd had a few, I decided to ask her to dance. You know, sort of test the water." His grinning gaze met Daryl's in the mirror.

"What happened?" Now he knew why Ashley wasn't waiting for him when he returned with their drinks.

Andre scratched his head, making his wild brown hair stand on end. "Can't 'member it all. It's been a while. But I remember she wanted me to drive her home." He rubbed his whiskered face. "She lived down by the lake then. Like I said, she about fucked my brains out as soon as we walked into her place. Damn near ruined my costume. I paid good money to rent the thing. I guess, considering how the night ended, it was worth every penny, huh?" He laughed again, but Daryl had a sinking sensation.

"Yeah." He forced a chuckle. "I forgot about the costume thing." Yeah, right. "I remember you saying you weren't going to pay to rent one. I didn't see you at the party. Which costume did you end up with?"

"Fucking phantom." He took another gulp and laughed at his wit. "Get it? Fucking phantom!"

Yeah, he got it.

"I hated the damn thing," Andre continued, taking another gulp. "I think it made Ashley wet." He gave a derisive laugh. "And that was about the last time she was, let me tell you. But she tried, I have to give her that. She moved in with me the very next day, fucking me at every opportunity. I never thought I'd dread getting a hard-on. Damn near wore me out that first year. When she started telling me how to do her, it was a cock shriveler. Then, when she started begging me to rent the damn costume, well, it was adios!"

"Did she say why she wanted you to wear the costume?" Daryl strove for nonchalance when all he wanted was to run for the door.

Andre shook his head, then motioned for another round. "Naw. Looking back, I think it was the only way she could get off. I sure as hell know she never came after that first night."

Damn. He'd made a major tactical error by not revealing his identity to Ashley. If what Andre said was true, and he had no reason to doubt it, Ashley could very well have thought he was Andre.

Ashley's words drifted through his mind. *Probably the best I've had, except for that first night with Andre . . .*

# 18

Ashley sat in the rapidly cooling water, flipping her phone shut in disgust when Daryl's voice mail clicked on again. Where was he? Was he having sex with the Angelina Jolie wannabe from the bar? She blinked back tears at the thought.

Still, if that's the kind of woman he was attracted to, it was obvious why she and Daryl had never hooked up during all the years they'd known each other.

She wracked her brain, trying to remember if he'd ever had a serious girlfriend. There was that one girl in college, Joan or Jillian or something like that. Ashley had run into them at the movies on campus once. Since she was between boyfriends, she'd been happy to see Daryl at her door the next day. Some friend she'd been. She'd never even asked about his date.

Just thinking about Daryl made her horny. How pathetic was that? Twisting the faucet, she added more hot water, then pushed the button to activate the whirlpool.

The force of the jets felt almost painful, doing nothing to relax her.

The bath gel came out in a blob, dripping off her loofah onto her breast. Her swipe served to smear the slick gel. In her attempt to get it off, she thought of Daryl and wished he were in the big tub with her, smoothing the gel over her eager body. She plucked at her erect nipple and felt an answering ache beneath the water.

An ache only Daryl could completely appease.

But her trusty whirlpool had helped take the edge off for the last two weeks.

With grim determination, she raised her left leg to rest on the lip of the tub, positioning the force of the jet by her hip directly at the spot aching for Daryl's touch.

Eyes closed, she imagined Daryl pleasuring her. Her hips bucked as the hot water lapped at her swollen clitoris. Her breath hitched, coming in fast pants. Close. She was so close to at least a temporary release, when the doorbell pealed.

She jerked upright. She wasn't expecting anyone. Closing her eyes, she slid back down, repositioning her leg for greatest stimulation. Immediately, she was back in the zone, poised on the brink, when the doorbell sounded again.

Crap.

There was only one person she wanted to see right now, and it was a pretty safe bet it wasn't him.

On the lip of the tub, her cell rang. She caught it before it toppled into the water.

Daryl. She punched the whirlpool off, silencing the jets.

"H-hello?"

"Hi. It's me. Is this a bad time?"

She was naked and needy. And missing him like crazy. Was it a bad time? It all depended on what constituted *bad*. "No. What's up?" She hoped she sounded casual, like she always had before . . . well, before everything that shattered her world.

"I need to talk to you."

"Talk." She sank back into the water, idly wondering if she could masturbate while he talked without him knowing. Just the sound of his voice made her wet. It wouldn't take much since she was already poised on the brink.

"Are you home?"

She sat up, water sloshing over the edge of the tub. "Yes. Do you want to come over?" What could she wear that would be enticing yet not say *take me*? Then again, the idea of him taking her up on what she'd love to offer had a certain appeal.

"I'm already here."

"What?" She stumbled getting out of the tub, shrieking the word in her haste.

"You didn't answer the door. I rang the bell. I thought maybe you were out. Or something."

*Or something?* Did he think she ran out and slept with someone just because she'd seen him with a date and couldn't cope? She hadn't thought of that. . . .

"Ash?"

"What?" Where the heck was her robe?

"Open the door."

"Hang on." She flipped the phone shut and wrapped a towel around her eager body. A glance in the mirror told her it was too late to do anything with her hair or makeup.

She ran for the door as fast as her bare feet would take her on the hardwood floor, skidding to a stop by the peephole.

Yep, there he was. Struck anew by his masculine beauty, she wondered how she'd never noticed until lately.

"I can see you looking at me." Daryl's voice sounded through the security door. "Open the door before your neighbors think I'm a pervert."

Her fingers fumbled with the chain and lock. Finally she threw open the door.

She'd come to a decision on her way to the door. She didn't want to talk. She didn't want to listen, either. She only wanted to feel.

And what she most wanted to feel was Daryl, naked and inside her.

"Ash, I need—"

Throwing herself into his arms, she silenced him with the deepest, wettest kiss she could muster. She needed, too, and right now, she needed him. She shoved the door shut.

Not breaking the kiss, she stripped him, scattering his clothing in her foyer, then walked him backward to the fluffy sectional in her living room, not stopping until they toppled to the cushions.

"I missed you!" She moved away to grab a condom from the pile she'd placed on the coffee table the day she came home from the beach, hoping Daryl would follow her.

Not wanting to talk, she scooted close to his face, pushing until her nipple filled his mouth. When he closed his mouth around it, she almost swooned, her knees weak with desire. Her hand shook so badly it took a few seconds to open the foil packet.

Reluctantly pulling her breast from his hot mouth, she sheathed him in two seconds flat and climbed on top, straddling his hips, not stopping until she sank home.

Daryl's hands cupped and massaged her aching breasts, his hips moving in a delicious counterpoint to hers, their labored breathing loud in the quiet room.

She climaxed three times, slipping and sliding on his hard abdomen before his muscles flexed for his final thrust.

Collapsing on his heaving chest, she placed soft kisses everywhere her lips could reach.

Daryl lay in the darkness, struggling to regain his breath as he stroked Ashley's damp hair. He loved her. He suspected, on some level, she probably loved him, too. He hadn't expected her to attack him when he stepped through the doorway, but he hadn't exactly fought her off. He sure hoped he hadn't made a tactical error.

She needed to know how he felt. She also needed to know he was the phantom lover at the Halloween party. Damn. How could he have been so stupid? He should have told her who he was from the get-go—or at least after their first mind-blowing sexual encounter.

"Ash, I missed you, too. I didn't like waking up alone at the beach house." He continued stroking her hair, composing his next words. It was important to say it just right. Quite possibly the most important speech of his life.

"I'm sorry I ran out like that." She did an all-over body hug that temporarily distracted him. "I had a lot to think about."

"Oh? And?"

"And I," she said, placing his hands on her breast, smiling down at him when he immediately flexed his fingers. "I came to an important conclusion."

*Say it. Say you love me.* "What's that?" Feigning nonchalance, he rubbed her beaded nipples with the pads of his thumbs.

She squirmed on his semierection. "I discovered I'm a sex addict."

His hands stopped caressing her breasts. "Oh?" *Shit.* "Maybe we shouldn't be doing this, then." A surge of satisfaction went through him when she clamped her hands over his, holding them in place.

"Wait. I'm not finished. I also made another discovery."

"You've been busy." *Tell me.*

"While I'm a sex addict, I discovered it's only with you. I'm a Daryl Garrett sex addict." She shrugged, her breasts rising and falling in a most distracting way.

"What do you think that means, Ash?" He was obviously going to have to make her spell it out.

Slipping from his recovered erection, she pulled up until she sat on his chest, her breasts practically suffocating him.

He inhaled the fresh scent of her soap, then took a tentative lick from each breast while he waited. As soon as she told him she loved him, they would move on to some serious makeup sex. He may even propose before the night was done. But first he needed to tell her about the phantom.

Her hips flexed with each swipe of his tongue. She teased him by circling his mouth with the tip of each breast, her wet center burning a hole in his chest. "I think," she said, dragging the tip of one breast along the seam of his mouth, "it means I was meant to be a lover."

He swallowed his disappointment, pressing his lips tightly shut, avoiding the temptation of her breast. Gently grasping her ribs, he set her back, creating a distance from the distraction of her delectable body. "Oh, yeah? Anyone in particular's lover, or just a lover in general?" At this point, he had no clue.

Plopping back, she glared at him, then grabbed his hands, placing them back on her chest. "Duh. A Daryl lover."

His heart soared. Lover was a start, wasn't it?

"Any particular Daryl, or just anyone named Daryl will do?" He loved teasing her. Could he settle for just being lovers? He wanted more, but this was more than he had a month ago.

"Don't be a weirdo." She sank back onto his renewed erection and gyrated her hips, eyes closed, holding his hands on her breasts.

He could live with being lovers.

For a while, anyway.

# 19

Daryl dried off, glancing down at his purple penis. Was he suffering the same fate as Andre, unable to sexually satisfy Ashley? No, he'd felt the flutter of her pulse, the change in her respiration. Her inner muscles convulsing. She wasn't faking her orgasms. But, despite their weeklong sexual marathon, Ashley seemed no closer to making a commitment than she'd been when they first got back together.

And he still hadn't told her about the phantom. Because of that, he'd waited, wanting to get a declaration of love before he revealed himself.

He'd thought he could live with being lovers. The idea of being a sex object had, at first, been exciting. Now it was tiring. Oh, he still got an instant hard-on whenever he was around her. That probably would never change.

But he wanted—he deserved—more.

Girding for battle, he dressed in the bathroom.

Ashley still lay in wanton abandon from their last lovemaking session. Sprawled naked on the rumpled sheets, she sent a silent subliminal message to his eager cock.

Being lovers gave him a sexual high he'd never imagined. But he needed to up the pressure to get Ashley to commit. Since she claimed to crave his lovemaking, maybe if he withheld it, she'd realize he was more than a convenient cock.

"Why are you dressed?" She propped up on her elbow, her heated gaze raking him from his freshly washed hair to his loafers and back again.

"It's Monday. I have appointments first thing this morning. I need to be there early to get some paperwork done." Paperwork he'd neglected during his weeklong sexual marathon.

She fondled her breast, plucking at the erect nipple.

"Come back to bed, Daryl," she said in a sexy whisper. "We can have a quickie. Or, if you can go in a little later, we can have some mind-blowing good-bye sex."

His gaze flew to the juncture of her thighs when her hand slid from her breast to her swollen folds. He swallowed and shifted in an attempt to adjust his suddenly-too-tight boxers.

Damn, it made him horny to watch her touch herself.

Averting his gaze, he cleared his throat. "Ash, cover up. Please. You're killing me."

"Are you already tired of being my lover?" She looked stricken.

His first thought was to strip and slide into bed and into her willing body, to prove he still desired her.

But he had to be strong.

"You know better than that. If we lived to be one hundred, I'd never get tired of loving you." He met her gaze. "And I do, you know. Love you. I've probably loved you since third grade, if I think about it honestly. That's why I'm going back to my place after work."

"But . . . I don't understand." He was relieved to see her pull the sheet up over her nudity. "If you love having sex with me—"

"I do, but it's not having sex, Ash. We're way beyond that.

It's making love. At least that's what it is for me. And I want more from you than sex." There, he'd said it.

Wrapping the sheet around her, she stood, glaring at him. "Why? We have a great sex life. We're best friends. Why can't you be happy with that?" She stomped to stand toe-to-toe. "You know my track record. You know I don't do well with committed relationships. Why are you pushing me?"

"Why are you denying your feelings?" he countered.

"Who says I'm denying them? Did you ever think, Daryl, maybe being lovers is all I have to offer?"

"Bullshit!"

"Keep your voice down! We've known each other since we were eight. You've seen me at my worst. How could you possibly be in love with me?"

"How could I not?" His voice was so low, it barely carried.

"Because a woman needs to maintain a little mystery. Because you know me too well, having seen me at my worst, on several occasions. That alone should preclude a serious relationship with me. Did you ever think maybe sex is all I can give? All I'm capable of giving? Isn't it enough that I want to sleep only with you and nobody else?"

"No, it's not."

He turned and walked toward the door, praying she would call him back.

She didn't.

"What are you doing?" Ashley trudged into the break room and poured a huge mug of coffee.

Amy looked up from the papers she'd been filling out. "Filing transfer papers. I'm transferring to the Austin office."

"What? Ow!" Ashley grabbed a napkin and dabbed at the scalding liquid she'd just sloshed on her hand. "Why?"

"Because I'm sick and tired of watching one of my best friends ruin her life. I can't stay and watch the carnage."

"Me?"

"You." Amy's dark head bent to her task.

"Don't go! I need you."

"No, you don't; you need Daryl." Amy pointed her pen at Ashley, then sighed. "But for some inexplicable reason, you're in denial. Maybe if I leave town, you'll realize what a mess you've made and fix it. I feel like I've been an enabler. I quit."

"Please stay." Ashley sank into the formed orange plastic chair across from Amy. "I'm just confused. As soon as I figure everything out, I'll be okay."

"What's to figure out, girlfriend? The guy's already told you he loves you. If you didn't love him, too, you wouldn't be such a pathetic mess. Admit it to him and yourself and let nature take its course. You're thinking too much."

"Speaking of thinking, I was doing just that last night."

"Uh-huh." Amy's head bobbed. "And what did you come up with now?"

"It's just a theory. . . ."

# 20

"Doctor Garrett? Are you listening to me?" Gerald Flowers's voice jerked Daryl back to his session.

"Sorry, I have a killer headache," he lied, rubbing his temple for effect. "What were you saying?"

"I said I was thinking of different ways to kill my wife and asked if you knew any poisons that would be undetectable." A grin flashed, revealing white teeth with a space in the middle. "Just yanking your chain, Doc. I just said I was going out of town next week, so I'd have to move my appointment."

"Oh." Relief washed through him. "So you and your wife are getting along better?"

"Yep." Mr. Flowers stood, offering his hand. "And I can't thank you enough. Mildred thanks you, too. In fact, we're taking your advice and taking the honeymoon we never had time for. That's where I'll be next week."

Daryl smiled for the first time since leaving Ashley's condo a week ago. "I'm glad things worked out."

Mr. Flowers gave a broad wink. "Sex with the woman you love does wonders. I highly recommend it. 'Bye!"

Daryl sat back down, swiveling his chair to look out the plate-glass window. A slight breeze stirred the tops of the crepe myrtle trees edging the parking lot, their bright pink blooms nodding in the late afternoon sun.

He thought of the breeze at the beach house and wished he could go back there with Ashley, this time being completely honest about his feelings. Honest about the phantom's true identity.

He picked up his phone, as he'd done a million times over the past week. Eight missed calls. Ashley. No messages.

If it was important, wouldn't she leave a message?

His phone chirped, indicating a text message. Ashley.

R U there? Call me.

His thumb hit her speed-dial number.

"Hi, you've reached Ashley Clark. I'm unable to come to the phone. Leave a message and I'll get back to you."

He waited for the beep. "It's me. Let's talk. Coco's at"—he paused to glance at his watch—"about seven? If that doesn't work for you, give me a call. Otherwise, I'll see you there."

He saw Ashley's Mustang convertible when he pulled into the parking lot a little before seven. Did the fact that she was there early mean anything? He took a deep breath and stepped out of his car.

Only one way to find out.

Regardless of the outcome, Ashley deserved to know the truth about the first time they'd made love.

He pushed through the doors, the delicious aromas of seared meat reminding him he'd missed lunch.

Ashley sat at a table in the corner, waving to him.

Maybe she'd changed her mind about being only lovers.

Maybe she thought he had.

She stood as he approached and gave him a quick hug, a friendly peck on the cheek.

He swallowed his disappointment.

Hell, what did he expect, her to strip naked and demand sex on the tablecloth?

Interesting fantasy . . . especially since he'd missed her so damn much the past week.

"We need to talk," they said in unison, then laughed.

"Ladies first," Ashley said, taking his hands in her cold ones. "I've missed you, Daryl. As a friend and a lover. And you were right. Despite my best intentions, I fell in love with you. Heck, I may have always loved you, too. I was just too stupid or stubborn to admit it." She squeezed his hands. "Forgive me? Please? I want you back. In my life and my bed."

"There's something you need to know before I say anything else." He let go of her hands to rake a hand through his hair, then heaved a sigh. "The only way to say this is to just come out with it."

"You've already moved on?" She looked stricken.

"What? Hell, no! If I can't have you, I don't want anyone. What do I have to do to convince you of that?"

"Shut up and kiss me?" She leaned closer, her lips puckered, waiting for his kiss.

He licked his lips. "I can't. Not now. Not until I tell you what I came to say."

"You don't find me attractive anymore? You decided you really don't love me?" His startled gaze met her twinkling one, and he finally relaxed a little. Maybe things would work out.

"Will you shut up and let me talk? It's hard enough for me—"

"Ah, but is it hard enough for me?" she teased.

He heaved a sigh and placed one hand over her smart mouth. "Shut. Up. I'm serious. I should have told you a long time ago. I think I may have figured out why you've had so many problems with committed relationships. And it may be sort of my fault."

She raised her eyebrows.

He nodded, wondering if it was safe to keep his hand so close to her teeth when he told her what he'd done.

What the hell. He deserved any punishment she dished out.

"I'm the phantom," he blurted out. "That night, years ago? At the costume party? That was me. The first phantom. The one who, you know, with you in the closet? I left to get drinks. I planned to tell you who I was when I came back. But you were gone." He shook his head. "I could never figure out how you could have had such hot sex with me and then moved in with my roommate the next day. Then, the other night, Andre mentioned he'd rented the same costume, and it suddenly became clear."

He leaned closer, his hand still covering her mouth, and begged her with his eyes to understand. "I'm so sorry, Ash. I should have told you right from the start. I guess I was hurt to see you with Andre. And, I swear, I didn't know about his costume until recently."

She pushed his hand away from her mouth and took a sip of water before meeting his gaze. "But you knew about the sex in the closet. You let me go on. You could have told me at any time. I'm especially thinking about my painful breakups, when I cried on your shoulder. You could have told me either of those times. Or how about when I asked why we'd never hooked up?"

"In my defense, I was angry by then. I thought you knew and were refusing to acknowledge it for some reason. Then I worried I'd somehow traumatized you and you'd repressed it."

"Get over yourself." She grinned over the edge of her glass, then set it on the starched tablecloth. "Okay, I've had my fun. You can stop the self-flagellation. I already figured it out."

"What? When?"

"After your huffy little sex object rant, when you walked out on me. I kept thinking I was missing something, that there was something you weren't telling me. Then I thought about how I've felt every time we made love. There was only one other time I'd felt like that. It was simply a matter of deductive reasoning, Doctor."

Relief coursed through him, causing him to slump for a moment. Reaching across the table, he took her hands. "And you still love me?"

"Daryl, sweetie, I've probably always loved you. I was just too blind to see it. Of course, thinking my most memorable sexual experience happened with another guy sort of threw me off track for a while. Andre was too easy. Connor was too difficult. It took me a while, but I finally realized you are the only one who is just right for me."

He kissed her fingers. "What can I do to make it up to you?"

"I figure you have two choices: you can either pay me exorbitant amounts of money to keep me from suing you . . ."

"Or? What's my other choice?"

"Well . . . you could marry me to shut me up."

"I'd never want to shut you up." He stood and tugged her to her feet, then pulled her into his arms. "But I definitely choose marriage." He kissed her, then pulled back and winked. "Besides, it's probably cheaper."

"Don't bet on it."

# STROKE OF MIDNIGHT

# 1

---

Beth Simpson stood on the edge of the upper deck of the yacht, blinking back tears as the medics loaded her nine-year-old student into the evacuation cage.

Squinting against the bright Gulf of Mexico sunshine, Ryan gave her the thumbs-up sign with his unbandaged hand.

"Wait," she called, hurrying over to the boy as he was being strapped in. She twisted her dive ring off her finger and pushed it onto Ryan's pudgy thumb.

"That's your favorite ring," he objected. "You always said you never took it off. I can't take it; it's yours." He struggled to get the ring off with his limited dexterity.

"No." She placed her hand over his, calming his movements. "You earned it down there." She swallowed a lump of emotion, recalling her horror when the wreck they'd been exploring folded in on her diving student. She should have gone first. It should have been her trapped beneath the wreckage. "You're a real diver now," she choked out.

The smile he beamed at her as he was lifted from the yacht told her she'd done the right thing.

"Beth," Ryan's dad, Jack Holms, said as he walked up to her.

"I want you to know we don't hold you responsible for Ryan's accident."

She sighed and forced a smile for her employer. "Thanks, I appreciate it, but I still feel responsible."

"Ryan said you told him to stay with you, and he disobeyed. He's fortunate all he suffered was a broken arm. He was worried I would fire you, I suspect." Mr. Holms looked distinctly uncomfortable.

"Are you firing me, sir?" It wouldn't be a surprise, since her student was being flown to a hospital. It had been a dream job while it lasted. She had no regrets. Spending her summer cruising around on a yacht and diving. Was that a cool summer job or what? She'd have done it for free, but the pay was pretty good. Good enough to pay for her last year of tuition at the University of Texas.

She held her breath. If Mr. Holms fired her, she'd have to find another job. The summer was half over; opportunities would be slim.

"Of course not!" He frowned. "Well, technically, I guess I have to release you from your contract, since Mrs. Holms is insisting we go home early. So, since I'm breaking our contract, I insist on paying the rest of the agreed-upon salary."

"Oh, Mr. Holms, I appreciate that, but it's really not necessary. We agreed on that amount because I'd be teaching your children to dive. Why don't we just part ways now and call it even?" While she appreciated his gesture, she would feel she hadn't earned the money.

"Too late. The money has already been transferred into your account." He held up his hand, stopping her refusal. "In return for paying the rest of your salary, I do have one more task for you. It's entirely up to you, though, and if you refuse, the money is still yours."

Unless he wanted sexual favors, she'd agree to whatever he asked. "Sure. What do you want me to do?"

"The yacht has been rented to another family, and I gave the crew their pay, so they're gone until the new people arrive. If you'll agree to pass the keys to the renters at midnight, three days from now, you can continue to enjoy the yacht until they arrive. Though the staff is gone, there's plenty of food. I'd really appreciate it if you'd stay."

"Of course I'll stay! Thank you for such a generous offer." Wow. A whole yacht to herself for three days. She should be paying them.

"Great. I left a list of contractors in the salon, in case you have any problems." He shook her hand enthusiastically. "We all had a great time and would love to hire you again next summer, if you're available," he said as he climbed down to the water taxi. He held up his hand, index finger and pinky extended, and called, "Go Texas! Hook 'em horns!" before the motorboat revved its engine and roared away.

Beth wandered around the empty yacht, peeking in closets, checking out the more-than-ample food supply, acquainting herself with the amenities.

It took less than an hour.

Slathering on sunscreen, she climbed up to the tanning deck with her paperback romance, prepared to bask in the sun and the luxury of the life of the idle rich.

The sun was really hot, with no clouds in sight. She didn't want to get sun poisoning. How long had she been up there, anyway? She looked at her watch, strapped to her insulated water jug. A whopping fifteen minutes had passed.

With a sigh, she flopped to her stomach. Twelve minutes later, she gave up and went to her quarters. After a quick shower, she wandered into the aft salon, where the Holmses hosted cocktail parties, and thought about making a pitcher of margaritas. But margaritas were no fun alone.

Sitting on the padded bench, she swung her leg and looked

out over the sparkling blue water. Maybe she would take the skiff to Crystal Key and check out the dive shop. She looked at her watch and slumped back on the thick pad with a sigh. Crystal Key would be shut down for siesta.

The yacht gently rocked, the soft sounds of waves lapping at her hull, calling to Beth.

She really wanted to go back down to the wreck. The silt would be settled by now. The sun was high, and the wreck was less than fifteen meters deep. She was a master diver.

And she knew better than to dive alone.

Grabbing a pair of binoculars, she headed back out to the deck. Maybe she'd spot a dive party and could join them.

Nothing but sparkling water greeted her.

Stripping to the bikini she always wore beneath her clothes, she dove into the water.

Five laps around the yacht later, she stopped to tread water, again scanning the Gulf for any signs of life.

If she held the bowline, she could snorkel alone. The thought cheered her as she headed for her quarters to grab her fins and snorkel.

Swimming out as far as her tether allowed, the edge of the wreck taunted her peripheral vision. Dipping below the surface only brought frustration. She really needed to get closer, deeper.

A movement caught her eye. Bubbles danced toward the surface. A diver. How had she missed seeing his buoy?

Beth kicked upward, breaking the surface with a gasp and scrambled up to the deck, tossing her fins on the chair. Her wet feet slipped on the warm decking as she headed for the compartment holding her equipment.

"Please don't leave until I get down there," she chanted to the unknown diver below the surface. "Please don't leave!"

Throwing on her tank, she fastened her weight vest after quickly checking her gauge and hoses and taking a quick hit of air to test her regulator.

Sitting on the rail, she spit into her mask, rubbing the lens hastily, then rinsing. Still no dive buoy in sight. She'd better take one. Fins on, feet beneath her, she held her secondary regulator and hose against her chest with her left hand. She put her regulator in her mouth and held it and her mask on with her right hand as she rolled backward into the warm water of the Gulf of Mexico.

Pausing while the water settled around her, caressing her, she squinted in the direction of the wrecked commercial fishing boat she and the Holms children had been exploring for the last few days.

Her heart plummeted. The wreck looked deserted. Did she dare swim closer to confirm?

While she argued with her better judgment, a stream of bubbles rose from the aft section of the old fishing boat.

Grinning, Beth sank deeper, then kicked out, anxious to join the dive.

Her hand touched the rough barnacle-edged bow, slowing her progress in order to peek around at her potential dive mates.

Make that mate. A lone diver moved slowly along the bottom of the wreck, searching inch by inch.

Curious, Beth held back, observing.

The diver knew what he was doing, as evidenced by the surety of his movement. Obviously experienced, she had to wonder why he chanced diving alone. Wait. She was alone, too. But at least she had a dive buoy. Where was his?

The diver looked up as she approached, nodding in greeting, strands of light hair floating out around his mask to give him a startled look.

She paused, allowing the silt she'd stirred to settle, then raised her hand.

The diver wrote on his dive slate, then held it up. *New here?*

Her hand automatically went to her hip. Crap. She'd forgotten her slate in her hurry to get below.

His eyes crinkled behind his mask, and he offered her his slate and pen.

Shaking her head in disgust at forgetting such a standard item, she wrote *Visiting*. She held the slate up, then passed it back and fell into line behind him as they made their way along the bottom edge of the wreck, occasionally tapping each other to point out interesting things or brightly colored fish.

The diver pointed at the dive computer on his arm. Beth glanced at the submersible pressure gauge on her wrist, surprised to see how much air she'd used, and nodded, pointing to the surface.

After the cool depths, the sun was blinding and hot when they broke the surface.

A few feet away, the diver blew water, then shoved his mask up, his grin white in his tanned skin. "Hi," he called, "I'm Will. Will King."

Beth shoved her mask up and brushed strings of wet hair from her face. "Hello, Will King. I'm Beth." She pulled on the anchor rope to free the buoy. "Where's your buoy?"

Will looked around. "Are you sure that's not mine?"

She tapped the side of the optic plastic where the yacht's name, *Salsa Time*, was stenciled beneath the larger diver logo.

He muttered something and pulled a Z-knife from his dive vest. "I'll be right back." He jackknifed and disappeared below the waves.

Beth treaded water for a few minutes, then decided he may not be coming back. Should she check on him?

While she debated, he popped up, spraying water as he shoved his mask up. A coil of rope was clutched in one hand. "Must have come loose and drifted away."

"Where's your boat?"

"Coming back for me around two."

She now noticed he wore two tanks. Obviously his prompt at the wreck had been for her sake. While she was thankful, it rankled to realize she'd let time get away from her like that. After all, she was not a novice.

"Where's yours?" he shouted across the water.

It took a second to locate the yacht. She pointed to it, about five hundred yards away from the dive site.

He allowed the water to bring him closer, his deep tan setting off the Caribbean blue of his eyes. "Is there a Mr. Beth on that thing who might feed me to the sharks if I asked you to have a drink with me?"

She smirked. "Are you carrying a flask, Will?"

"Okay, you twisted my arm. I'll have a drink with you." He winked. "But the next time is on me."

She smiled as they made their way to *Salsa Time*.

Once on deck, they dropped their gear. Beth handed Will a towel from the supply chest as she toweled her hair.

"Dive much?" Will tossed his towel into the bin she'd indicated.

"Every chance I get, for the last fifteen years." She grinned back as him. "I was a Dolphin then a Junior-certified rec diver before I became an instructor."

He nodded,then fixed her with a hard stare, surprising her. "Then you, of all people, should know better than to dive alone."

"Me? You were down there by yourself, too. At least I had the sense to use a buoy."

"Mine was there when I went down," he shot back. "Besides, I live here. I've logged hundreds if not thousands of hours in these waters. My heart about stopped when I saw your shapely behind bobbing at the bow of that boat."

He saw that? "How long were you watching me before you acknowledged me?"

"Long enough." He glanced around. "And now," he said, advancing on her, "here we are, alone, on your fancy boat." He tsked. "You believe in taking risks, don't you? Or do you enjoy living dangerously?"

# 2
———————

Beth swallowed, fighting the urge to take a step back. Although his words scared the bejesus out of her, a second look in his blue eyes told her he wanted to scare her. She also knew desire when she saw it.

With his fit body and golden tan, he could easily inspire the female equivalent of a wet dream.

She knew she'd been isolated too long from eligible members of the opposite sex, but the idea of the specimen before her finding her attractive shot a thrill through her.

Not that she would encourage him or even consider getting involved with someone when she would be leaving in three days.

Still, the look in his eyes was flattering. Which was why she decided to ignore his insult regarding her actions and offer him a drink.

Smiling sweetly, she walked toward the bar as she asked, "What would you like to drink? I make a mean margarita and more than adequate daiquiris. There are also bottles of single-serving wine and just about every kind of beer in the cooler. Feel free to help yourself."

Feeling smug, she poured a generous amount of Cuervo Gold into the margarita maker and reached for the heavy bottle of mixer.

Will watched the play of pectoral muscle over the skimpy cup of Beth's bikini. He'd prefer to drink his margarita from her hot little body. He reeled in his libido. Visitors were off limits. He'd have a drink to be sociable and then be on his way, even if it meant swimming back to Crystal Key.

"Iced tea sounds good. Got any of that?" He swallowed a laugh at the shocked look on her sun-kissed face. Did she think he'd get liquored up and have his way with her?

Though appealing, it wasn't bloody likely.

Closing her mouth, she nodded. "Sweet and unsweet, bottles and cans. Also in the fridge. Fresh lemon, lime, and orange wedges are in the plastic container on the top shelf." She reached beneath the bar and handed him a tall glass. "The ice maker is to the right of the beverage cooler."

He popped the top of an unsweet tea and poured it into the ice-filled glass. A wedge of orange followed. He grinned, his white teeth flashing. "All the comforts of home." He took a long swig and sighed.

Great. He probably thought she was an alcoholic. She jabbed the power button. The margarita machine did its thing, its whirring drowning out any possible conversation. Pausing it, she added a ladle of strawberries in heavy syrup. The blending resumed as she glanced at her guest while she rimmed her glass with sugar, then poured her concoction.

He waited until she sat before choosing a seat on the opposite end of the padded bench. "Nice," he said, indicating the yacht with a wave of his glass. "Is this yours?"

What the heck? "Sure." She shrugged, avoiding eye contact. "Why else would I be on board?"

He nodded and took another long drink. "Where are the staff and crew?"

"Below."

"Bullshit." At her widened eyes, he said, "I may not move in the same circles as you, but I know a boat this size has staff and crew, and someone would have greeted us if they'd been aboard."

Licking the sugar from the rim of her glass bought a few seconds for her to formulate her story. "Fine. The truth is they all have the day off. We just met; I wasn't sure I wanted you to know we were alone." Catching what she'd just admitted, she hurried on. "But they'll be back any time, so don't get any ideas."

His heated gaze licked her from her toes to her hip. Funny, she never felt exposed in a bikini before she met him.

She blinked and he was sitting closer. A lot closer, the heat of his hip against hers informed her.

"Do you just cruise around all summer?"

Hastily swallowing her mouthful of margarita, she had to push her tongue into the roof of her mouth to stop the brain freeze. "Um, I guess. Well, when I don't have classes. I'm a senior at Texas."

He frowned. "And you already own a yacht? Or does it belong to your family? How old are you?"

"Twenty-four." She ignored the yacht question, preferring to lie as little as possible. "I took a couple of years off to travel before I went to college, if you're wondering."

"That's good." He leaned closer, pinning her against the back cushion.

"W-why?" Dang, he was hot. If he didn't back off soon, she didn't want to think about what she might be capable of doing, after being out to sea for so long.

"Because," he said, his breath hot against her lips, "I don't want to kiss jailbait."

She squeaked when his mouth covered hers, shocked at the sensation zipping through her sex-deprived body when their lips touched.

Then his tongue slid between her lips to sweep her mouth, marauding her senses.

Deep within, a dam burst. She pulled him closer, one hand holding his head while the other gripped his back, holding him tight.

He wasn't exactly fighting her off.

In a flash, her bikini top hit the area rug, his hot hands wedging up to cup and squeeze her bare breasts.

More. She squirmed against his hardness until she sat on his lap, her legs wrapped securely around his waist. Her hips bucked of their own volition, the feel of his hard ridge against her aching folds feeling so good it almost made her climax.

She couldn't remember the last time she'd had sex, didn't want to try. Right now, her main concern was ending her dry spell.

It didn't matter that he thought she owned the yacht. It didn't matter that they'd just met. It didn't matter if they were alone and he could potentially do whatever he chose without fear of being caught. It was a two-way street, and right now, she had some pretty definite ideas about what she would like to do to him.

He tore his mouth from hers and tried to speak, but she shoved him downward until her breast filled his mouth, groaning and writhing with each strong draw of his mouth.

Bending her back over his arm, he continued his assault on her breasts, his hips thrusting and grinding against her softness.

Was this considered dry humping? She was far from dry. Whatever it was, she liked it. She wanted more.

When she pulled away from his mouth and sat up, rising on her knees to reach down and tug his suit from his lean hips, his hands on her wrists stopped her.

"We can't," he said, panting the words.

Shameless, she brushed her erect nipples across his chest, her hips grinding her aching folds against his covered erection. "Sure we can," she whispered back, reaching for his elastic waistband.

He shuddered, took a deep breath, and looked her in the eyes. "No. We can't. I have a policy. A strict policy about tourists."

"What policy is that?" She trailed nibbling kisses up his neck, then sucked his earlobe.

He groaned and broke contact. "A no-fuck policy."

# 3

----

Humiliation seared her cheeks. Stumbling from his lap, she groped for her top, too embarrassed to look at him. "We wouldn't want to compromise your policy, would we?"

"Beth, I . . ." He reached for her, but she shoved him aside while she pulled on her top. "Beth—"

"Stop. Whatever it is you're going to say, I don't want to hear it." Standing, she looked out the window at the water, blinking back embarrassed tears. "Your gear is by the ladder. Don't forget to grab it when you leave."

"Let me make it up to you," he said from behind her.

She whirled on him. "Make it up to me? Why would you want to do that?" Her eyes widened. "A pity fuck? Oh, hell, no! I'm not that desperate! Get out."

He glanced at his watch. "My boat will be back soon, but I don't want to leave you like this. You took what I said wrong or I didn't say it right. Although fucking of any kind, with you, would not be a hardship," he said with a grin. "I meant, let me make it up to you by taking you to dinner. How about it? You have to eat," he reminded her. "I know a great place on the beach. I could be back to pick you up in a couple of hours. What do you say?" He leaned closer and whispered, "Say yes."

Her hurt and outrage deflated. What the heck? He was right; she did have to eat. And since saying she was no cook was putting it mildly, dinner out was probably a good idea. But she didn't want to give in too easily. After all, the guy had turned her down when she'd been almost naked and begging. "All right. Fine. But don't pick me up. I'll meet you there." She snatched a pad and pen from the drawer by the door, pushing it at him. "Write down where and when. And directions. Please."

His lips twitched, but he took the pad and wrote down directions, then handed it back. "See you in a couple of hours," he said, brushing a light kiss on her forehead as he walked toward the deck.

A splash soon followed.

She glanced down at the pad. "Nick's Seafood and Beach Bar. I like seafood." Her reflection in the salon mirror made her gasp. She had a lot of work to do before she met her date if she had any hope of being presentable.

Gathering her clothing, she moved into the master stateroom, justifying it by the fact that it had a bigger bathroom and was the only one with a tub. After all, what difference did it make? She would be the only one on board for the next three days. She may as well make the most of it and be comfortable.

While the big bathtub was filling, she retrieved the pitcher of margaritas and her glass. Naked, she was padding to the oval tub, glass in hand, when she spotted several vials on a little mirror tray next to the tub.

"Gardenia," she read, then removed the stopper and took a big whiff. "Oh, yeah, I'll take some of that." But the little bottle was slick, slipping from her grasp when she began pouring the oil. "Crap!" Hanging on to the side of the tub, she fished out the near-empty bottle while the heady scent of fresh gardenias permeated the air.

Her nose immediately started running, and her eyes burned. "Whoa, that's some heavy-duty gardenia." She coughed as she lowered into the hot, fragrant water. A push of the button to activate the jets caused the floral scent to explode into the room, all but choking her with its cloying sweetness.

"Oh, Lord," she wheezed, "I'm being asphyxiated, death by gardenia!" Running more water only aggravated the problem.

Funny, she'd always envisioned the romantic ambience of taking a whirlpool bath, soaking in elegant perfumed water, surrounded by candles.

Reality was much different, and she had a feeling if she dared light a candle, the fumes would ignite.

Eyes and nose streaming, she finished her bath in record time and flipped the drain, all but sprinting from the room, wrapped in a bath sheet.

Bath sheets were another luxury she'd looked forward to experiencing. The reality . . . not so much, since she was too short and kept tripping over the towel.

Flopping onto the bare mattress of the king-size bed, she enjoyed the soft breeze of the ceiling fan, hoping it would dissipate some of the gardenia scent clinging to her skin.

Restless again, she searched until she found the Egyptian cotton sheets and made the bed. She'd just finished smoothing the quilted silk bedspread when she looked at the tiny brass clock on the nightstand.

"Oh, no! That can't be right!" Rushing to her pile of clothes, she dug until she found her watch. Crap. It was the right time. She sniffed her gardenia-scented arm and coughed. No time to try showering it off.

A little gel worked into her short brown hair, tinted moisturizer, a swipe of mascara and blush were all done at landspeed-record time. A quick floss and brushing of her teeth, tinted ChapStick application, along with a swipe of antiperspirant and she was ready to shimmy into her sundress.

Heels or no heels? She was taking the dinghy. Climbing in and out would be easier without heels. Rubber flip-flops wouldn't do, though, so she dug in her bag until she found some that looked a little less . . . flip-floppy.

She did a quick turn in the three-way mirror in the dressing area, deciding she cleaned up pretty well. Scooping up her clothes, she stuffed them in the tall wicker hamper in the bathroom, then glanced at the neatly made bed.

Why had she made the bed? She planned to sleep there, but did she plan to do something else there if the evening went well? Maybe . . .

"Ugh. Get it out of your head. Will is probably not nearly as sexy as you thought he was this afternoon. You were just lonely. It's a common occurrence in situations like this, I'm sure." Stuffing her license and debit card in her purse, she headed for the door, determined to keep her cool and have a nice evening, regardless of how it ended.

And determined to ignore the little voice telling her she was still lonely.

# 4

---

Will arrived early at his restaurant, Nick's, to apprise the staff of his date. Maybe it was wrong, but he ordered everyone to keep mum about his ownership.

He'd done well, parlaying his modest inheritance to buy and expand Nick's restaurant and bar into the wildly profitable business it was, but he didn't spread news of his success around. Success that had enabled him to fulfill a lifelong dream: opening a dive shop.

King's Diving Castle was not only successful, but it was also the only dive shop on Crystal Key. Popular among residents and tourists alike, business was flourishing. And, thanks to his expert staff, he was able to spend more time doing the thing he loved most: diving.

But, despite his success, he knew it was small potatoes compared to the things Beth must be surrounded with every day.

And when Will King couldn't compete, he didn't play the game.

Which was the real reason he'd left Beth half naked on the yacht instead of satisfying them both. Okay, that may not have been a particularly brilliant idea, especially when he'd been re-gretting it for the last few hours, counting the minutes until he could see her again. Then what? The lady was clearly out of his league. What would she see in a guy whose best outfit was a wet suit?

But that didn't keep him from wanting her.

"Okay," he said to Korine, his hostess, "remember, tonight I'm just a customer."

Korine did an eye-roll. "How will we know which one is your special lady, boss man?"

"She's short." He held his hand at midchest level. "About this tall. Dark hair—"

"Cut short? Good tan?" Korine nodded toward the door. "I think she just walked in."

He turned and had to catch his breath. His late granddad's voice echoed in his head: *Go get her, boy. She's the one.*

Beth smiled and made her way toward where he stood, rooted to the floor next to the hostess stand. Her modest, dark, peach-colored sundress set off her tan and seemed to glow in the dim lights of the bar. Or maybe it was the woman wearing it.

He stepped forward, grasping her arm, and brushed a chaste kiss across her temple. Tiny diamonds sparkled from her ear-lobes, drawing him like a moth to a flame.

He could be in deep trouble with this woman.

He couldn't wait.

"How many tonight, sir?" Korine's voice broke into his trancelike state.

"What? Oh, um. Two, please."

"Your usual table?"

"I eat here a lot. Alone," he hurried to say when he saw Beth's dark eyes widen.

As his grandfather would say, he saw the devilment in Korine's eyes as she turned to lead them to the secluded table near the window overlooking the harbor. It was easily the best table in the place, but not his usual. For that he was grateful, since he didn't think it would make a very good impression to sit in the back, next to the kitchen door. Korine had a wicked sense of humor.

She returned to the table after they had ordered, a waiter in her wake, carrying a linen-wrapped ice bucket. "Champagne," she said with a smile, pouring the sparkling rose liquid into crystal flutes. She winked at Will. "Compliments of the management."

"Wow." Beth took a sip. "Yum. What a nice thing for the management to do! Do you know who ordered it? Maybe we could call him over to say thanks."

He watched Beth's mouth caress the edge of the champagne glass and clamped his jaw when his dick twitched in response. "Ah, I don't see him around," he finally replied. Of course he wasn't around; he was playing customer.

The food was great, as usual, which made him proud. The service was better. Attentive but unobtrusive, their server anticipated their every need.

Will made a mental note to commend the waiter.

"I'm stuffed." Beth leaned back against the red leather booth and sighed. "I can't eat another bite," she said when the waiter approached with the dessert tray.

"You have to try the chocolate turtle cheesecake; it's a customer favorite." At her quick look, he hurried to say, "Or that's what I've heard, anyway. How about splitting a piece?"

Reluctantly, she agreed but ended up taking only a couple of bites.

"You didn't like it?" He took another bite and a sip of coffee.

"I loved it. But, like I said, I'm stuffed. If I keep eating like that, I won't be able to fit into my bathing suits."

An image of her, topless, flashed in his mind. If he had his way, she'd stay naked. Completely naked.

Tourist or not, he knew in that instant, he was going to break his own rule.

He was going to have sex with a tourist. And, if at all possible, as often as possible for however long she stayed in Crystal Key.

He'd worry about the wisdom of it later.

"What?" Beth set her cup on the saucer and blotted her mouth. "Do I have something on my face?"

"Hmm? No, why?"

"You were staring at my mouth."

"I was?" He made a covert adjustment and leaned forward, taking her hand. "Maybe that's because I was thinking about kissing you."

"Here?" Her voice squeaked.

Smiling, he stood, pulling her to her feet. "All over," he said in a low voice as he steered her toward the exit. He leaned close to her ear and whispered, "But not in public."

She stopped, lagging back as they got to the door. "Aren't you going to pay for dinner?"

Damn.

"They have my card on file; they'll just bill me," he said, pulling her onto the sidewalk.

"You must be a very good customer," she said, falling into step beside him.

"You have no idea," he muttered. Louder, he said, "Would you like a quick tour of our booming metropolis?"

They took a few steps before she answered. "I think I'll take a rain check. It's dark, plus I'm really kind of tired. I think I'm going to call it a night."

"No problem. I'll take you home." He turned and walked in the direction of the marina.

"Thanks, but I brought the dinghy."

"It's dark and you're tired. I insist. Just let me swing by my place to get my boat key. I live by the marina, so it's not even out of our way."

Boy, he wasn't kidding about it being close, she thought a

few minutes later when he unlocked the door of a beach house located on the other side of the dock from the bay.

"I bought this place because it had a dock for my boat," he said, flipping the light switch. A modest chandelier illuminated the small navy-blue-marble-tiled entry. "I figured it would save a lot of time. Whenever I wanted to get away, my boat would be right there, ready."

"Do you find you need to get away a lot?" She glanced around, wondering where his bedroom was and if he planned to take her there.

Dangerous thoughts. Must be the champagne talking. "Will, thank you for dinner. I had a great time. But I really do need to head back. It's not necessary for you to go to all the trouble of taking your boat out, then having to come back, when I'm perfectly capable of going back the way I came."

He paused in his search of the drawer in his hall table, then straightened and walked toward her.

Dang, he was hot. Tall and yummy-looking in khakis, an ecru linen sports coat, and an open-neck pale yellow shirt.

He shrugged out of his jacket and hung it on the back of a chair by the door, then pulled her into his arms.

Whatever aftershave he wore made her mouth water. It had to be strong in order for her to smell it over her gardenia stench.

He nuzzled her neck. "You smell so good. Like fresh flowers."

*Tell me about it.*

He kissed his way up her neck to her ear. "It makes me want to lick you. All over."

She could live with that. Her knees threatened to buckle. Maybe going home alone was not such a great idea after all. She pushed out of his embrace and reached for the door.

"Well, if you insist, I guess it would be nice—if you took me home, I mean." Although the idea of Will kissing her all over certainly had merit. "We can tie the dinghy to your boat, right?" He nodded. "And, since you'll be going to the trouble of taking me back to *Salsa Time,* the least I can do is offer you a nightcap."

"What's the most you would do?" he teased as he locked his door on their way out.

"Don't push your luck, King."

# 5

---

"Your staff is still not aboard?" Will looked around the lounge while Beth popped the cork on another bottle of champagne.

She looked up from pouring. "Um, no, I mean, I guess they've already turned in for the night."

"Hmm. I'd have thought at least one of them would have waited up for you. After all, you're their boss."

Wracking her brain, she tried to remember if the staff usually hung around until the Holms were in bed. Since she usually retired by the time the children called it a night, she had no idea. "Oh, um, we're very informal around here." She shrugged and handed him a champagne flute. "I'm pretty self-sufficient. If I need anything, I can always buzz them."

"They're not here, are they?" He took her glass and set it on the bar with his, then tilted her face.

Crap. Now what? At least part of the truth was better than an outright lie. "No, I gave them some time off."

"Were you afraid to tell me?" His mouth was so close now, she could feel his breath on her lips.

"Not really." She licked her lips. "I just didn't see the point."

"Liar," he whispered into her mouth as he leaned into the kiss.

Holy crap. She'd forgotten the potency of Will's kisses. Tiny droplets of perspiration popped out all over her body. Was she glistening?

Regardless, her muscles were rapidly taking on the consistency of overcooked spaghetti. Her knees refused to hold her weight. Had his arms not been clutching her, she knew she'd slide to his feet, a pathetic puddle of needy goo.

Not a pretty picture, but there you have it.

He slid his hand up to push the ribbon straps from her shoulders.

Weak, she clung to his lips while gripping the sides of his shirt. It was either that or fall over. Plus, there was the fact that she didn't want the semiorgasmic kiss to end.

Reality hit her square in the face about the same time her most expensive silk dress hit the floor.

It wasn't fear of intimacy. It wasn't fear of being seen naked— she knew she was in fairly decent shape. It wasn't even fear of someone seeing her underwear. A part of her had planned for just such an opportunity, so she had donned her prettiest undergarments.

It was the extra secret in her Victoria's Secret, the little glob packets she'd found in the bathroom drawer that she'd impetuously stuck into the cups of her strapless bra to give her girls an added *oomph*.

In hindsight, it had been a stupid thing to do. The guy had already seen her breasts. Besides which, to be totally honest, she'd hoped they'd end up naked after dinner.

In the back of her mind, she must have also planned to undress herself, either in the dark or in the privacy of the bathroom.

Yes, that must have been her plan, she thought, easing out of

Will's embrace. Changing in the bathroom, alone, then making a grand entrance in . . . well, something sexy and spectacular.

The only problem with that plan was the sexiest thing she owned now lay warming her feet. She usually slept in old T-shirts or, if it was really hot or she was sunburned, just in a thong.

*Note to self: buy lingerie.*

"Let's take this to my cabin," she said, dousing the lights.

Unfortunately, she was a fraction of a second too late. Her words were scarcely out of her mouth before she felt the hooks at her back release.

Her bra, thanks to its extra packing, shot away from her like a slingshot, knocking their champagne glasses across the bar.

"Crap!" She dove toward the sound, her eyes rapidly adjusting to the moonlight. "It's okay," she called from where she crouched behind the bar. "They didn't break." Thank goodness. Grabbing a bar towel, she mopped the sticky trails from the cabinet doors as much as possible, then tried to soak up the liquid on the bar mat.

"Do I make you nervous?" Will's voice ruffled the hair by her ear, making her shriek and jump. Her head smacked the underside of the bar. "Are you okay?"

Arm around her, his hand suspiciously close to the underside of her breast, he eased her to a standing position.

"Well?" Arms around her again, he swayed from side to side.

Eyes clenched shut, she burrowed against the solid wall of his chest, inhaling the subtle scent of fabric softener and aftershave. It was a potent combination. She had no problem with staying right where she was, but it probably wasn't going to happen.

Gathering her courage, she looked up at him. If possible, he was even better-looking in the filtered moonlight. "I think I've done about all the damage I can in here. Let's see what I can do to the bedroom."

A low sexy chuckle sent goose bumps down her spine. No doubt about it, she also wanted to see what he could do in the bedroom.

He eased her around the bar, moving toward the door she indicated, which led to the hallway, then stopped abruptly. "Wait. I stepped on something."

"It's okay." She tugged when he bent. "I'm sure it's nothing important. We can check it out later."

"Turn on the light. I want to see what it is."

*Do we have to?* "I'm sure it's nothing." Tug, tug.

"Whatever it is, it's cold and gooey."

"Here, give it to me!" Feeling in the shadow, she snatched the slippery glob out of his hand, trying to think how she was going to explain to Mrs. Holms that Will had killed her cleavage, and tossed it in the general vicinity of the trash behind the bar. "There. Done." She pulled him down the corridor. "Now, where were we?"

She'd gone too far to quit now. Dang it, she was going to get laid if it killed her.

Moonlight shining through the window gilded the room where it reflected on the silk bedspread and the deep wood of the built-ins.

Along their walk down the corridor, Beth had removed Will's shirt. When he let out a low whistle upon seeing the master suite, she knew how he felt, looking at his tanned chest.

Wasting no time, she plastered her bare chest against his and licked the base of his throat.

"What are you doing?" he said on a laugh, hugging her close.

"Trying to get your attention." On tiptoe, she nipped the tip of his chin. "Is it working?"

"Oh, yeah." He bent his knees, scooped her off her feet, and carried her to the bed, where he followed her down to the silky softness.

The silk at her back made her squirm almost as much as what Will was doing to her front.

After another toe-curling kiss, he licked and kissed his way down her receptive body, pausing along the way at all the interesting parts.

He circled her navel with the tip of his tongue, then kissed each hip bone while sliding his hands under her hips to cup her buttocks.

His growl vibrated a place deep within her.

He nipped the tender skin just above Beth's pubic bone, eliciting a moan. "God, I love a woman in a thong." He had a strong suspicion he literally loved the woman spread before him but didn't want to freak her out. Not yet, anyway.

Her abdomen contracted beneath his lips as she tried to sit up, reaching toward his waistband. "One of us has on too many clothes," she said.

"You're right." Hooking his fingers beneath the thin side straps of her thong, he pulled them from her in one quick move. Her skin was baby soft and smooth. Everywhere. His fingers traced the fine white stripe of her tan line, which widened just enough to cover her hairless pussy.

A dark spot, low on her abdomen, very low, caught his eye. "What's that?" He touched the tip of his finger to it and felt her recoil.

Her hand shot to the spot, hiding it. "Nothing." Sitting up, she reached for his zipper. "Your turn. Take them off."

He shook his head, then, in case she couldn't see him, he said, "Not yet, darlin'."

Grasping an ankle in each hand, he toppled her to her back as he pulled her toward the edge of the big mattress until he could place her ankles over his shoulders, deliberately making her vulnerable to him.

Before she could react, he lowered his head, swiping his tongue along her sweet-scented folds. She moaned, arching her hips.

He smiled against her flesh, then tickled her with the tip of his tongue.

She squirmed on the bed, arching her hips, tilting her pelvis higher.

Clasping the tops of her thighs, he dipped his head again, sucking her into his mouth, rolling her engorged nubbin with his tongue, then sucking it deeper into his mouth. Again and again he performed the act he'd wanted to do with her since he first saw her in her barely-there bathing suit, the current beneath the water jiggling her breasts like a siren calling to him.

But it wasn't a siren; it was Beth herself. Her pure sexuality had him wanting to beat on his chest, drag her to his cave, and claim her as his mate.

Beneath his hands, the muscles of her silky thighs vibrated. The tender flesh against his mouth softened and swelled, becoming slick with her desire.

He fluttered his tongue against her swollen flesh, eliciting a moan. Her excited breathing matched his, echoing in the room.

Spreading her legs wider, he speared her with his tongue, wiggling it deep within her.

She let out a strangled cry, her back arching off the mattress, her sweet climax filling his mouth while her muscles contracted around his tongue.

He petted her until she settled down, then quickly stripped. When he reached for her, the mystery spot again snagged his attention.

*What don't you want me to see, Beth?* He flipped on the sconce next to the bed. Still too dark, her abdomen fell in shadow.

She opened her eyes when he scooped her off the spread and turned back the covers. "About time you undressed," she said, stretching to kiss his neck. Her shoulders shivered. "Let's hurry up and get under the covers."

Holding her high, he paused on his way to do just that, staring at the tiny burgundy letters tattooed low on her otherwise-perfect skin.

A capital *T* with a smaller capital *A* and *M* on either side.

He must have shown his shock, because she gasped and quickly covered the spot.

Not wanting to get into a discussion while standing naked in the lamplight, he slid her beneath the covers and followed her in.

He reached to turn off the light, then gathered her close before speaking. "I thought you said you went to Texas."

She stiffened against him, but he refused to allow her to put distance between them. Finally, she relaxed against his side, where—as far as he was concerned—she belonged.

"I do go to UT," she said in the dark, her breath warming the side of his neck, making it difficult to concentrate on her words. Especially when his body was so happy to be next to her. Especially when they were both naked.

"Then why the tattoo?"

Her shrug nudged his armpit. "I was young and stupid."

"No offense, but you'd have to be a special kind of stupid to get that tattoo when you went to Texas."

Laughing, she gave his shoulder a soft punch. "I wasn't that stupid!" She sighed. "I was young and thought I was in love. It was spring break, my senior year of high school. My boyfriend was already at A&M. I assumed I'd be joining him the following year." Her deep breath pushed her breasts against his ribs. "Only, I didn't realize I'd already been replaced."

"What an asshole. I can't believe you were even involved with such a loser." He trailed kisses along her hairline, sliding his excited body along hers as he stroked her breasts.

A contented sigh escaped her, her flesh relaxing into his as she stroked his abdomen, her hand going lower with every movement. "I don't want to talk about the past," she said, licking his collar bone. "Let's just say I vowed to never have anything to do with A&M or Aggies again." Her hand closed around his erection, which was less happy than it had been mere seconds ago but still glad to see her. "I can think of other things I'd rather be doing, can't you?"

"Absolutely," he said, squeezing her breast. He was going to make love to her until they both couldn't walk straight.

Then he'd go home and hide every trace of his alma mater, Texas A&M.

# 6

---

Morning sunshine washed the bed in a pink glow. Beth stretched, smiling as delicious memories of the night before danced through her mind.

A warm mouth covered her nipple, drawing it deeply into its heat. The faint smell of shampoo from their shower a few hours ago wafted up to her.

While he sucked, his hands stroked her instantly primed body from his position between her legs. The bump of his erection against her inner thigh told her he'd already donned a condom.

She bit back a smile, wondering how many they had left. They'd fornicated like Energizer Bunnies all night long.

Not that she was complaining. She had three days to indulge in whatever she desired. Diving and screwing Will's brains out sounded like the perfect vacation. . . .

"It's about time you woke up," he said in an early morning, intimate-sounding voice. "I was beginning to think you were unconscious."

Drifting in a half-sleep state, she vaguely recalled feeling some very sexy tingles before she came fully awake. She stretched, arching her back, enjoying the intimate wake-up massage she was getting. "You've been awake a while," she said, glancing at his sheathed erection. "Did you start playing without me?"

He grinned down at her, eyes twinkling. "Nope, not me. I'm a firm believer in playing *with* you." He slid his finger into her wetness, causing her hips to buck in an involuntary response.

She arched again, plucking at her nipples, feeling especially hedonistic for so early in the morning.

When her breath caught, she realized he had brought her to the edge of a promising climax. She opened her eyes to find him in the same place, his busy hands now still. "Why did you stop?"

"I want you to come while I'm inside you."

Gazes locked, she spread her legs wider and pulled him into her embrace as he slid into her welcoming body.

She honored his request.


Limp from being thoroughly satisfied, Beth lolled against the side of the whirlpool tub, letting the hot water soothe muscles that she hadn't used in a while. The all-over body wash Will was lovingly performing barely registered. Was there such a thing as sexual exhaustion?

While her personal vibrator helped take the edge off her sexual frustration, she couldn't honestly remember being so sated until she'd slept with Will.

"Much better than a vibrator," she mumbled.

"Excuse me?"

She lifted heavy lids. Did she say that out loud? She licked her lips, suddenly aware of the sexy way his soapy hands were moving on and in her body. "Um, I said you were much better than a vibrator. Much, much—aah!—better!" His fingers wiggled deep within her, setting off renewed sexual interest.

He revolved his hand, his thumb flicking her nub to screaming awareness. "Can your vibrator do this?" He leaned close, his hand still embedded, and nipped at her breast with the tips of his teeth.

Her climax took her by surprise, nearly drowning her in its delicious sensations. She sagged on the edge of the tub as residual aftershocks made her shiver.

The jets fired up, jostling her relaxed body.

"Or this?" Will pulled her from the side of the tub, arranging her like a rag doll with one leg hitched along the back side of the tub, the force of the jets vibrating her labia and clitoris in a very interesting way.

Hello. Suddenly alert, sleep was the furthest thing from her mind.

Within seconds, her hips were undulating. She tried to stay still, casting a guilty and somewhat embarrassed glance at Will.

He smiled and winked. "It's okay, baby, let it go. I love watching you come." He reached to tilt her hips a little more.

The action must have tripped an internal switch, because she came to instant screaming awareness as her whole body responded.

He patted her still-throbbing folds. "That was hot. But I think you could still manage at least a couple more." Switching her position to a jet on the other side of the tub, he massaged her clit to life before he directed the jet at her from a slightly different angle.

The results were remarkably similar, with her screaming her release within seconds.

Slumped against the side of the tub, one leg still hitched on the side, Beth sat with her eyes closed while she waited for her breathing to slow to normal, her heart to stop trying to break through her ribs.

She was dimly aware of the jets quieting, the gentle slosh and splash of water as Will climbed from the tub. Content, she would willingly stay until her skin shriveled.

"Here we go." Will's disgustingly cheerful voice almost startled her as he gently lowered her leg, then lifted her from the tub.

When did he drain the water?

"Look what I found!" He held up a bottle of the now-hated gardenia oil. She knew she should have thrown the rest of the bottle away.

She wanted to tell him not to come near her with that stuff but lacked the strength. Instead, she hung on his arm while he dried her off, then allowed him to carry her into the attached massage room and stretch her out on the draped table like a sacrificial virgin.

The thought brought a smile to her lips. After what she and Will had done last night and again this morning, the term certainly did not apply to her.

The cloying scent of gardenia filled the room. Before she could voice an objection, his hands smoothed the junk over her abdomen and over and around her breasts with sure, smooth strokes.

"Okay, sweet thing, roll over before I'm overcome with lust. I don't think that table will hold us both."

She rolled over and tried not to gag at the smell wafting around her. After all, he meant well. Not to mention the fact that he was sexy as all get-out, standing buck naked beside the massage table.

"Ah-ah," he said, "I saw that look." He gave a playful slap to her behind. "No more massage for you. Well, not right now, anyway. Besides, we're burning daylight." He waggled his eyebrows at her when she sat up, gripping the sheet around her nudity. "Even in paradise, there are schedules to maintain."

"What schedules? I'm on vacation." She hopped down and walked to the wardrobe where she'd hung her robe.

"I took zee lib-erty of planning mademoiselle's day."

She snickered. "Cut out the fake French accent; it's creeping me out."

"Okay. Here's the plan." He stepped into his wrinkled box-ers. "How about you make us some breakfast while I finish getting dressed? Then, while you make yourself even more gor-geous, I'll run back home and pack us a lunch. And why, you may ask, am I packing our lunch?"

"Okay, I'll bite. Why are you packing a lunch?"

"I'm glad you asked!" He winked. "Because we are going for a picnic and snorkeling. I know the perfect spot. Gorgeous and deserted." He lowered his voice. "You could even snorkel in the nude if you wanted."

"What about you?"

"Oh, yeah, I want you to snorkel nude. Ow!" He made a big production of rubbing his arm. "You're a dangerous woman." He turned her toward the door and patted her butt. "Now go get breakfast going. I'm starving!"

She took two wrong turns but finally found the galley. The thing she'd thought was the galley was sort of a pantry-microwave area. With a start, she realized she'd never been in several of the rooms. Including the kitchen, er, galley.

Too soon, Will came whistling down the hall. "Hey, hot stuff," he called, "talk me in! I'm lost!"

She knew the feeling. "In here. Follow the sound of my voice." Frantically, she glanced around the kitchen. It could easily be a professional chef's dream.

It was more like her nightmare.

She couldn't even find the refrigerator, she realized after opening several wrong doors. Whose bright idea was it to blend all the appliances in with the cabinetry?

"Aha!" Relief washed through her when she opened another cabinet, and a light came on as cold air wafted out.

She picked up as many eggs as she could fit in her hand. She never ate eggs. How many should she cook?

"Aha what?" Will's voice, directly behind her, startled her.

With a shriek, she jumped and the eggs made their escape.

In slow motion, she watched as five eggs went up above her head and came down with a cracking splat, cool egg guts splashing her bare feet and ankles.

Will hopped back. "Is this some kind of weird culinary skill I don't know about, where you throw stuff on the floor?"

She forced a returning smile. "Yeah, all the great chefs do it, I hear." She glanced down at her feet. "That was your breakfast."

"Thanks. Good job, but I prefer mine a tad more done." He started opening and closing drawers and cupboards. "Where is the bread? Let's just grab a piece of toast and get going."

Beth looked around, trying to remember if she'd seen a loaf of bread. Stalling, she reached into the refrigerator and pulled out some whipped butter for their toast. Assuming there was a toaster.

Will watched Beth and realized she had no better idea of where things were than he did. Poor little rich girl. She'd probably had servants taking care of her throughout her entire life and was lost without them.

The thought was sobering. How could he compete with that? Although he'd done well and was doing better every day, he was far from being flush enough to have servants. After Beth had fallen asleep in the early morning hours, he'd lain awake, scared spitless because he had a sneaking suspicion he'd just become a statistic: he'd fallen in love at first sight.

What he was going to do about it, he hadn't a clue. He just knew he wanted to spend as much time with her as possible and hope things worked out the way he wanted.

He wanted his own happily ever after.

And he was pretty sure he wanted it with Beth.

# 7
---

Beth was ready and waiting on deck when Will came roaring up in his sleek boat.

He cut the engine and threw the bowline loop over the docking post. After securing it, he hopped out and glanced up. "Ready?"

Nodding, she grabbed her gear bag and stepped onto the ladder, acutely aware of Will's eyes on her hot-pink-bikini-clad rear as she backed down.

"Nice suit." He winked as he helped her aboard.

"Thanks." She took in his ripped T-shirt and cutoffs. "Wish I could say the same."

"What?" He held his arms out to his sides. "What's wrong with what I'm wearing?"

"Nothing." She slid her sunglasses down to cover her eyes. "If you're planning to do yard work." Stashing her bag behind the seat, she sat down and propped her bare feet on the dash. "What are you waiting for?" She grinned up at him. "Oh, I get it, you planned for me to take the helm?"

Biting her lip to hide her laughter, she watched him untie and then scramble to the captain's chair to fire up the engine.

When their takeoff roar had subsided, she shouted, "How far out are we going?"

"Not far," he yelled back, glancing over. "There's a great little island not far from here. The lee side has a protected bay for sweet snorkeling."

Within minutes, they roared up to the tip of a barrier island and banked port. White sand sparkled along the azure water. Their wake caught up to them, gently rocking the boat.

Will stood and handed her an oar. "I retracted the motor. We'll have to paddle the rest of the way, then anchor about twenty meters from shore."

Nodding, she took the oar and dipped it in the water, waiting for him to be seated. A diver, a skilled lover, and a protector of the ocean's ecosystem. What a guy.

They dropped anchor and prepared to disembark.

Beth slung her bag over her shoulder. "Do I need my water socks?" She peered over the starboard side and smiled at the antics of a knot of monkfish.

"No, just kind of watch where you're stepping. There's a sharp drop-off about five meters port, but if we walk straight toward the beach, it's not much above our knees."

"Do you need me to carry anything?"

Picking up his gear bag, he hefted a huge cooler and smiled. "No, thanks, I got it." He waited until she had her feet under her in the warm water, then jumped out, holding the cooler high above his head.

Beth blinked away the saltwater spray from his jump and licked her lips. "This is deeper than just above the knee," she pointed out as they trudged toward shore, her shirt floating out around her armpits. "Good thing I wore a bathing suit." She looked pointedly at his attire.

"My suit's under my clothes."

"Smooth move."

His chuckle followed her as she slipped beneath the shallow surf and swam until her knees scraped sand. Much faster and more efficient than walking against the resistance of the water.

Slogging to shore, she turned and saw Will trudging into the shallow water, holding the cooler balanced on his head.

For the next few minutes, she admired the play of muscle with each sure step he took, his long stride eating up the distance.

She glanced around as he approached and dropped the cooler to the sand. "Boy, you weren't kidding when you said this beach was secluded. It's as though we're the only ones here."

He paused from opening the lid of the giant cooler. "We probably are."

"Where is everyone? I can't believe no one knows about this place. It's gorgeous!"

"They know about it. But for some reason, no one comes here. Hungry?" He started handing her containers.

"Starving!" Sex always made her hungry. After last night's marathon session, it was amazing she hadn't passed out from malnutrition. "What's for lunch?"

"I packed a little of everything, since I didn't know what you'd like," he hedged. Actually, he hadn't packed the cooler; one of his staff had done it. He opened a square container and sniffed. "Seafood salad. There are crackers and utensils in the compartment under the lid. Grab some for me, too. Please." He opened a large insulated square. "All right! Fried chicken."

"You sound surprised. I thought you packed it."

Damn. "All right, you caught me. I had it packed at Nick's. They have great deals on boxed lunches." Like free, when you own the place.

"I'm not complaining." She grabbed a chicken leg. "Hurry up, I'm starving!"

"Eat." Digging around in the bottom, he brought out two cans of iced tea. "Sweet or unsweet with lemon?"

"Sweet, please." Accepting the can, she popped the top and took a long swallow. "Ah! That's good. Did you ever wonder why everything tastes better at the beach?"

He grinned and handed her a plate and utensils, then passed the various containers. "I hate to break it to you, but we may be in the minority for feeling that way. Not everyone has an affinity for water. Me, I'd sleep in it if I could."

Her laugh startled some seagulls. "I have."

"Get out. Where?" Swallowing the rest of his piece of chicken, he spooned a small mountain of seafood salad onto his plate.

"I kid you not." She nodded when he held up the serving spoon, and he shoveled a pile of seafood salad onto her plate. "I spent so much time in our pool as a kid, my parents used to try to scare me and say they thought they saw gills forming."

"How cool would that have been?"

She nodded. "I know! I used to watch *Aquaman* on TV and prayed I could have gills and be able to live underwater."

"Me too!" He drained his tea and reached for another can. "But how did you sleep in the water?"

"Well, I guess technically I didn't. But every summer, the day before school started, my folks allowed me to spend the night in the pool. We had a huge float, about the width of a king-size bed. My sister and I slept on it. Sort of like camping."

"Is she a diver now, too?"

Her smile faded. "No." She scraped her plate off by the edge of the water and watched the hungry seagulls swoop down and gobble it up. "Sarah doesn't have much use for the water these days." She looked out across the water and took a deep breath of sea air. "She lost her husband and kids in a boating accident a few years ago."

"God. I'm sorry. I can't imagine what that would be like."

"I came as close as I ever would want to be to knowing, living through it with her." Sniffing, she wiped her eyes and smiled.

"So, what's the name of this island, and where are all the people?"

"It's uninhabited. It's just a small barrier island. This is the only decent stretch of beach."

"Does it have a name?"

"Bear Island."

"Are you kidding me?" Her gaze swept the dense vegetation edging the beach. "Is it because there are, ah, bears?"

He shrugged and popped a black olive into his mouth and chewed. "Used to be, I guess." His voice was low as he bent over the cooler, pushing containers around. "I've never seen any, though."

"How often have you been here?"

"Will you stop looking like that? I've been to this beach more times than I can count, ever since I was a kid." He tugged her to sit next to him on the blanket he'd spread over the hot sand. "If there were bears, I'd have seen them. Here. Have some cheesecake and put the bears out of your mind."

She took a begrudging bite, her gaze darting back and forth along the trees while she chewed.

"Want some strawberries on—oh, here, take another piece of cheesecake."

"Don't laugh at me," she said around a plump strawberry, swiping at the juice escaping from her mouth. "I always eat when I'm scared." She swallowed. "What are you doing?"

"Taking off my clothes so they can dry out. If you want, you can hang your shirt on the other end of the cooler so it can dry, too."

Bending to the task, he stepped out of his cutoffs, flipping them up with his foot and catching them midair, a self-satisfied smirk on his face.

*Why do guys think dorky stuff like that is cool?* She shook her head and bit back a smile.

"Go ahead," he said, shaking out his shirt and draping it over the cooler. "Strip."

"That could have a different connotation than what you meant."

"I wouldn't mind."

Neither would she. But, for now, she just hung her T-shirt on the cooler.

"Okay, ready to show me this great snorkeling site?" After shaking sand from her gear bag, she turned as she reached for her fins.

Will lay stretched out on the blanket, as naked as the day he was born, only with sunglasses on.

And a lot sexier.

# 8

Mouth suddenly dry, she swallowed, her pulse pounding. "I thought we were going snorkeling."

One side of his mouth quirked. He slowly shook his head, sunlight flashing from the lenses of his Oakleys. "We need to wait a while after we eat. You should know that."

"Oh, what a crock. We'll be snorkeling, for goodness sake, barely under the water most of the time. It's not like we're going to get the bends. Snorkeling isn't that rigorous."

He lay back on the blanket. "Well, I'm going to take a little siesta, so you're out of luck, because I won't be showing you around until later."

Hands on hips, she stared for a minute. "You're kidding, right?" She pointed. "The Gulf is right there. I could probably find it by myself."

In reply, he turned over, flashing a breathtaking set of buns. "If that's what you want. Before you go, though, would you rub some sunscreen on me? Wouldn't want to burn anything . . . important."

The sight of his firm buttocks and the opportunity to touch

them again, up close and personal, pushed imminent thoughts of snorkeling from her mind.

"Okay," she said in a resigned tone, "where's the sunscreen?"

His hand stopped her from dropping to her knees on the blanket beside him. "This is a no-sand zone."

"Excuse me?"

"No-sand zone," he repeated. "You just schlepped through the sand. You'll contaminate the tanning area."

"Oh, for pity's sake. How do you expect me to rub sunscreen on you if I'm not allowed on the blanket?"

"Only one way. Naked." He raised his sunglasses and looked up at her. "Strip off the contamination—in this case, your bikini—before you step onto the blanket. And make sure you dust off your feet first."

Her nipples began tingling at the thought of what might occur if she followed his instructions. But she didn't want to make it too easy for him. "What do I get out of it?" she asked, slipping the straps from her shoulders.

"I'd be happy to apply suntan oil to you, too, of course. We wouldn't want you to burn anything important, either."

"So this is all strictly for preventive measure?" She stepped out of her bottoms, relishing the soft feel of the Gulf breeze on her bikini area.

"Absolutely. The sunscreen is in the side pocket of my bag." He turned his face into his folded arms.

Beth glanced around the deserted beach and squinted up into the trees and underbrush. "You're sure this place is uninhabited?"

"Yep. And if you get the oil for us, I can make it downright *uninhibited,* too." He grinned over at her.

Squirting a liberal amount of oil onto his broad back, she smoothed it down in long strokes. Strokes that slid over the firm swells of his buttocks.

He jumped when she stuck her hand between his legs, her oiled fingertips brushing his sack. "That's not my back."

"I know, but I figured you'd consider that some of the *important* things you wouldn't want burned. Now relax."

"Good point." He settled his head in his folded arms and tried to relax, but it was difficult knowing Beth knelt, naked, close enough to touch.

And he really wanted to touch.

"Maybe I should turn over and let you do my front," he suggested after trying not to squirm when she insisted on doing a thorough massage of his butt. He wasn't sure how much more he could take. Plus, the idea of applying oil to every inch of Beth's delectable body was exciting him. A lot.

"Not yet."

More sunscreen puddled on his back. Followed immediately by what felt like Beth's breasts, slipping and sliding on his oiled skin.

He held perfectly still, naming off standard dive gear, specialty dive gear, and qualifications for every dive certification in his mind. It didn't take his mind off the fact that a naked woman was rolling around in oil on his equally naked back.

Or the fact that they were naked on a deserted beach. Or the fact that he had a zipper compartment full of condoms.

When her smooth mound rubbed against the lower swell of his butt cheek, he could take no more.

With a growl, he flipped over, catching her before she toppled to the blanket, pinning her well-oiled nudity to his primed-for-action body.

"Kiss me," he said against her laughing mouth, the distinctive smell of coconut oil swirling with her gardenia-scented skin.

"I thought you wanted me to oil your front. Or I could always share." Executing a little shimmy to demonstrate, she rubbed her slick breasts against his chest, exciting every nerve ending in his body in the process.

"Or you could shut up and kiss me." Before she made another smart-assed reply, he covered her mouth in the deepest, most carnal kiss he could muster, given his overwhelming need to claim her body.

His excitement ratcheted up another notch when she sighed and noticeably relaxed against him, as though she were melting into his skin.

Oh, yeah, he liked that idea.

Slapping around on the blanket, he finally closed his hand over the edge of his gear bag and groped until he found the zip pocket.

Sheathed and ready for action, he paused, looking down at her smiling face. He could easily imagine spending the rest of his life looking at her smile.

Any doubt or reservation he may have had floated away on the ocean breeze.

He loved her.

Of course, he couldn't tell her that. Not yet. First he had to tell her about Nick's and the dive shop. And tell her he was an Aggie. To anyone other than a Texan, it wouldn't be a big deal. But to a Texan, especially one who went to UT, it could very well be a deal breaker. And when you added in her personal history, it was doubly dubious. But he had to be completely honest with her, show her what she was getting into if she returned his love.

He glanced down at the tiny Texas A&M tattoo. She'd loved an Aggie once who had betrayed her.

Would she be willing to take a chance on this one?

# 9

Beth dodged a jellyfish, then tapped a warning hand on Will's leg as they made their way to shore.

"Tide's going back out," Will pointed out as they took slogging, fin-covered steps toward the beach. "We need to get packed up and back to the boat or we'll be stranded in the shallow water."

She nodded, watching where she stepped, since jellyfish corpses were already beginning to wash up on the edge of the shore, a sure sign the tide was going out.

The romantic part of her would love being stranded on the beach overnight with Will. But the realistic part knew the reality would be far from romantic.

"Or we could wait it out, camp on the beach." He leaned close as they walked to the blanket. "Make love under the stars."

"We ate all the food, remember? All we have are some olives and a couple cans of beer." Lifting her bag, she began stuffing her gear inside.

"We can always fish for our dinner and breakfast."

Pausing, she turned to him. "Okay, I have a confession to make. I love the water, and I love diving, but I'm really a girly-girl. I don't do well with roughing it."

He watched Beth's expressive face. Of course she didn't do well with roughing it. She'd had everything done for her all her life.

Life with him could be a real culture shock.

He picked up the cooler and tossed her shirt to her. "Then we'd better get a move on," he said, trudging out into the water.

He noticed she followed several paces behind. Was she thinking about their differences, too?

Beth made a face at Will's back, the increased current dragging her steps. He'd had a real mood change after she'd announced being a girly-girl. He could have at least tried to change her mind.

Then again, she totally understood why he couldn't waste too much time if he didn't want his boat to be grounded for a while.

But now what? Would he just drop her off and zip back to Crystal Key and his swinging bachelor life there? Sure, she knew Crystal Key wasn't exactly a hot singles spot, but she'd been with Will. She'd seen the way women looked at him. Even the hostess at the restaurant had looked at him differently than she'd looked at other male patrons.

"Hey," she called as they climbed into the boat. "Do you think the dive shop will still be open? I need another regulator. Is it full service, or will I have to order one?"

He paused and looked at his watch. "It should still be open. If not, I know the owner. We can pick up a regulator for you."

"I guess that's one of the perks of living on an island, knowing everyone." With a grunt, she threw her bag into the boat, then hoisted her leg and climbed aboard.

She'd scarcely taken her seat when Will roared the motor and banked the boat starboard, leaving their little secluded beach obscured by a plume of water when she looked back to say good-bye.

"How about dinner and a movie tonight?" Will gripped her hand tightly as he helped her from the boat at the slip by his house.

She looked down and said, "I don't think I'm dressed for it. Or did you mean later, after I've had a chance to go back and clean up?"

His laughter startled some pigeons from a nearby flowerbed. "I saw a media room at your place. I thought I'd pick up a DVD and some food and we could eat there, then watch a movie."

The media room. She'd only been in it once and had totally forgotten its existence. "Oh. Right. The media room." She gave a little laugh. "I assumed you meant an actual theater."

"That's a good idea, but Crystal Key doesn't have one."

She nodded, falling in step beside him as they made their way to his house.

"You don't have a DVD player?" she asked when he'd unlocked the door and motioned for her to enter before picking up the cooler. It would be easier to just stay there and grab something to eat when they went to the dive shop.

"Sure, I have one." He disappeared through a door to the left, leaving her standing on the marble entry tile. "But I don't have a media room. It would be better at your place."

Of course it would. What could compare to a tricked-out media room on a frigging yacht? Her good mood evaporated. Was Will using her for the yacht? Could at least part of his attraction to her be because he thought she was rich? How would he feel when he found out she had no more money than him? She glanced around. Though small, the house was richly deco-

rated, with good-quality furniture. Mental photos of her mea-
gerly furnished apartment flashed through her mind. Will probably had more money.

How would the reality of her financial status impact their
relationship? And, she realized, she desperately wanted a relationship with Will.

Of course, the problem with that was her living in Austin. It
was too late to register for summer school at UT, but if she
doubled up on her classes, she could easily graduate in December.
If she found a job on Crystal Key, she could work and explore
her feelings for Will, go back to school in September, then come
back for good after the holidays. Assuming things worked out
the way she hoped. Assuming Will wanted her in his life.

And all those assumptions hinged on how he would react
when she told him the truth about the yacht.

Maybe later that night, after they'd watched the movie, she'd
find the right time to break the news.

Maybe.

Or she could just let nature take its course and tell him the
following day, after she turned the boat over to the next occu-
pants. Yes, that was a better idea. There would be more time
then.

"Beth?" Will stood before her, dressed in cargo shorts and a
blue tank top beneath an unbuttoned, brightly printed shirt. "I
asked if you're ready to go?"

"Oh! Ah, yeah, sure." They stepped out into the sunset.
"Are we driving?"

He grinned and turned her to the right, following the stone
path away from the marina. "I don't own a car. There's no need.
Everything here is within walking distance."

She laughed. "Everything's in walking distance, if you have
the time."

"True." He chuckled. "I hadn't thought about it like that,
but you're right."

They made a right onto a store-lined street. "How about some ice cream?" He pointed to an ice-cream shop a few doors down. "Hooper has the best on the island. Handmade every morning."

"Sounds like a plan. But . . . do you know what time the dive shop closes? If we're going wreck diving tomorrow, I'd really like a new spare regulator."

"Plenty of time," he assured her, holding the door for her to enter the ice-cream parlor.

"Agh." Beth held her stomach and leaned back in the red vinyl booth. "I can't believe I polished off that whole thing." She groaned. "It was huge! Why didn't you warn me?"

After wiping his mouth with the paper napkin, he shook his head and smiled. "What did you think something called the Sampler Trough would be?"

"I dunno. I couldn't make up my mind, and when I saw I could get a sampler with every flavor, it seemed like a good idea. The word *sampler* was a misnomer. Those were not sample-size scoops!"

"And yet you managed to scarf it all down," he noted as she waddled from the store.

"How kind of you to point that out." She struggled to keep up with him, hoping the exercise would negate the megacalorie trough of ice cream she'd ingested. "Darn!" The dive shop was dark, obviously closed for the night. "I knew we should have come here first."

"Hey, I said I knew the owner." He pulled her back toward the street and pointed to the sign above the shop.

KING'S DIVING CASTLE.

"A relative?"

His smile flashed in the burgeoning darkness. "You could say that." He dangled a keyring in front of her face, then unlocked the door and punched in a code on the alarm pad. "It's mine."

"You own your own dive shop?" How cool was that? "That has to be the best job in the world." She lovingly ran her hand over a display of wet suits. "I'd love to own a dive shop."

"Buy one." He strode to a cabinet and pulled out a few regulators. "Take these and try them out."

*Buy one.* Her heart sank. He thought she could just go out and buy anything she pleased, including a business.

She needed to tell him the truth.

"Crap," she said instead. "I forgot my debit card. I have some cash, though, um, back at the boat." *In my locker.*

"You mean your yacht. It's okay to call it that. It's what it is. You can't help it if you're loaded." He winked. "I kind of dig it."

"Can I just pay for the regulator when we go back to watch the movie?" She did not want to discuss her perceived wealth. Or lack thereof. Not yet, anyway.

"I meant what I said when I told you to take them. If you decide you want one, keep it. On me." When she started to argue, he said, "Or pay me then, how's that?" Before she could answer, he swept the store with his outstretched arm. "So, what do you think of my place?"

"It's fabulous," she finally choked out. "I can't believe how much stock you have." She peered into the glass case next to the cash register and couldn't prevent a little gasp. "I used to have a ring just like that."

"Oh? Probably not just like that. It's fairly cheap, sterling silver and enamel. I've seen them in platinum with pearl inlays and rubies."

"No, mine was just like that. For ten years, it never left my finger."

He glanced at her bare hand, and she stopped rubbing the spot where the ring had resided. "How did you lose it?"

"I didn't. I gave it away." She shrugged. "It's a long story." And to tell it meant she had to tell him about her summer job.

He shoved the regulators in a King's Diving Castle reusable bag and jerked the drawstring shut. "Let's go find a DVD before they're all rented."

Ernie's Barbershop and Video Rental was a few doors down from the dive shop.

"That's an odd combination," she commented, looking up at the sign.

Will smirked. "That's small-town life. Especially on an island. We also have Russell's Law Firm and Car Stereo Installation as well as Consuela's Optical and Plumbing." He held up his hand as they walked through the automatic door. "I kid you not."

"I've never been in a video place with an automatic door." She glanced at the darkened side where the barber chairs stood as they proceeded down the well-lit aisle lined with DVDs.

"It used to be a Piggly Wiggly supermarket."

"Where is the market now?" She picked up a DVD and read the back of the case.

"Gone. If we need more than what we can get at the two convenience stores, we have to go to the mainland." He picked up a copy of *Fool's Gold*. "How about this? Or have you seen it?"

"I saw it, but I love it. I wouldn't mind seeing it again. I have to confess, when I was snooping around the wrecked fishing boat, I thought about how the characters in this movie had devoted so many years to their quest of finding a sunken treasure ship."

He laughed. "Yeah, well, don't expect to find anything on *The Tarpin*. It sank about fifty years ago and was picked clean of anything before we were born."

Her shoulders slumped. "Shoot. I wasn't looking for treasure, just to find something that hadn't been touched since it sank. When I first started diving, I found an old corroded coin.

I imagined all kinds of scenarios, from lost pirate booty to the sinking of a *Titanic*-type ocean liner. Just the idea of touching something that had last been held years, if not centuries, ago was thrilling. I was hooked from that point on."

"A lot of divers feel that way."

"Don't you?" She skipped along next to him as they made their way down the street.

"Well, I guess. But what pulled me into it from the beginning was the sense of peace I get underwater. I can't describe it. Yeah, it's pretty with all the tropical fish and underwater vegetation. But it's not even that." He shrugged. "I think it's just the absolute quiet that gets to me." Holding the door for her at the Clucky Chicken takeout, he said, "Having grown up with four rowdy brothers, quiet was a scarce commodity around our house. Maybe that was the attraction of diving. It was my escape."

"Wow. It was just my sister and me. I can't even imagine what it was like to have a brother, much less four of them."

He brushed a kiss on her forehead as she walked past him. "Boys run in my family." *So you'd better get used to the idea.*

A busty blonde behind the counter flashed a megawatt smile at Will. The smile slid away when she spotted Beth.

Will draped his arm around Beth's shoulder and whispered in her ear, "Play along. I'll explain later."

"Hey, Roxi," he said with a smile, drawing Beth closer. "Have you met my fiancée?"

# 10

_____

"Fiancée?" Roxi's green eyes flashed. Her knuckles were white where she gripped the top of the cash register. Her gaze narrowed on Beth. "Since when?" she asked in a malevolent tone.

"Doesn't matter," Will continued, obviously ignorant of the contentious body language the blonde was fairly shouting. "Give me a large bucket of extra crispy, a dozen biscuits with honey, a pint of cole slaw and . . ." He looked down at Beth, who looked ready to bolt. "You want any fries, hon?"

She vigorously shook her head while covertly pinching a plug out of his ribs. He'd definitely have a mark tomorrow.

Keeping an eye on Roxi to make sure she didn't spit in their food, he dug in his pocket with his free hand until he found his Visa.

He wasn't born yesterday. He knew if he relaxed his hold on Beth, she'd sprint for the door.

Not that he'd blame her. Roxi had glaring down to a fine art. And if looks could kill . . . Well, he'd be a widower before he could become a groom.

Gathering their bags of food in one hand, Beth firmly clamped to his side, he nodded at Roxi and headed for the door.

"She's not your usual victim. What happened? Did you knock her up, King?" Roxi's belligerent voice gave him pause as they stepped out the door.

He felt Beth stiffen when he called back, "Not yet, but I'm working on it." Never breaking stride, he hurried down the street.

As expected, Beth broke away before they'd passed the next store. "You're working on it?" she sputtered. "Working on it? What the hell does that mean? Besides the fact that it's none of her dang business, we've always used protection." She stopped, hands on hips, and narrowed her eyes. "You didn't do anything funny with the condoms, did you? Did you?"

He knew he should remain calm and try to reassure her, but son of a bitch! "What the hell are you implying?"

"What the hell were *you* implying, back there at the chicken place?" she shot back. "And fiancée? Fiancée? We hardly know each other! What is this, some sicko game?" Her eyes widened. "Oh! Have you and what's-her-name been doing the wild monkey dance? You have, haven't you? No wonder she looked like she wanted to tear my hair out. Am I disrupting your romance? Or am I just a brief intermission?"

"Shut. Up." Jaw clenched, he strode toward his boat, holding their dinner and movie in one hand, his other hand clamped around her wrist as he pulled her along.

"You want the truth?" he half growled "You got it. The brief time I spent with Roxi—and I do mean brief—ended almost a year ago. I'm embarrassed it even happened. It meant nothing, just a physical release. It's not something I'm proud of, but it's the truth."

Since meeting Beth, he realized what making love really was, and he wished he could erase his past up until the moment they met.

He sighed and pulled Beth into his arms, the weight of their dinner hanging on his arm, shoving her closer. He awkwardly rubbed her stiff back until he felt her relax a little.

"I have a past," he said. "regardless of whether or not I'm proud of it. Everyone has a past. Beth, you with the rival college tattoo on your sexy abdomen, of all people, should realize that."

They made the ride to the yacht in record time. Also in silence.

As soon as he'd tied off, he jumped out of the boat and hefted her into his arms. "I swear, I'll never put you in a spot like I did tonight, okay? I don't want to fight," he said against her mouth, then told her with his kiss what he wanted to do.

By the time he pulled away, they were both breathing heavily.

"Let's forget everything except having dinner, watching a movie and having a good time," Beth said, her lips brushing his with each word. "I don't want to fight, either."

Beth wiped her hands and tossed the napkin into the empty chicken bucket as the credits scrolled on the big-screen TV. She flopped back in the media lounger. "That was fun."

"Even though you'd already seen it?" Will regarded her while he finished his bottle of beer.

"Yeah. I always watch movies I enjoy more than once. I see little things I missed the first time." She sighed. "I wish we could find a treasure like that."

"Babe, that's fiction. Most wreck dives come up empty. And the few lost treasures are always found by the professional reclamation divers."

"I know. But still . . . I can always dream, right?"

"Why get greedy?" He waved his empty bottle, encompassing the opulent media room. "You're obviously set for life. You don't need to dive for treasure."

*Tell him,* her mind urged, *tell him now.*

"Whoa." Will frowned, interrupting her as he waved his bottle. "What's that?"

She followed his gaze and did a mental groan when she saw the picture of his hand and beer bottle moving on the giant screen. She'd forgotten about Mr. Holms and his dumb idea of having a video camera click on to monitor activity in the media room if the DVD wasn't turned off immediately after a movie ended.

But she couldn't explain it without telling Will about the Holmses.

"It's a video camera." Duh. "It's over there." She nodded toward the side wall. "It's motion activated, set to run if the TV is on video and no DVD is playing." There. She'd told the truth. Well, part of it at least.

"Oh, yeah?" Will folded up the armrest between them and reached for her, pulling her into his lap while he watched their video image on the big screen. "How cool is that?"

Shocked at his reaction, she didn't object when he pulled her top off along with her T-shirt, baring her to the waist. At least, that was her reason for not objecting.

He turned her slightly, plumping her breast in a kneading motion. His erection stirred against her hip. "Look," he whispered. "Look how sexy you are, how pretty your nipple is. Is there any way we can zoom in closer?" He licked the tip of her nipple, causing it to pucker in the air-conditioning, while he watched the screen. Her breath hitched.

"Um, I don't know." She groped for the remote, surprised at how turned on she was getting by sitting on his lap and watching him lick her nipple in high definition. "Here's a little blue button that says 'zoom.'" She pressed it and gasped when her breast took on giant proportions.

Will's laugh filled the room. "Oh, yeah, we're going to have some fun with this!" He set her back on the cushion next to him and shucked his shorts, his erection popping free. "Check it out!"

Embarrassment heated her cheeks, but she squirmed at the sight of his humongous penis filling the screen. It was lude; it was ridiculous; it was beyond raunchy.

And she couldn't tear her gaze from it.

Before she could censor her actions, she pushed her breasts to cup his erection, her eyes locked on their big-screen image.

He moved his hips as they watched his penis slide in and out of her cleavage.

Their gazes met.

He pulled her to her feet and into his kiss while he rubbed suggestively against her abdomen. His hands slid down to push her bikini from her hips. He dropped to his knees, his lips trailing fiery kisses along the exposed trail.

His warm hand on her abdomen, he pushed her back into her seat. He stroked down the inside of her thigh to her ankle, then lifted her foot to the back of the seat in front of her.

Her moist, exposed folds filled the screen.

She watched, her breath coming in shallow pants as his tongue circled and lapped and prodded her giant genitalia.

Will's head obscured her view. He sucked her clit into his mouth, setting off tiny electric currents to her extremities. Since she couldn't really see anything on the TV at the moment, anyway, she closed her eyes, savoring the sensations zipping through her body.

Her climax snuck up on her, pulling her under in its fierceness.

Gasping for air, she barely had time to register what was happening when her peripheral vision snagged on Will's giant penis, sheathed and ready for action, as it approached her slick, engorged folds.

Fascinated, she watched him enter her. Sure, she'd watched the act several times, but never in eighty-inch, high-definition, living color. Tingles began again as his tip penetrated, followed by the smooth lunge, stretching her to accommodate his girth. Her juices kicked in at the dual turn-on of watching their actions on the screen and experiencing the sensations deep within her body.

Talk about the ultimate viewing pleasure.

"Is it recording?" he asked in huffing pants as his hips began moving faster.

"I. Don't. Know," she answered, each word punctuated by a hard thrust she felt deep within. But she did know one thing.

If it was, she wanted a copy.

# 11

_____

After their marathon sex session in the media room, they staggered to the master stateroom and collapsed into bed.

Chilled from making the trip au naturel, Beth scooted close to Will, snuggling against his warm, fit body.

*Tell him,* her conscience screamed. *You're falling for him; he needs to know before things go any further.*

He turned to his side, dragging her along, spooning her, his hand possessively covering her breast.

She sighed in contentment, a feeling of peace washing over her. She'd tell him in a minute. After she rested a little and caught her breath . . .

It was still dark when she woke, thrilled to feel Will's arms banding her back to his chest while he pumped into her already-willing flesh. Her hips moved of their own accord, meeting his thrusts, grinding against his heat. It was a pleasant way to wake up, a midnight quickie.

Smiling in the dark, she placed her hand over his on her breasts, surprised to feel arousal stirring again when he squeezed her nipple.

Their thrusts increased in speed and force. Will rolled her to her stomach, pounding into her willing body. His hands gripped her hips, pulling her to her knees, where he continued his forceful thrusts.

The tip of his penis kissed her uterus, setting off an ache deep within her abdomen.

She rocked against him, grinding, seeking more as she pushed up with her arms. On all fours, she had more leverage, pushing and rocking with each thrust.

The soft slapping sound of their flesh meeting echoed in the quiet room.

Feeling her climax nearing, she pounded against him, ferocious in her need. With a raw cry, she tumbled over into the sea of satisfaction, welcoming the drowning sensation as she floated down.

Will found his release almost immediately, his hips bucking faster and harder as he pumped into her sated body. His muscles stiffened, his arms holding her up off the mattress in a vise-like grip. He roared his completion and collapsed, pinning her to the mattress.

Sunlight streamed through the window when she opened her eyes again. Beside her, Will stirred and pulled her close, his morning stubble prickling the back of her neck.

Her eyes widened when she glanced over at the little brass clock.

"Will." She reached back, tapping his bare hip. "Will. What time do you have to open the shop?"

"Don't." His voice was muffled, vibrating the skin on her neck as he pulled her back against him. "Taking the day off to dive with you."

"So you're just closing for the day to go diving?" While personally thrilling, it wasn't a very wise business plan.

"Nope." He kissed her neck. "Chris, my assistant, is opening." The hand fondling her breast slid downward.

She grabbed his forearm, halting the roving hand, then scooted toward the side of the bed, away from his warmth. Away from temptation.

Pulling the blanket from the bed, she wrapped it around her nudity while she waited for Will to blink her into focus.

"Coffee should be ready," she said, reaching into the closet for her robe. "Want some?"

Will jackknifed to a sitting position and sniffed. "I smell it. Where is it?"

She laughed and tossed her blanket to him, then tied her robe. "It's in the coffee bar." She pointed toward the bathroom. "In there, in the dressing area. I made a fresh pot yesterday and set the timer."

Sitting up, he yawned and scratched his stomach. "Um. I bought a coffeemaker with a timer, but I always forget to use it. It's easier to just make it when I want it."

"Not after you get used to it. I use mine every day." Of course, it was the one in her apartment at home, but it was technically the truth.

A smile creased his stubbled cheeks. "Why don't you just have one of your servants bring you a fresh pot each morning?"

"They have more important things to do than wait on me," she snapped. Again, true. Especially since she was their coworker. *Tell him.*

"Did you want to go back to *The Tarpin* wreck today?" Will called to Beth from the bedroom when she went to pour their coffee. He located his shorts and stepped into them. "There's really not much to see. It's basically used as a habitat and for beginning divers to explore. Besides . . ."

"Besides? Besides what?" The cup was warm to the touch when she handed it to him. "I didn't know if you wanted anything in it. There's all kinds of stuff on the coffee bar."

"No, I only drink cream in it after dinner. But thanks." Taking a bracing sip, he sighed and looked at the woman he'd decided to marry. "We can dive, if you want, but I'd rather go somewhere that didn't require tanks." Leaning close, he brushed a kiss on her cheek, then winked. "Just in case."

His finger, beneath the opening of her robe, traced the edge of her nipple. The action gave her all kinds of ideas that would be difficult to do with tanks strapped to their backs and regulators in their mouths.

Clearing her throat, she found her voice. "There's a roof-deck pool and spa. Or we could go snorkeling again."

"I like the idea of being lazy and hanging around in the pool. Naked."

"I'll make sure I bring lots of sunscreen."

"I'll make sure to bring lots of condoms."

Beth rolled to her back on the double air mattress, grabbing the edge to keep from falling into the water, thanks to her well-oiled body.

Will had rubbed suntan oil into places that would never see the sun, then used his body to make sure it was thoroughly rubbed in.

The result was two condoms used in the first hour in the pool.

Floating in companionable silence in the blazing sun, Will reached over to idly rub her breast.

"Again?" Her muscles already felt like overcooked spaghetti. But, deep within, moisture surged, a sure indication she'd be a willing participant for round three.

"Not yet," he mumbled. "I'm just petting. I like touching you."

"Good. Because I like touching you, too." She rolled to her side, stroking more oil on his penis.

He made a playful growl. "You're playing with fire, woman."

"Good thing I'm wearing lots of sunscreen," she teased, then tapped the head of his recovering erection. "Down, boy. I was just making sure you didn't burn anything important."

"Good to know you have your priorities straight." He rolled over, grabbing her, pinning her beneath him. "Whoa! You'd better hold on to me or I'm apt to slide off from all this oil."

Her giggle sent sparks through him. "You're blocking my rays. You wouldn't want me to get an uneven tan, would you?"

Her shriek as she hit the cool water of the pool startled the seagulls circling overhead in search of food.

Sputtering, she broke the surface. "That was sneaky! I thought you were getting turned on; then you pushed me in!"

"I figured you needed to cool off before you wore me out." On his stomach, head resting on his folded arms, he closed his eyes.

After taking a moment to admire his prime rear, she gripped the edge of the float and gave it a yank.

A minor tsunami rolled through the pool with the force of his splash as he toppled into the water.

Quiet, he treaded water, his eyes trained on her. After a minute or so, he began moving toward her. Slowly and deliberately.

Trying to appear casual, she edged back.

But he was too quick, grasping her ankles before she could get out of range. His pull jerked her under. Water rushed into her ears, burned her nose, and threatened to gag her.

Choking and wheezing, she scarcely noticed when he lifted her to the float, her legs bent at the knees, feet dangling in the water on either side of his ribs.

He kicked out, pulling the raft to the shallow end, then stood chest-deep in the water between her legs.

Recovered, she opened her eyes, squinting at him in the bright sunlight. "What are you doing?"

"Taking advantage of your nudity." His mouth came down

on her, short-circuiting cohesive thought processes for quite a while.

The day passed in a sensual blur of foreplay and sex. Too soon, the sun was setting.

Weak from a day spent in the sun and water, they continued their sexual gluttony indoors until hunger forced them to dress and motor to the village in search of a real meal.

Despite Will's objections, Beth held firm and took the yacht's dinghy. She didn't want to depend on him to get her back to the yacht if they lost track of time.

"Let's just grab something to go from Nick's and eat at my place," Will suggested as they strolled down the darkened street, his arm slung casually over her shoulder, his hand more than occasionally dipping into her T-shirt to pet her braless breast. He tweaked her erect nipple. "I don't want anyone to see this but me."

Since he'd convinced her to not only go braless, but also pantyless, she had no problems with not dining in public. Especially since tonight could possibly be their last night together.

Subdued by that thought, she was scarcely aware of picking up their order and walking back to Will's beach house.

"Let's eat at the table," he suggested, ushering her into the coolness of his home. "I don't know about you, but I'm starving. If I don't get some sustenance, I may not be able to get it up again today." Lifting her top, he placed a kiss on each nipple, then pulled the shirt back down. "I even have some candles." He left her side, then paused at the doorway, batting his eyelids. "I look better in candlelight."

"You're such a dork."

"But you love me," he called from the other room.

Yes, she was beginning to suspect she really did love him.

There were a couple of problems with that, though. First off, how was she going to tell him the truth about the yacht?

Stupid, stupid, stupid. She should have just come clean about it from the get-go. But, in her defense, they'd just met. She'd thought it safer to assume the persona of a yacht owner with a staff who could show up at any time. And later . . . well, later, she'd just been a coward, plain and simple.

The second problem was the fact that she had to be back at the yacht by midnight to transfer the keys. Then she had to pack her belongings and catch her flight. Unless tonight went better than anticipated and Will offered her a job and begged her to stay. Since he thought she was one of the idle rich, the chances of that were slim to none.

Which took her right back to problem number one.

Sighing, she gave a little shake and tried relaxation techniques she'd learned in yoga class.

A glow announced Will's return with two fat candles resting on thick, carved pedestals.

"Have a seat," he said after placing the candles in the center of the table. "I'm just going to transfer the food to platters."

That's when she noticed the table was already set. "When did you set the table?" she called.

"I didn't. It comes that way."

"What do you mean, it comes that way?" she asked when he reentered the little dining room, carrying two large platters.

"Marta, my cleaning lady, sets it before she leaves. She calls it 'staging.'"

"How often is that?" What did Marta look like? She hoped she was a hag.

He shrugged as he dished up shrimp jambalaya and dirty rice. "Three times a week, I think."

"You think? You don't know?" Appetite gone, she waited.

"Eat." He took a seat at the other end of the table.

Smart man. He obviously knew he was in danger.

Heaving a sigh, he placed his fork on the edge of his plate. "She used to clean once a week, but she complained, saying I was a pig and she was going to have to charge more if I didn't let her come twice a week. Then her husband left her, and she couldn't find a regular job. I didn't really need her the two times a week, but I told her if she needed more money, I'd pay her more. She refused. I told her I needed her to clean three times a week, minimum. She seemed okay with that."

"But you don't know, exactly, how many times she cleans your house?" It boggled the mind.

"No, I don't. It's no big deal, Beth. She needs the money. I have plenty. I leave it on the entry table every Monday. When I notice it's gone, I replace it. In return, my house is always clean, my laundry is done, and my table is set." He chewed and swallowed. "In all, not a bad deal."

It wasn't. And if he didn't know when she came, obviously she wasn't providing sexual services in addition to housecleaning.

Maybe she could choke down a little jambalaya after all.

The first bite left a trail of fire all the way to her stomach. Her eyes teared. Her nose ran. She drained a glass of ice water without coming up for air. "Hot!" She reached for his glass and drained it as well.

"Sorry." He got up and refilled her glass, which she promptly drained. "I should have warned you—they add a couple shots of extra Tabasco to my order."

"A warning would have been nice," she finally rasped out.

Swiftly clearing the table, he said, "I had them put in cheesecake for dessert."

Swiping at her watery eyes, she perked up. "I could eat cheesecake."

When he returned, he took the chair next to her as he set a gigantic piece of cheesecake, covered in strawberry topping and whipped cream, at each of their places.

"Thanks for agreeing to eat in." He swallowed, his eyes intense, burning holes in her shirt.

The look immediately made her nipples pucker beneath the soft cotton.

Her bite of cheesecake hung around in her throat for a few seconds, preventing speech. Finally she was able to swallow. "It's nice. Private." *And I'm not wearing underwear, which is convenient, in case you get any ideas.*

Nodding, he put his fork on his plate and reached for her hand. "I had a great time today. Thank you."

"I should be thanking you," she said, worrying he was about to dump her. "You've made the last few days exciting." She swallowed around the lump forming in her throat. "I'll think of you whenever I watch a movie." Or go in a pool. Or dive. Or snorkel. Or, heck, just breathe.

"You talk like you're leaving. Fall semester doesn't start until, like, September, right? You'll be around until then. I mean, if you're just going to be cruising around on your yacht, you may as well hang out around Crystal Key."

"Actually, I—"

"We can have a lot more dinners like this," he said, scooting closer, turning her chair toward him. "I had a great idea, for you to not wear underwear." His hand snaked up her skirt, tickling her labia. "Brilliant, even," he said in a gruff whisper, plunging his finger deep within her wetness.

She gasped, dragging air into her starving lungs. Her back arched. How could she leave him, leave this?

"And eating here was another stroke of genius," he continued, shoving her top up. "I couldn't have done this in a restaurant." He bent, taking a nipple into his mouth and sucking deeply, while deep within her he moved his talented fingers.

Just the thought of him doing the things he was doing in a public place was enough to make her body spasm in a fierce orgasm, drenching his hand and the edge of her skirt.

Acting quickly, he relieved her of her soggy skirt and tossed her shirt across the room.

Naked, she shivered at the intense look on his handsome face as he lifted her to the table.

He reached for his cheesecake and took a fat dollop of whipped cream on his index finger, then dragged it over each of her sensitized nipples.

When he'd thoroughly licked her clean, he smiled.

"What?" she whispered.

He pulled his shirt off and flung it toward hers, then stepped out of his shorts.

"I was just thinking how much I wanted to do this the last time we were at Nick's."

She swallowed, eyes wide, as he approached. "Wh-what?"

"Strip you bare and lay you out on the table as my own private feast." He nudged her thighs apart and bent to swipe his tongue over her moisture. "Then," he said, stepping between her legs, massaging her vibrating thighs, "then I'd climb up on the table with you and fuck—" *Clunk!* "Oh, shit!"

Flames engulfed the table within seconds of him snatching her out of harm's way.

## 12

"Who knew cheesecake was so flammable?" Beth mused, wrapped in a blanket, sitting next to Will as the firemen finished up.

"It was probably the combination of fat and the liquor in the strawberry sauce."

Turning, she forced a smile. "Liquor? Were you trying to get me liquored up and have your way with me?" Placing her hand at her throat, she batted her eyelashes to let him know she was joking.

His mouth quirked in a small smile. "Yeah, how'd I do?"

"It was working . . . until everything went up in flames." Unable to stop the laughter bubbling up, she put her hand over her mouth.

His laughter joined hers, and soon they were leaning against each other, dissolved in hysterics.

"You reached a whole new level of being hot and bothered," he said through guffaws.

They'd already been checked by the EMT crew, so it was just a matter of thanking the firemen who'd responded.

After the trucks left, they made their way back into Will's house, studiously averting their eyes from the bright yellow caution tape across the charred door of the dining room.

"I want to sleep with you, but I'll understand if you want me to take you home."

In answer, she dropped her blanket, then shoved his from his naked body. "Let's go to bed," she whispered.

A quick shower to get rid of the smoke smell turned into much more as Will soaped and rinsed every inch of Beth's body.

She came twice before he entered her from behind, pushing her breasts flat against the glass of his shower enclosure.

*Tell him, tell him, tell him,* her conscience told her with each of Will's thrusts.

A shudder coursed through her body, tightening her muscles, blotting every thought from her mind except the exquisite feel of his body in hers, the rightness of the act they shared, as her climax overcame her.

Limp from the force of her orgasm, she lay draped over Will's arms as he carried her to his bed.

Cool sheets caressed her bare back while Will caressed her front, heating her up again until her desire burned white hot.

He stroked oil over her breasts, between her thighs, kissing her strategically until she was writhing on the sheets, begging for release.

Begging for him.

Hushing her fretful murmurs with soft words she couldn't decipher in her agitated state, he finally slid up her slick body until his erection probed her willing flesh and slid home.

They sighed.

In silence, he slid against her. In. Out. In. His hands gently stroked her damp hair, his thumbs stroking the tops of her ears. His mouth kissed hers, driving her desire into overload.

His thrusts increased in tempo, his breathing harsh against

her ear, his arms clutching her tightly to him, their hearts dancing a passionate, thumping tango.

In an instant, they reached their release.

He collapsed on her, a welcome weight, their hearts beating against each other. The sound of their labored breathing filled the room.

Beth lay, staring into the darkness, long after Will's breathing told her he slept.

Had she imagined his gruff words of love? Were they just spoken in the heat of the moment? She had never declared love while in the throes of passion, but she'd heard it happened with some people.

Her mind replayed their lovemaking. She wiped a tear away at the remembered intensity. And the tenderness.

*Tell him.*

She loved Will King.

And she couldn't tell him how she felt until she told him the truth.

In his sleep, Will tugged her close. Sighing, she closed her eyes. She'd rest for a few minutes, then wake him up and tell him.

And then tell him good-bye.

The internal alarm clock that always told Beth when she needed to surface had her jackknifing in Will's bed. Oblivious, he slept next to her.

A glance at the clock confirmed her fears. Less than half an hour remained until she had to be aboard the yacht.

Borrowing a shirt and shorts from Will, cinched with one of his belts, she searched in vain for a piece of paper to leave a note.

Another glance at the clock had her heading for the door. She'd just have to come back as soon as possible and tell him everything, pleading her case.

Hopping into the dinghy, she started the engine and motored toward the yacht, glancing back as Will's house grew smaller.

She refused to allow herself to think part of her allure may have been her perceived wealth.

While fairly small, business-wise, Will's shop appeared to be doing well. It may not need her perceived money, but her expertise would be an asset. While she could use the money working at the dive shop would bring in, she knew in her heart she'd work for free. She'd work for love.

As soon as she turned over the yacht, she'd pack her belongings and get someone to bring her back. Doing a timeline in her head, she figured she had plenty of time to confess and plead her case before her flight. If Will refused to listen, she would board the plane and take back memories. She had no choice.

Will rolled over, his hand connecting with cool sheets, and realized what had woken him from his sated sleep.

Beth was gone.

There was no point in calling to her. He knew, in his heart, he was alone in the house.

Still, he raised to look out at the dock, not surprised to see the dinghy gone.

No wonder she had insisted on taking the damn thing. Had she planned on making a quick, subversive getaway? He flopped back on the pillow and closed his eyes.

It didn't matter. He loved her. And, in spite of the short time they'd known each other, he felt certain she loved him, too.

She'd be back.

Even if he had to drag her back.

It was where she belonged.

He rolled over and smiled against the pillow.

If things went as planned, by the same time the next night, he would be an engaged man.

# 13

When Beth returned to *Salsa Time* and turned over the keys, she quickly packed her belongings and then paced while she practiced what she was going to say to Will.

Kenny, the steward, knocked on her open door. "Beth, the water taxi is here."

"Great." She picked up her suitcase and dive bag, then looked around. "Thanks. I'm ready to go."

"That's all you have?"

"I travel light. My dive gear is crated and already waiting at the airport." By planning ahead, she would be prepared if things didn't pan out with Will.

"Beth?" Kenny glanced down the deserted hall, then lowered his voice as he reached into the inner pocket of his uniform blouse. "I have something I think you might want."

"What? Did I forget something in the owner's suite?" She mentally ticked off everything she'd packed.

Kenny smiled. Something flashed in his hand. A CD or DVD in a clear plastic case. "It's the master copy from the video camera in the media room." He pressed the case into her hand and whispered, "Don't worry. It's the only copy, and I already deleted it from the camera." He winked. "I didn't think you would want it hanging around here."

Cheeks flaming, she gave him a quick thank-you hug. As she made her way topside, judiciously avoiding eye contact with other staff members, she was sure she heard a few snickers but kept walking.

Things didn't go as Will planned.

A minor problem at the bank required Will's personal attention.

On his way to the jewelry store to pick out a ring for Beth, his cell rang.

"It's super busy, dude," Chris's voice echoed in his ear, conversations in the background making it hard to hear. "I need help, pronto!"

"Chris, you're going to have to handle it." He waited for a delivery truck, then crossed the street.

"But the shipment was here when I got here, and I haven't even had a chance to open the boxes. I have a dive class scheduled in an hour—"

"Cancel it. Give them a free lesson. Whatever."

"But—"

"Chris, listen to me. Cancel the fucking class!" Disconnecting, he averted his gaze from two old ladies, dressed in muumuus, who stood staring at him.

"Now what?" He was tempted to throw the phone in the storm drain when it immediately rang again. NICK'S SEAFOOD appeared on the readout. Great. What now? "Speak," he barked.

Korine's strident voice vibrated the earpiece. "You'd better get your fine little white fanny over here, boss! The assholes at the LiquorMart are trying to fuck us over again." A male voice grumbled in the background. "Shut the fuck up, asshole! I'm talking to the boss. Don't you walk out of here, or I'll blow your ass to kingdom come."

"Korine! Are you packing again? You know what happened last time."

"Hunh. It wasn't like it was concealed," she argued. "I have it right here, in plain sight."

"You don't have a permit."

"Permits are just a technicality."

He sighed and gave a last longing look at the jewelry store. So near, and yet so far. "Don't do anything until I get there."

Chaos was the only way to describe the scene at Nick's. Obscenities were flowing freely on both sides as Korine held the LiquorMart driver's face pressed to the exposed brick wall, the business end of a very large handgun at the base of his skull.

From the kitchen came the sounds of the chefs' semiweekly screaming match, their foreign obscenities echoing from the appliances.

The waitstaff and busboys looked as nervous as cats in a room full of rocking chairs, jumping and twitching at every little sound.

It took some doing, but he finally convinced Korine to put down her gun. Sorting out the liquor order took a little longer. He noticed the delivery guy kept a wary eye on Korine during their entire discussion.

"Okay," he said an hour later, extending his hand to the man. "I'm glad that's settled." He leaned closer. "And I'm sorry about the little, ah, misunderstanding." He shot Korine a reproachful look.

"Now, if you think you can manage," he told Korine after the delivery man left, "I have some important business to take care of."

"Huh." Korine did an eye-roll, the gold sparkles in her liberally applied eye shadow flashing with reflected light. "I bet it's with that little girl you were wining and dining night before last." She nodded. "Yeah, I saw you looking all googly-eyed at her. I don't know what she sees in your sorry ass, but if that's what blows your skirt up, so be it. Go on. Get on out of here."

Feldman's Jewelry shop was the only one on the island, but Will was pleased to find they had an extensive selection.

Maybe too extensive, he decided, after looking at every ring in the store. He glanced at his watch. He'd planned to be engaged by now.

"This one is pretty," Mr. Feldman said, extracting yet another ring from the showcase. "I don't know any girl who'd turn her nose up at this ring." He handed it to Will, then rocked back on his heels. "Tell you what. Seeing as how you're a fellow business owner, I'll give you the ring at cost, if you take it today. If your girlfriend decides she doesn't like it, find a new girlfriend." He laughed. "No! Kidding! Seriously, if for some insane reason she doesn't like it, she can come back and exchange it."

They agreed on the price, and Will handed over his card and signed.

The ring burning a hole in his pocket, he ran home for a quick shower and another shave before heading out to the yacht.

After changing clothes three times, he was on his way, the wind whistling by him as he headed full throttle across the waves.

*Salsa Time* was not where he left it.

Grabbing his binoculars, he scanned three hundred sixty degrees of nothing but blue water. Where the hell was it?

"Time's flying, King, think! Where would a boat that size be able to anchor?" The answer, assuming *Salsa Time* was still in the area, was a select number of coves. Bearing a sharp starboard, he headed for the first one, his hull barely touching the tops of the waves.

He breathed a sigh of relief as he rounded the tip of a barrier island and saw *Salsa Time* anchored in the deepest part of the protected body of water.

Jumping to the slip, he cast on his bowline and lurched up the ladder.

"Oh!" A pretty older lady in a polka-dot swimsuit with an old-fashioned skirt sloshed her drink when Will jumped down onto the deck.

"Where's Beth?"

"Who? I don't know who you are, but you can't go in there," she said when he strode to the sliding glass door of the aft salon. She picked up a walkie-talkie. "Kenny! Leonard! Someone get out here immediately! We have an intruder!"

Three men in white uniform jackets headed his way across the salon.

Will held up his hand. "I'm just here to talk to the owner—"

"The owner lives in Maui. You're trespassing," the largest of the men, one with no neck, said in a gravelly voice. "Leave before we throw you overboard."

"No, you don't understand. I need—"

"And we need you to leave," the taller of the three said.

"I'm not leaving until I talk to Beth," he said, dodging them and heading for the stairs leading to the sleeping quarters.

Tall Guy grabbed the edge of Will's shirt, halting his progress. "Beth? Beth Simpson?"

"Um, yes?" How had he not even known her last name?

"Kenny!" No Neck grabbed Tall Guy's arm. "Privileged information, man. You could lose your job."

"It's okay," Tall Guy said, shaking off No Neck's hold. "I know who he is. I mean, I've seen him around. He's a friend of Beth's."

"You call her by her first name?" Seemed kind of odd, considering the formality of their uniforms.

"Why wouldn't we call a staff member by her first name?"

"Staff member?" She'd said she owned the yacht.

"Yeah." Tall Guy looked over his shoulder and lowered his voice. "She worked as the diving instructor for the previous tenants. When they left early, she was out of a job, lucky girl. The new family isn't much fun."

Shoving aside the relief he felt at the realization he wouldn't have to ask Beth to lower her standard of living, he fought the panic his next thought provoked. "Where did she go?"

Tall Guy shrugged. "Home, I guess. Left for the airport this morning. But I heard her making a call to change her departure. I don't know when her flight leaves, but you may still be able to catch her."

"Thank you!" He pumped Tall Guy's hand and ran for the ladder.

Jumping from his boat as soon as it bumped the rubber surrounding his dock, he ran for the house, dialing directory assistance on the way.

Crystal Key Airport was small, with only one ticketing counter. As luck would have it, he knew the attendant who answered and was able to convince her to check and see if Beth had left the island.

"No," Roberta, an old girlfriend from high school, whispered into the phone. "She hasn't checked in yet."

"What time is her flight?" He paced the entry hall.

"I'm sorry, sir, I can't give you that information."

"Damn it, Berta, I have to know!"

"She was here earlier and checked her bags, but she hasn't checked in at the gate," Roberta whispered. "According to the itinerary, she changed her flight, but I can't get into the screen for the update without a supervisor to key in the access code. I'm sorry," she said in a normal voice.

"Thanks. I appreciate what you were able to tell me. Can you tell me when the next flight takes off?"

"Yes, sir," came her chirpy reply. "There's one more flight out for the mainland tonight, at eleven fifty-five. But you need to allow at least an hour for check-in."

After thanking Roberta, he resumed pacing, raking his hands through his hair.

Where could Beth be? He had less than four hours to find her.

He tried Nick's first, with no luck. Along the way to the dive shop, he stopped at Hooper's ice-cream shop, the video store, and walked through just about every place they'd seen when they were together.

No Beth.

Defeated, he trudged toward the dive shop. Something about being around diving equipment soothed him. Maybe he'd luck out and Beth would be there, since she shared his affinity for diving.

No surprise to find the store empty. It seemed to be the way his luck was running.

Jack, his part-timer, looked up from counting money. "Hey, boss man, I didn't expect to see you tonight. Did your lady catch up with you?"

Will's heart stumbled. "Beth? Beth was here?"

Jack nodded. "Shit. Now I have to start counting all over again." He looked up at Will. "Oh, yeah, that was her. Beth. She came in a couple times this morning." He grinned, exposing a mouthful of braces. "She's hot."

Fists clenched, Will spoke slowly. "Beth. You said she was here. Did she say where she was going?"

Nodding, Jack held up his finger. "Okay, I may not be exact on the money thing, but I'm close. Beth? Oh, yeah, she was on her way to the airport. Said she had a plane to catch for home."

"Did she say when her flight was?" Will could barely choke out the words.

"Sorry. I didn't listen too close after she told me she wanted to talk to you. Tonight, I think."

Will knocked over a display on his way to the door, then ran smack into Chris.

"Dude!" Chris said, steadying Will. "Where you going?"

"Beth!" Will and Jack said.

"Did you give Will her note?" Chris asked Jack, stopping Will in his tracks.

"Oh, man, I totally forgot." Jack picked up and put down several pieces of paper. "It's here somewhere."

"I saw you put it in the register, dude."

"Oh, yeah. Right." Jack opened the register and pulled out a folded piece of paper. "Sorry, I forgot," he said, holding the paper out to Will.

He ripped it from Jack's grasp and unfolded it, his hands shaking.

> *Will,*
> *Something funny happened while I was in Crystal Key. I fell in love. But you probably already know that. I'm not who you think I am. But, by now, you probably already know that, too. I switched my flight to tomorrow. If you're willing to listen to my lame explanation, meet me at Nick's at midnight.*
> *All my love, Beth*

Will's feet floated on the old cobblestone walk on the way to Nick's. He wasn't sure, but he thought he may have kissed Jack.

A glance at his watch had him picking up the pace. He wanted everything to be perfect when Beth arrived.

Beth paused to wipe her sweating hands on her denim mini-skirt, then pushed open the door to Nick's, her heart in her throat.

What if it was too late? What if Will hated her for lying to him?

She took a deep breath. If he could hate her so easily, he wasn't the man for her, despite what her aching heart may try to tell her.

The hostess grinned when Beth walked in and motioned toward the bar, where a bottle of champagne chilling in a silver bucket with two crystal flutes were waiting.

And Will.

He smiled and stood as she approached. That was a good sign, wasn't it?

"Hello, Beth." He just stood there.

Blinking back tears, she said, "I can explain—"

In the next heartbeat, he was holding her, covering her face with kisses.

Behind him, she saw the hostess dabbing a tissue to her eyes.

"It doesn't matter." He placed a lingering kiss on her lips. "Nothing matters except I love you. And you love me."

"But I lied. I—"

"I wasn't totally honest with you, either, sweetheart."

"I don't understand. You don't own the dive shop?" Not that she cared, but she'd sort of been counting on working there if they stayed together.

"No, I own the dive shop. But I also own this place. And the bar next door." He shrugged. "As for you not owning *Salsa Time*, babe, you have no idea how relieved I am! I mean, I make a decent living, but—" Her hand on his mouth silenced him.

"Shh. It doesn't matter. Heck, I'd live on your boat or even camp out on the beach, as long as we're together."

"The beach, huh? That's a pretty tall order for a girly-girl. Ow! If I agree to finance your education and marry you, will you stop abusing my poor arm?"

She sobered. "Is that a proposal?"

He took a box from the jacket draped on the barstool next to him.

Blinking back tears, she looked at the ring nestled in black velvet, a pearl-and-ruby version of her dive ring.

Will dropped to one knee, amid hoots from the staff and customers. "Damn straight. So, what do you say?"

Dropping to her knees in front of him, she slid her arms around his neck. "What took you so long?"